After Dinner Conversation
"Best of 2025"

Philosophy | Ethics Short Story Fiction

After Dinner Conversation – "Best Of" 2025

After Dinner Conversation publishes fictional stories that explore ethical and philosophical questions in an informal manner. The purpose of these stories is to generate thoughtful discussion in an open and easily accessible manner.

Names, characters, businesses, organizations, places, events, and incidents are either the product of the author's imagination or are used fictitiously. Any resemblance to actual persons, living or dead, events, or locales is entirely coincidental. The magazine is published monthly in print and electronic format.

ISBN# 979-8-9924170-9-8 (Digital)
ISBN# 979-8-9946899-0-5 (Print)

Library of Congress Control Number: 2026932849

Copyright © 2026 After Dinner Conversation®
Editor in Chief: *Kolby Granville*
Story Editor: *R. K. H. Ndong*
Copy Editors: *Stephen Repsys & Kate Bocassi*
Cover Design: *Shawn Winchester*
Design, layout, and discussion questions by After Dinner Conversation.

https://www.afterdinnerconversation.com

After Dinner Conversation is an award-winning independent nonprofit publisher. We believe in fostering meaningful discussions among friends, family, and students to enhance humanity through truth-seeking, reflection, and respectful debate. To achieve this, we publish philosophical and ethical short story fiction accompanied by discussion questions.

* * *

Recent Awards
- *Ranked #20 "Fish List of Indie Lit Mags 2026"*
- *Rated "Top Lit Mag Editor(s) 2025" by Chill Subs*
- *Rated "Most Popular Fiction Magazine 2024" by Chill Subs*
- *Rated "Top 10 LitMag of 2023, 2024" by Chill Subs*
- *Rated #1 "The Very Best Literary Magazine" by Ranker*
- *Rated Top 50 "Fiction" on Substack*

Table Of Contents

On Ice

Laura Mullen

* * *

Content Disclosure: None

* * *

Jacob keeps calling. The phone buzzes at inconvenient times, interrupting my morning meditation, a call with my therapist, my weekly team meeting. I silence the calls, but his name threads through my mind, interrupting my train of thought, demanding attention.

Please answer. We need to talk.

The text messages pile up as well, though I have muted notifications on his missives, protecting me from the onslaught. Dr. Novali notices my eyes darting to the screen midway through our Wednesday session, my voice catching mid-story, derailing me. She looks at the phone but doesn't ask.

"Jacob," I offer. The name is heavy with history and innuendo, and Dr. Novali raises her eyebrows.

"Have you been talking to Jacob again?"

I haven't, I assure her, and I try not to read into her tone.

Jacob has only recently stopped being the main character in my therapy sessions. I assume Dr. Novali is not eager to resurrect the topic of our failed relationship.

Before bed I scroll through dating apps on my phone, rereading long message chains I have started and abandoned with men I avoid meeting in real life. Dr. Novali says my engagement on these platforms counts as self-care, and so I swipe right and left, respond to direct messages, pretend I am interested in future moments. When Jacob calls, I am startled. Jacob's familiar face—his smile, his stubble—displaces the profile of the man I had been considering (Brandon: he likes boats and beer). I throw the phone across the bed, panicked.

"CeCe?" His voice is muffled, and I realize I have inadvertently answered the phone. I crawl from beneath the covers to retrieve it, planning to hang up, but I hear his voice. "Don't hang up."

His voice. His voice. Deep and throaty, as familiar as the voice of my mother, as distinct as any I have heard. He should record audiobooks, do voice-overs or movies or radio shows. Even two years later, his voice is intoxicating. I lift the phone to my ear, thirsty for more, but say nothing.

"CeCe, can you hear me? I don't know if you can hear me." I imagine him pulling the phone away to confirm the timer on the call is still going. I open my mouth to speak but find I cannot. "CeCe, we should talk. I think we should talk. I don't know if you got the letter from Coastal, but if you did, you need to read it. We need to make some decisions, and I have a question for you."

Still, I say nothing. I did get the letter. It was a bill, actually, accompanied by a letter. When it arrived, I set it aside, a problem for another day. It wasn't the money. Six hundred dollars wouldn't break the bank, though when I paid it each year, I wondered why I was continuing to do so, whether Jacob even knew I did. It was illogical to preserve these embryos for a future that wasn't coming.

"I got it," I say, and I hear him exhale.

"You're there. Hi. Thanks for answering."

"Hi." My voice is higher than I intend, and I realize I haven't spoken in several hours. I am surprised he receives the bills or the letters from Coastal Fertility. I wonder when he called them to update his address. The embryos are half his, I suppose, though I alone have funded them.

"How are you?"

I contemplate responses to this question. I am well. I was recently promoted at work. I am in therapy. I have morning rituals I follow with the devout rigor of a religious convert. I have my friends, my work, and my nephews nearby. I am well. If I tell him I am well he will be relieved to know he did not break me. I say nothing.

He allows a long moment to pass before he speaks. "You sound good. I'm good too. I'm back in Syracuse, you know." I do know. I ran into Mitchell—once our friend, now Jacob's friend—a year ago. Mitchell told me Jacob moved. Jacob met someone. Jacob was doing well.

"I heard."

Silence expands and I try to imagine what I will do when this call ends. How will I put it out of my mind, calm down, find sleep? What ritual will keep my mind from spinning, my thoughts from spiraling down, down, down?

"What do you want?" I ask, and I hate the harshness in my voice. I want to be peaceful and magnanimous, not a raw open wound oozing through the phone. And yet, I sound angry. I am angry. Still.

"Did you pay the bill?"

"Not yet."

"Are you going to?"

"I don't know."

"Did you read the letter?" The letter, included in the envelope with the bill, informed me I could either pay the six-hundred-dollar annual fee to keep our seven embryos frozen, or I could opt to destroy them. The South Carolina legislature was considering a bill that would change IVF by categorizing embryos as human beings. The new law would make it a crime to destroy them. If that happens, I may be signing up to pay the six-hundred-dollar fee in perpetuity to avoid criminal charges. Or, of course, I could use them. Septo-mom.

"I'm gonna have them destroyed," I say, though I wasn't sure of it before this moment. "We aren't going to use them; I don't know why I have even saved them this long." Even as I speak, I am not sure whether I hope he will protest.

Jacob is silent and I'm surprised. I do expect him to agree, to express gratitude for making this easy, letting him off the hook, once and for all.

"I can pay it," Jacob says.

"Why?"

"I just—I may want to use them someday."

"What?"

"I mean, I may want to use them. I do want to use them."

"You want to use them? To have a baby? We haven't spoken in two years." And yet, a bubble of possibility is rising within me. I have let go of Jacob, of our life together, but with only one sentence he springs the hinge on the hope stowed deep down in my subconscious.

"No, I mean. That's not what I mean."

The surge shifts into something else—confusion? rage?—as the possibilities of his meaning trickle into my brain. "What do you mean?"

"I mean..." He pauses and I wait. "*I* want to use them. I'm seeing someone. I've been seeing someone since I moved back up here, and... it's serious. And we want kids. Someday. But, she can't—she is older. But I think we want kids. And she is open to using our embryos."

"Our embryos." Somehow, in my wildest dreams, this hasn't occurred to me. Jacob and I were together for six years before we froze the embryos. I was thirty-four, the realities of my biological clock settling over me. I wanted kids, and I wanted Jacob. I had a good, steady job and a man I loved. But he wasn't ready. The reasons, those stated and those silent, were plentiful.

Jacob worked in construction, scraping together projects, bringing on bursts of cash followed by droughts between jobs. An injury could sideline him for weeks, and years of playing rugby had left him with a bad back. He needed to find something steady, a job with benefits. He needed to be worthy of me, of our potential children. He needed a cortisone shot, one big job, a new certification—and, it turned out, a different woman. Still, back then I heard *reasons* rather than excuses, and I pushed him to make the embryos. To preserve the option.

"Hopefully we won't ever need them," I had said. "When we are ready, hopefully, I'll just get pregnant naturally. This is just a precaution, so we have the option." I had watched my friends struggle through miscarriages and IVF, through cycles of hope and loss and pain. He listened to me describe it, of course, but his knowledge wasn't intimate. Still, he agreed, and we went through the process, the hormone injections, the extraction, the insemination, and genetic testing. In the end, we got seven—a great yield—and I relaxed. The future could take its time.

"No," I say now. "You can't use them."

I try to conjure the woman Jacob is *seeing*. The woman he is ready to have children with. The woman he gets out of bed for each day. By the time we ended, Jacob hadn't gotten out of bed or left the house in months. He wouldn't see a therapist, wouldn't go to physical therapy, or take medication. He was in quicksand, slipping beneath the grains with a resignation that seemed intentional. He would rather sink to the depths of the hole than rise to the heights of my expectations.

Jacob had always struggled with depression. Years of therapy have helped me to see the darkness was a part of what made him attractive. My urge to save him, my satisfaction in being the light in someone's life. I liked to be his one good thing. It was a role that made sense to me. Until it didn't.

Dr. Novali would say I was repeating a pattern. I had seen my father make sacrifices to support my mother through her battle with cancer—a valiant, eight-year struggle that ended in defeat. And then it was me who learned to swallow my desires in the interest of the family. I needed to be home after school for Evan and Jade. I needed to stay close to home rather than flee far for college. My value was equal to my contributions. It never occurred to me that it should be different.

It didn't start that way with Jacob. When we met, I was working in publishing, eager to climb the ladder, thrilled to work in the literary world with so many others whose lives had also been shaped more by characters and plots than actual human interaction. When we met, he was happy and hopeful, planning a home remodeling business that would give him financial and creative freedom. We could see our futures unfolding, side-by-side, a gorgeous pursuit of our separate dreams. Jacob didn't have a bad day for the first year we were together, and when the first one arrived, my response was a reflex. A work trip canceled, a conference missed, emails delayed. It felt good to take care of him. It felt good to be needed, for a while.

Eventually, his needs grew heavy. I was not a young girl trapped in my childhood home. I had glimpsed another version of life, experienced joy derived from dreams and talent. His bad days were repeated, sometimes growing into weeks and months, a crushing heaviness I bore with silent fury, tallying the friendships, the plans, the future we were losing. Still, I said nothing. I longed for change; I was terrified of losing him.

Jacob is talking again. "I know it's a big deal, and it's probably a surprise, and—we can talk. We should talk. I want you to meet Adrienne. You'll like her. And we can work out whatever you want; we can work it out."

"No."

"CeCe, please consider it. Please think about it."

"No. No. Those are mine. You can't use them."

"But you've been paying to keep them frozen. Were you thinking you would use them someday?"

"I don't know. Maybe. I didn't think about it."

"Well. But. I mean. You did keep them." He says it as though this is evidence to support some theory. The truth rises in me and I swallow it. I don't say: *I kept them for us.* I don't tell him I am keeping them frozen to keep the ember alive. It is too sad. Too pathetic.

"So you're ready to have kids now?" I hear the bite in my tone, and it sounds petty. Resentful.

"Yeah. I'm sorry, CeCe. I'm sorry."

I hang up the phone, simmering with the indignity of the conversation, of the entire situation. Jacob is doing *well*. I had imagined him across town, living in a dim basement apartment, eating ramen and Cheetos and cans of peas, playing *Call of Duty* late into the night. I had pictured him gaining weight, losing money, feeling miserable. Sometimes I had imagined his funeral, myself—grieving—embraced by his family and friends. I pictured him realizing, one day, what he had lost, and coming to claim it. Even when Mitchell told me Jacob moved and met someone, I resisted the reality.

Now I imagine Adrienne. How old could she be? I am thirty-eight. Jacob is forty. Adrienne wants to implant my young egg into her body. How old is she? I picture crow's-feet and gray roots, his strong hands massaging her slackening skin. *No.* I haul myself out of bed and down the stairs, unearthing the Coastal letter and the bill.

Did you think of using them? I haven't. But I have taken comfort in their existence. Their existence allows me to turn down dates, to brand the last two years as "rebuilding years" for focusing on myself. *It's the year of Cecelia*, I say each January, as though I am in charge of my life. As though I am alone by choice.

I lift the Coastal Fertility envelope from the mail tray on the marble countertop and reread the letter, considering my options. Seven embryos. If it were an even number, perhaps we could split them, each able to do what we wish. A friend once pointed out all seven of our embryos are technically twins, conceived at the same time. We could birth a basketball team of siblings, raised in different states, different homes. It would be a scientific study of nature versus nurture. Would they be depressives and martyrs like Jacob and I? Or could we nurture that out of them?

I could use them myself—have the baby Jacob and I had intended, raise him or her on my own. It wouldn't be a betrayal of Jacob. I wouldn't do it with another man, implant the embryo into someone else's body, pretend a third person plays some part in the biology of our creation. I would do it alone. Would it bring Jacob back to me—a creature made from our two halves, a baby sleeping in the sunlit second-floor back bedroom we always said would be a nursery?

I put the letter down again and wedge my feet into the sneakers near the front door. It is late but I need to move, to sweat the conversation with Jacob out of my mind. My phone dings while I am running, my heart racing, perspiration pouring down my face and chest. I ignore it, not ready to see any more from Jacob.

When I slow to a walk near my house, I look at my phone and see the notification was not from Jacob after all. It was Matt R., from my dating app. Matt R. wants to meet. Matt R. thinks we have a lot in common.

"Sure Matt," I type, though Matt and I surely do not have anything in common. "Let's have coffee tomorrow."

"How about I make you dinner at my place?"

The exchange—the push and pull of plans and power—is already exhausting. How do people do this? "How about coffee?" I reiterate, and he relents. I hope he drinks coffee. In our last year together, Jacob renounced caffeine, blaming it for the rise and fall of his psyche. Coffee became my guilty pleasure, sipped furtively at work, scrubbed from my breath before I walked in the door.

"Coffee sounds good. See you tomorrow."

I shower and then crawl back into bed to indulge in my worst habit: getting drunk on nostalgia. On my phone, I scroll through pictures of Jacob and me from years ago, searching for signs of what would come. But, as usual, there are no signs. There are no photos of the piles of laundry, the unwashed dishes, the disappointment I felt when I walked in the door at the end of each and every day, month after month. The pictures are bright, a portrait of a happy couple.

Why her? I text Jacob before I can help myself. It is embarrassing to ask and yet, it is all I can think of. Who is this Adrienne? What about her lets him rise each day with hope for the future?

He doesn't reply, and I think this is a gift. Or maybe he's just gone to sleep.

* * *

When I meet Matt for coffee the next morning, I am pleasantly surprised to find he is a clean-shaven freelance journalist who was previously married to his college girlfriend. (I have found divorcees are better than bachelors, at my age.) He orders a black coffee and swallows it like medicine. Like me, he has been on the apps for three years, and like me, he appears bored by the predictability of each question and each answer.

"Do you want kids?" he asks as though he already knows my response.

I nod, because I have always wanted kids. It isn't a hard question. It's just become hard to say it out loud, as the years have passed, the possibility dimming.

Matt says he wants kids *someday*, a familiar code indicating he is no different than the hundred dates that preceded him. Nonetheless, his sense of humor is self-deprecating and disarming, he pauses to consider before answering my questions and leans in to listen intently when I speak. He tells me he started cycling as a way to release tension, a recommendation from his therapist, and I am intrigued by this man who is curious and confident enough to seek help. We plan to meet for dinner the following weekend, giving each of us four days to formulate a plausible reason to cancel.

It is two days later when Jacob's reply to my question arrives. *I don't know.* And although I am in the middle of a meeting with my team, I read it and then go off camera, surprised by the tears that fall. I don't know what I wanted him to say. I don't know what words would be a salve.

Later that evening, alone in my house, I see I have a new email from Coastal Fertility.

Please complete the attached form to indicate your consent to destroy Embryos #74832, #27483, #37281...

I read it several times. I have not yet asked for the embryos to be destroyed. This must be Jacob's doing, and it feels like an act of love. One last kindness, a concession to my wishes. How do they destroy embryos? I imagine them thawing, softening, becoming vulnerable. I close the email, not sure whether I am ready to give up on the potential those blobs of DNA represent.

I think of Matt's question, of the clarity I felt when I nodded my head. I want kids. I am just afraid it won't happen for me. Wanting has become a dangerous, vulnerable thing.

In the morning, I call Coastal Fertility and wait on hold for a surprisingly long time before a woman answers, her voice strained. She introduces herself as Susan and apologizes for the wait. "Obviously we are experiencing a much higher than usual call volume." I imagine the other women calling in—the women desperate for babies, the women who froze embryos before going through chemo, the women who had tried everything else before emptying their savings for Coastal Fertility—somehow, I never thought of them before.

"I wanted to know whether it was possible to preserve some of my embryos but not all of them," I say, and Susan explains the change it will cause in my billing, the method they use to select which to preserve, the timing for destruction. It echoes the roadmap that guided my past experience: a literal application of *survival of the fittest*. Four years earlier nineteen eggs were harvested from my thirty-four-year-old uterus, thirteen of which survived insemination. After genetic testing, only seven remained viable, deemed optimal specimens. The others were destroyed, though it hadn't felt like murder.

"My ex requested that all seven embryos be destroyed. If I consent, but decide to retain one or two, will he be notified that some have been retained?"

"He will be notified if you attempt to use the embryos while they are in our care because his name is on the account, but honestly, if I were you, I would transfer whichever ones you want to keep out of the state. I don't know how long we will be able to stay open with the way the laws are changing. The doctors are worried about their own liability."

"How would that work?"

She explains the intricacies of exporting the embryos and it is clear she has given the speech many times.

I tell her I will think it over and hang up, letting the possibilities settle over me. I look again at the email requesting my consent. I imagine Jacob's conversation with Adrienne, the way he settles into his chair before delivering bad news, looking down while he speaks and then looking up, into my—her—eyes to gauge the reaction. Had Adrienne really wanted this—to carry his ex-girlfriend's baby in her body? We'd never even

met. What did she know of me—who was I in the story Jacob told? Maybe a part of her would be relieved to take this option off the table. Maybe not. Would she show her dismay? My disappointment used to deflate him, so I hid my desires, my successes, my expectations. I buried myself in the hope of resurrecting him.

When Jacob left, I was bereft. For two years, I have inventoried the opportunities I missed, the ways I went wrong, the love I let slip through my fingers. I've relived the day he left—the day he rallied himself to pack bags, to say goodbye—countless times, imagining the fierce pressure of his arms around me, the hug I didn't believe would be our last. I had waited and begged and promised I would change. I had committed to demanding less, accepting his depression, his limitations. But still he left.

I imagine Adrienne—whoever she is—now bearing the burden of Jacob's emotions. I feel a heaviness that may be jealousy or may be something else. Empathy? Maybe. For a moment I am Adrienne, sitting on a sofa in a room far north of here, the sky outside eternally gray. I hold my breath as I consider my response, measure my reaction before revealing it, a habit too entrenched to erase. I see myself cross the room to Jacob, sit on his lap, collapse into the hard warmth of him, luxuriate in his embrace. I feel his release, relief. But when the Adrienne version of me stands, she is heavy with all that went unsaid. She must wonder whether he will be happy without children. Wonder how he can love her and also want children who are half of me. She must yearn for him to see the feelings she cannot voice.

I look at the phone in front of me. I could call Jacob and talk it through. I could explain my reservations, my fears, my need to keep a sliver of hope alive for the future I once thought I owned. He would listen and sigh deeply, unable to make a decision, unable to give me what I want. He will not surprise me. I don't call him.

With a blue pen, I mark up the consent form before I sign it, modifying it to reflect my own preferences—the only ones that matter anymore. I use my phone to scan and email it back to Coastal Fertility. I find I am relieved. Almost grateful for the unilateral decision. I don't have to live in reaction to him anymore. I don't have to accept his open arms, his broad chest—his good intentions—as consolation for his shortcomings. I can make a choice without apology or explanation. This is the silver lining to my loss: when Jacob left, he released me. He gifted me a freedom I have refused to see, my back to the door for all this time.

I hesitate before I text Jacob, indulging in a fantasy of defiance. If I didn't text him, would he ever ask? Probably not. But I reach out anyway, another pesky habit, the need for a period at the end of a paragraph.

All done. I write. Because what's done is done.

* * *

I am reviewing a presentation for work when my personal email dings. Coastal Fertility has sent me an extraction form for the two remaining embryos. I open the PDF and fill it out. Both embryos will be transferred to a clinic in Pennsylvania. When I sign, I release the clinic from liability in the event the embryos are damaged during their transition. Susan assured me the embryos would remain in a deep freeze through the transfer, unscathed by the shifting landscape, but now I contemplate car crashes and broken cooling systems.

I have a date with Matt the next evening. We meet for

dinner and stay for dessert, ordering decaf cappuccinos to extend our time together. We talk about our jobs, our families of origin, our hobbies—he wants me to try cycling with him, and it occurs to me that relationships can open doors, push you out of your comfort zone. I confess that bikes hurt my butt.

"But you'll get used to it after a few times. You have to keep riding through that pain."

"I'll get used to the pain? Or it will stop hurting?"

He laughs like I'm joking. "It stops hurting. You just can't give up after the first time or you won't get to the other side of it."

Conversation turns to the week ahead and the week we just finished. Fueled by the bottle of wine we drank, or maybe just the sense of intimacy we have created at our candlelit corner table, I tell him about the embryos, the need to move them out of the state. I focus on the absurdity of the situation to avoid the pinch of pain the topic raises in me.

"Can you imagine wanting to use the embryos in some other woman? I mean, she has never even met me."

Matt nods thoughtfully, considering. Perhaps he, like me, is trying to picture this woman. "Did you say yes?"

"No. I said no."

"Are you planning to use them?"

"I don't know. Not right now." I want to tell him that I destroyed some—but only some—of them, that I kept two as a nest egg for myself, an insurance policy. But I don't go into the details.

"It's kind of lovely," he observes, and I wonder where he is going with this. "The potential they represent. The possibility. If one of you were to pass away, you could leave a legacy with those embryos."

I wonder if I can be with a man who says *pass away* instead of *die*. His impulse to sugarcoat is suddenly repulsive. I wish I hadn't told him about the embryos. I moved too fast. The only thing less sexy than the harsh realities of fertility planning is a man's opinion on the topic.

"Well, hopefully, no one dies any time soon." I look for the waiter, suddenly desperate to leave. I picture my embryos preparing for their trip, moving north into a new climate, resilient when confronted with transition.

* * *

Three days later Matt texts me a news article about a South Carolina fertility clinic torched by political protestors. *Good thing you're getting your little guys out of dodge,* he writes.

I click through the link, annoyed by his use of the phrase *little guys* to describe a pile of cells. The picture that comes up on the screen is familiar, and my breath catches. It is not *some* fertility clinic. It is Coastal Fertility, still standing, though the windows are blown out, the insides clearly charred.

I freeze, holding my breath as I scroll through the article. No one was harmed. The fire was set in the middle of the night, and the culprit has already been identified: Marjorie Maynor, the leader of a local True Patriots group who was a loud voice on the issue of fetal personhood. She is in custody, apparently unavailable for a quote. The paper dug up old talking points from her Facebook page where she decried IVF as legalized murder and wrote lengthy rants about God's intentions. The article includes a link to her personal page and the page of True Patriots.

Matt sends a follow-up article in which a representative for the True Patriots praises Marjorie Maynor's vigilante approach to justice and appears surprised that the facility not only conducted fertility treatments but also housed embryos. *I hope yours are all right,* Matt texts.

I want to send the article to Jacob, but Jacob thinks the embryos were already destroyed. I consider replying to Matt but don't want to try to explain the sharp wound opening inside of me as I review images of the scorched facility. I call Coastal, hoping to talk with Susan, but get a busy tone. I wonder whether my last two embryos were extracted before the match was struck. Maybe they are safe in Pennsylvania.

I've avoided imagining the possibilities the two remaining embryos represent. Their preservation somehow made it possible for me to let go of the future I had attached to the seven test tubes Jacob and I had created.

I dial the clinic again and am again met with only a flat beep, droning into my ear. I won't have answers today. I may not tomorrow. I rest my phone on the counter and turn on the television. On the local news, Marjorie Maynor's face looks haggard. I try to direct my anger in her direction, the villain in this tale. But I can't rouse myself to hate her. I feel something else, something dull and empty I can't quite name.

I turn the television off and go out the back door to the shed, where my bike rests against a wall, tires deflated, a layer of grimy dust covering the bright red bars I once admired. I touch the seat tentatively, its firm confidence a threat, and wheel it into the sunlight, using my sleeve to remove some of the black crust from the frame. There is a pump in the shed, and I fill the tires, using more strength than I expected. The exertion is soothing.

I bought this bike three years earlier, an initiative to get Jacob out of the house, to give us a shared hobby. He had mounted his with a grimace and made it a few blocks before stopping and walking it home. I apologized, seeing my miscalculation, and walked home beside him. It was hot that day, the sun punishing, and I longed to climb onto my new bike and feel the wind in my hair, to soar over routes that took ages to walk. But it felt like bragging, my ability to fly.

I mount the bike unsteadily, pedaling down my driveway and out to the street. I want to stay on the sidewalk, protected from passing cars and the tyranny of traffic laws, but I veer into the street instead, living dangerously. My neighborhood breezes by, familiar facades a flash in the passing scenery.

When I get to Coastal Fertility, I am drenched in sweat, the humidity oppressive and draining. I let my bike fall to the ground and sit on the curb to survey the scene in front of me. There is yellow tape around the building, one car still in the parking lot, trapped by the ongoing investigation. I run my fingers over the spikes of grass lining the curb, appreciating their tough resilience, their consistency. My finger catches on a stem, softer and juicier than its neighboring growth, and I close my fingers around it, snapping it, lifting the yellow dandelion head to my nose. I recall vaguely that a yellow flower can reveal a love of butter or evolve into a puff you blow on to make a wish.

Before I mount my bike, I cross the street to rest the flower on the curb in front of the burned-out building, gently exhaling the last of my wishes for this place. The ride home feels longer than the ride there, and I know when I wake in the morning I will ache.

I snap a picture of my bike and text it to Matt. *Got her out of retirement this morning.*

His response is almost immediate. *Nice! If you aren't too sore tomorrow, let me show you my favorite trail.*

I go back outside and look at the bike, still dirty. When I touch the seat, the handlebars, I imagine the bike is humming its gratitude in my direction, preening, hoping to be touched and used.

"What do you think?" I ask it out loud. "Should we ride again?"

* * *

It is nearly a month before someone answers the phone at Coastal Fertility, a young man who I picture wearing a suit in a skyscraper, the undertaker for the facility's carcass. I read out all seven embryo numbers from the letter I had received, bracing to learn their fate.

"Yeah, I have the records. It looks like the three slated for destruction were lost in the fire, but the four selected for relocation had already been removed. They should be safely in New York by now."

It takes me a moment to understand what he is saying. Four? New York? "You mean Pennsylvania. Two in Pennsylvania."

"Oh yes. I'm sorry. Two in Pennsylvania"—I release the breath I had held. That makes more sense. He continues—"and two in Syracuse, New York."

"I'm sorry. I only requested the transfer of two embryos. To Pennsylvania. Who requested the other two?" Though of course, I know. The voice on the phone confirms that Jacob filed the request for removal the day after I did. I look back through our messages. He must have done it when he received my text message.

All done, I had written.

And he thought I was.

* * *

Discussion Questions

1. What are the factors that cause a person to "move on" after a breakup? Why is Cecelia having so much trouble moving on?
2. What individual rights should Cecelia and Jacob have to the fertilized eggs being retained? Would you support a law enshrining those rights, or should they be rights based on the conversation between the two parties?
3. Cecelia has been going to therapy for two years related to her breakup with Jacob. Is the fact that she is still struggling with their breakup proof the therapy isn't working? How do you know if therapy is working?
4. If either Cecelia or Jacob used one of the fertilized eggs with a new partner to make a baby, do they have an obligation to tell the other? Would you rather know, or not know, you have your biological child out in the world? Why or why not?
5. If Jacob was the one struggling with depression and other issues, why is he the one that ended the relationship? What (*if anything*) does that tell you about each of them and their relationship?

* * *

The Apath

A.J. Parker

* * *

<u>Content Disclosure</u>: Sexual Situations; Depiction of Drug Use; Substance Addiction Themes; Strong Language

* * *

The line to buy Happiness was long.

Finn walked past expectant guests waiting to get into the sharp, white building. A procession of people curled around the corner, hair glinting like plastic, skin as smooth as rubber. Marcus's Delights sold only the best emotions. Everyone knew that. The storefront was all glass, so it could boast of its fluttery, color-changing light. Crystal vials sparkled on purple cushions, and the edible items on display were fresh out of the oven. Even the pills were put in dainty little bottles, rubbed spotless to be chic enough for uptown folk. The product was kept in locked glass cases like fine jewelry.

Finn continued down the street until his feet transitioned to cobbled sidewalk. He knew he was close to Mammy's when the buildings around him grew rickety and gray, and the sky was striped with animated billboards and electric wires.

"Out to run errands, Finn?" Elephant, the security guard, asked from his ripped barstool. His accent was an oscillating blend of Irish and British. He was all shoulders, torso, and arms, beefier than any man Finn had seen. Elephant was a staple at Mammy's, more decoration than anything else. An electrified, holographic gate to a darkened staircase was the real barrier to entry.

"Only for your best," Finn said, to which Elephant gave a hearty laugh and replied, "Not that you could afford it."

"Careful there, or I might go to Harry's instead."

"Ho ho ho," Elephant said. "Somebody call True Designs."

"Why? They're already listening."

"That's enough of that. Go on in, boy."

Elephant waved a palm over a keypad, and the gate retracted. This was always Finn's favorite part—walking the roughened stairs. There was nothing but possibility there as the distance shortened between him and what he wanted to feel. There were no lines or diligent security cameras, no boasting glass-front windows. Who knew what he was going to get? As he climbed the scuffed steps, it was just him, the dying lightbulb above, and the peeling charcoal walls.

When he entered, his least favorite employee was working the register. Mariana was a fixture at Mammy's, too, but not a decoration. Her hair was a ruffled white and gray, which complemented her beady brown eyes. She wore a permanent frown. It was just the two of them inside the store. He nodded to her respectfully, but she ignored him as she sorted a jar full of Mixed Emotion lollipops.

Mammy's didn't put their product on display like Marcus's Delights. At Mammy's, vials upon vials dotted the walls, gripped by a claw, each labeled respectively. There was no organization to it, no luxury to it. He skimmed the wall—neon green for Jealousy, gray for Nervousness, amethyst for Awareness, orange for Frustration. He was surprised they hadn't been shut down by the National Health Service yet, but as long as Mammy's kept their "True Designs merchandise sold here" sign up in the window, their asses were covered. Even if that merchandise was only candy.

Old felt jewelry holders decorated the dinged-up tables in the middle of the room. Tiny baggies squeezed into the place earrings would go. Individually bubble-wrapped pills filled the sunken necklace compartments. Flavored candies sat in the ring holders. It seemed laughable compared to Marcus's. Finn picked up a small bag of Distraction before carrying on.

He found himself in front of the wall again. Yellow for Panic. Crimson for Vengeance. Fuchsia for Enthusiasm. You wouldn't find any Happiness there. It was a secondhand shop full of cheap knockoffs and watered-down products.

Who would buy the bad emotions? That was the public debate, at first. The answer was simple. The ones who couldn't afford any better.

Finn hovered in front of a swirling blue and gray vial. He checked the price tag.

"Ten pounds sterling," the cashier said, startling him. "Knocked down the price. It's just been sitting there, collecting dust."

He picked it off the wall. When he was done perusing the store, he set his collection of items onto the checkout counter.

"Would that be all?"

"And one of those." He pointed to the lollipops in front of the register. She added it to his purchase. He paid with his wrist chip and then dug a hand into the candy jar. He peeled the wrapper off. Her eyes widened as he placed the lollipop into his mouth, crunching the wrapper in his fist.

"Didn't you want to check what you got?"

"Thanks." He took his bag and left.

When he was outside, far out of Elephant's sight, he uncrumpled the wrapper. The groovy pink lettering on the foil read "Desire."

He gave a dry laugh and kept sucking.

* * *

Sarah didn't say no when he invited her over. They did lines of her leftover Intrigue.

"Do you feel it?" she asked as they sat on the sagging brown couch. His apartment's yellowing walls shimmered. He could see the individual nicks the place had collected over the years, thin lines on the floor from dragged furniture and scuffed corners from negligence.

"Yeah," he said, though his pupils were already dilated.

"Yeah?" she asked again.

"Yeah."

He kissed her first because he knew women liked that. Everything about her was vibrant. The blond at the base of her mascaraed eyelashes. The stained pink bra she wore, peeking out from behind her tank top. He squished her skin between his fingers, feeling peach fuzz. She was a marvel of mediocrity. He dug his fingers into the outside of her thighs and worked his hands up her supple body. She groaned. It was guttural and ugly. He took her chin in both his hands.

"What are you doing?" she asked as he titled her head side to side.

"I just wanted to get a good look at you."

She blushed as he examined the unkempt hairs around her

eyebrows and the faded tattoo on her collarbone. Her roots were dark from poor maintenance, and her rosy lipstick had been smudged. He pinned her shoulder down against the couch where she sat, freeing his other hand, as his lips found her neck. She tilted her head back and closed her eyes, moaning.

She was interesting, wasn't she?

* * *

"It's no fun anymore, is it?" Finn waved the smoke away, the artificial tobacco leaving a burnt taste in his mouth. His friend's kitchen was crowded with partygoers, most of whom had become onlookers to Finn's monologue. Music pulsed in the background. Sarah giggled as he pointed at her with the cigarette between his long fingers. "They keep us alive longer so they can sell us more things. We used to just die, you know."

He had tried a real cigarette only once (he was mates with an antiques collector), but it wasn't hard to figure out why they had been discontinued. The curl of poisoned tobacco was addictive, the taste terribly good. This imitation was just a mouthfeel: thick, flavored water vapor and a smokey taste. Unregulated feelings were the only dangerous thing left in the world.

Sarah opened her mouth and waited, her pink tongue on display. He popped the cigarette in as he leaned against the fridge, one leg propped up.

"Wouldn't you rather be alive?" she asked, mouth full. She blew smoke directly into Finn's face and giggled again. He watched her tongue play with the end of the cigarette.

Finn liked Sarah. He liked her thick Northern accent and her crispy yellow hair. He liked her uneven teeth. She was the furthest you could get from the plastic sheen of the New Designs uptown who sold out for new hair and new skin and new teeth. Sarah wasn't very smart, but that's what he liked best about her.

"Bloody hell," Freud interrupted. "I shouldn't have given you that Energy shot when you came in."

"You know what counters Energy?" Xi said as he lounged against the back doorframe. His shock of black hair was impeccably clean and his beige skin, impeccably smooth. Cool air wafted in through the screen door. Finn took his cigarette back and grinned, leaving the smoke in Sarah's mouth behind.

The screen door creaked shut as they transitioned to the overcrowded townhome's porch. Xi looked clean in silver pants and a matching silver overcoat. Underneath it, he wore the black button-up all the coders were required to wear to the office. It was the best way to differentiate bot from person. Xi could afford to live uptown—he had access to the best products because of it.

"You've taken this before, right?" Xi asked as they sat on the back porch. Moths buzzed at the light above them. The yard was tiny, squishing them between the hot water unit and the trash cans. Though it was significantly quieter outside, the neighbors were used to Freud's rowdiness by now.

"Yes," Finn lied.

Xi took out the small vial. When he unscrewed the lid, a dropper came out. "Let's see what a wee bit of Calm can do for you."

"Couldn't shell out for the proper stuff? Tranquility, Serenity, Bullshitery?"

"Now that's above my pay grade. Cheers."

Xi twisted his mouth, head leaning back, as he put the drops into his eyes. Xi passed it to Finn, who followed suit. He sniffed when he sat up, blinking the clear liquid away. It stung at first, but nothing Finn wasn't used to. That's how you knew it was real and not the diluted kind they sold at Mammy's.

Xi stared at the sky. It was one of those nights where the constellations were blinking in and out sporadically. Someone would have to call maintenance to reprogram the drones. Xi snorted and shook his head.

"All that taxpayer money and they can't even get the fucking stars to work."

"Let the Design girls worry about it. They're the ones who believe in that shit." Finn passed the cigarette to Xi, letting out smoke. All he could think about was what it was missing.

"I'm sure you dream of getting one of those New Design girls underneath you, eh?"

"Never."

"Never?

"There's something unnatural about them, isn't there?"

"And this is natural?" Xi asked, waving the fake cigarette around.

"It's affordable," Finn said. He took the vial from where it sat on the steps next to them.

"You know not to take too much, right?"

"I'm not a dumbass."

It had been plastered up on flashing billboards and portable screens his whole life. "Get emotional. On occasion." The pretty model would smile, teeth too white, as she held out a bright yellow tab in her palm. She swallowed it with as little thought as she would a painkiller, and afterward, put her thumb up, laughing as she said, "It's *occasionally* good!"

They even named their parent company "The Occasion Corporation," as if that covered their asses when the lawsuits trickled in. They had created a feat of science. A way to heighten emotions. A way to maintain them. The warning labels weren't big enough, so they made them bigger. The more of an emotion you took, the less of it you could feel on your own later. Their lawyers made a fortune, but once the product was out there, it couldn't be taken back, only regulated.

Finn didn't mind. He didn't have a lot of use for Calm in his life. He put two more splashes in each eye. When he blinked his vision clear, everything in front of him was smooth and pastel. It wasn't black outside; it was a dark cerulean. He looked at his hands. They gleamed like he had moisturized them. Everything was slow and syrupy. Peaceful. He liked the way the stairs creaked as he shuffled his weight and how Xi's jacket shimmered underneath the fuzzy light.

"Finnnn," Sarah drawled as she cracked open the screen door. "Are you having fun without me?"

She came down to him and when she sat, she sat in his lap, wrapping her legs around him. Her tights rippled as her dress rode up.

"That's my cue," Xi said, slipping the vial into his pocket. He took the cigarette with him. Finn cursed silently.

The doors clicked shut in succession, two layers protecting them from the racket inside.

"Why did you have to do that?"

"Do what?" She was curling the sides of his hair in her fingers, even though it was too short.

"I was having a good conversation."

"As good as this?" She kissed his neck. A constellation winked in and out above him. He kept his eyes trained on it. Her pressure was muted, as if a feather was brushing up against him instead. His mouth tasted like coconut water, and if Sarah hadn't touched him with her frozen hands, he was sure his skin would've felt toasty with sun.

She started undoing his belt.

"Sarah. Somebody could come out."

"So? You love me, right?"

He blinked.

She sat back when he didn't answer. He couldn't afford Love. She knew that.

"That wasn't rhetorical, you know."

"Sarah..."

She waited, giving him a second chance. He didn't take it.

"I can't believe you," she said, wiping tears from her face. She pushed her body off his, not bothering to fix his belt. The doors slammed shut behind her once, then twice.

Finn felt fine where he was. The stairs were a hammock, and the dirt below him, soft sand. Why would he want Love ruining his life? He was fine with his run-of-the-mill emotions. The last time he took Happiness, his left eye hadn't stopped twitching for a week.

A star blinked in and out. He watched, waiting for it to happen again.

* * *

Finn was on his way to Mammy's the next day when he saw Elephant arguing with someone. A small girl was pouting, arms crossed tight, as Elephant gestured to the street.

"First time?" he asked the girl as he approached. Her clothes were grungy, and her synthetic black hair unkempt, but still, something bothered him. She was short and dirtied with makeup, but she had the unblemished complexion of a New Design. Her green eyes were big, accentuated by her thick lower lashes. Her lips were plush and the most perfect coral color. Her cheeks were round and smooth, and the space between her eyebrows, hairless. Underneath that baggy shirt...

She said nothing.

"Mammy's is referral only," Elephant grunted, crossing his arms back.

"That's why she was waiting for me. I'm her referral." Finn smiled, all teeth. "You know, Harry's is doing a two-for-one on mid-tier emotions right now."

Elephant scrutinized Finn before he waved down the barrier. "You're lucky I like you."

"You didn't have to do that," the girl said as they climbed the stairs.

"I don't mind."

He knew how desperate someone needed to be to end up at Mammy's, the cheapest shop in town. He also knew how much she must've spent to get her new skin and new features. He wanted to press her, but he also didn't want to scare her off.

"I'm Finn, by the way."

She hesitated before she replied. "Elsbeth."

"Need a tour?" he said as he held the door open for her. She gravitated toward the multicolored wall, laden with breakable emotions. Finn moved to her side. They stared at the array of colors.

"I'm going to try them all at some point."

"Yeah?" She was incredulous.

"You know what they say." He spread his arms out at the display. "Try everything once."

She looked at the wall. "Even... belittlement?"

"That one, I'd only try if the big kids were doing it too."

Her lips perked into a smile. Finn left her as he picked up his usual stash: a dropper of Charm, five tabs of Distraction, and a baggie full of powdered Adequacy. At the checkout counter, he took a handful of lollipops for good measure.

On their way out, Elsbeth pulled a vial from her bag.

"What's that?"

"No cheating," she said, wrapping it in his palm. The sloshing liquid was indistinguishable between yellow and orange. "Everything once, right?"

She left him next to Elephant. He opened his palm.

Curiosity.

"Oh, you're in trouble, aren't you?" Elephant asked.

* * *

Finn paid a pound for a vial of Love off a woman on Seventh Street. He knew it would taste terrible, and the color looked more beige than pink, but he wanted to try it. He couldn't afford the real stuff—never could and never would—but he'd grown used to Mammy's watered-down products, so what difference was something off the street?

He tossed it down his throat and continued his evening stroll through the metallic city. It was bitter at first, almost like Anger, but it had a sweet aftertaste. He hoped it wasn't laced with anything. He'd heard of Love-Exhilaration trips gone wrong, and that wasn't to mention the Happiness-Fear combo that killed a couple kids a year ago.

His sensations were heightened. He rubbed his pointer finger and his thumb together to test it. You could learn a lot about how an emotion was affecting you by how things felt. He could detect his own fingerprints, sense the dirt underneath his nails. The dose lasted him fifteen minutes, and it was mostly warmth and heart palpitations. He liked the Calm droplets better. Love's jittery feeling unnerved him.

He didn't think about Sarah once. Instead, he pictured Elsbeth, those big doe eyes and the black seeping from her hair.

He wondered what Elsbeth had been like before the Re-Design. He wondered what she would feel like between his pointer finger and his thumb. Wondered what she'd feel like on Love. When he got home, he had a nibble of Boredom to level himself out.

The problem, though, was that everything tasted like chalk after Love, even the cheap stuff.

* * *

The next time he went to Mammy's, Elsbeth was smoking on the corner of the block. It was one of those new devices that made you feel like you were somewhere else, something about how it interacted with neurotransmitters and microchips. He had canceled his subscription to most of the chip's features months ago, but devices like that cost so much upfront, they worked for free.

"Want to try it?" she asked.

Today she was wearing ripped black tights and a T-shirt so big, it was a dress. Her boots were fancy leather, but the shoelaces were fraying. Her black hair had been tied back messily. He took a hit.

When he closed his eyes, he was in a dark, misty forest. Pine needles and dead leaves crunched underfoot. It smelled of evergreen. He couldn't see more than a couple meters in front of him as a dense fog approached. When he opened his eyes, the smell was the only thing that lingered.

"You're new around here, aren't you?" he asked.

"What gave it away?"

Her perfectly sculpted brow. Her faded freckles. Her expensive shoes. Her voice, the manufactured cadence somehow both soft and gritty. She sighed. "I was having some trouble at home. Needed a break, you know? How about you?

You seem to know the place well. What brought you to Mammy's?"

He leaned against the wall, scratchy brick on his back, and laughed. "No one else would sell to me."

Her eyebrows perked up. "You're an Apath?"

"I don't like that word."

Many people had tried to use that term with him over the years. The doctors. (He didn't go back). His mates. (They were teasing, so it didn't really count). His parents. (They were just tired of him spending their money). Sarah. (As she moaned his name while they were high on Greed). Shop owners. (Selling to an Apath was license for closure).

"So, you can't feel anything without them?" Elsbeth asked.

"I wouldn't say that. I feel the wind on my cheek. I feel the wall biting into my back. I feel your arm close to mine."

She adjusted so there was more space between them. "And now?"

"I feel like you want to be an Apath. But New Designs don't need to, do they? They have everything built in."

She recoiled. "That's not true. We pay just like the rest of you."

Finn laughed. "At discounted prices."

"It's microdosing," she argued. "Nobody gets addicted."

"Is that why you left?" She snapped off the wall, but he continued. "It wasn't enough anymore. Nobody uptown would sell to the New Design girl. Nobody downtown wants to be caught dead with one, lest the department shuts them down. But you found out Mammy's doesn't care."

Her nostrils flared. He took her device once more, inhaling the foggy pinewood forest. It was dark and mystical. It filled his lungs with cedar. She could've chosen anywhere, anywhere in the world, but she picked there. He didn't have to ask why.

She liked the darkness. They had that in common.

As he exhaled, he handed it back to her with a folded-up note from his pocket.

"If you want to feel—really feel—you know where to find me."

* * *

Someone had scored Delight, and it was going around like a disease.

"Now this is the good stuff, eh?" Freud said as Finn came up from the kitchen table, wiping his nose. "Thank God for Xi and his rich mates."

Finn grinned. They were all secondary schoolmates, still living in the same neighborhood they used to tussle in. He was grateful for it. Who else would he get his real emotions from? They were on their way to becoming Apaths themselves, so they couldn't say anything.

Finn reached into his pocket, grabbing a fistful of lollipops, and then slammed them down onto the dusty table.

"What the fuck is this?" Freud asked when he saw the pile.

"Have you ever heard of roulette?" Finn was arranging them in a straight line, turning them over so their labels weren't visible. "Bottom of the millennium tradition. They did it with all sorts of things, I think."

The screen door creaked open and in came Sarah. Her eyeliner was smeared, and the tiny ensemble she wore, disheveled. They hadn't talked since the porch last time. Besides, she was dragging some new bloke in by the hand. She gave Finn a nasty side-eye.

The Delight was making him delirious as he shuffled the lollipops around, laughing.

"Go ahead," he told Freud. The man frowned but reached for the fifth down the line. He turned it over. It was Annoyance.

Finn cackled.

"You and your bloody lollis," Freud muttered as he unwrapped the bright red sphere, placing it in his mouth. His face contorted. "It's too salty. Your turn."

Finn swiveled his choice around so Freud could see. It was Confidence.

"Oh, fuck you," the man said.

Finn popped it into his mouth. It burned, but the pain faded after a couple seconds. It was tangerine colored and tasted like fruit too. As much as he hated True Designs and everything they stood for, they had mastered their recipes.

"Finn," Xi said from behind him. "Someone's looking for you."

Elsbeth stood by Xi's side. She had put something shimmery on her eyelids, and her hair fell onto her face in coquettish layers. Her black lace dress hugged her constructed frame just right. She was angelic, all dark lines and creamy flesh. Standing next to the No Designs (a name Finn and his friends had made up for themselves), she was an airbrushed painting.

Sarah caught notice, her glare sharpening.

"You came," he said when Xi had stepped away. Elsbeth took the lollipop from his mouth and placed it in her own. Her voice held an alluring cadence as she said, "Don't make me regret it."

Everything was beautiful at Freud's. The music was loud and pumping. He took Elsbeth's hand in his, and they danced together. Her skin felt like skin. Her breath, like breath. When he examined her side profile, he noticed dead skin peppering the arches of her eyebrows. Her green eyes were marred by flakes of yellow.

But everything was beautiful. She was beautiful, pressed into him.

"So, Elsbeth," he asked. "What made you become a New Design?"

She pursed her lips together. If she wanted to play it off, she was in the wrong part of town.

"I didn't really have a choice," she conceded. "My parents work in the Influence sector. There's not much to want for when you have everything."

Maybe the statement would've revolted him if the Delight hadn't hit.

"So, *Finn*," she enunciated. "What made you become an Apath?"

He stole the lollipop back from her.

"A shitty childhood," he lied. It was boredom, more than anything. A deadbeat job in data collection and a string of disinteresting romantic entanglements. His parents thought kicking him out of the house would help, but it just made him lazier as he rented out his brother's place, who let him be late on his payments. Relics of the past were the only things Finn was truly interested in.

He hesitated. "Maybe I didn't have a choice, either."

When the lollipop had dissolved, he took her out to the porch, making sure both doors were shut tightly behind them, and then gave her his last line of Elation. How many emotions had he mixed at this point? It didn't matter. He craved the unpredictable outcome at the end of each night.

When he put her onto his lap, her pupils were huge, and her hair caught in his mouth. His vision was bright and distorted, filled with the twinkle of the inconsistent stars and the flash of

Elsbeth's pale neck. He was bursting with fire from the stimulants, a combination of bad interplay in his liver and utter gratification.

"Feel it yet?" he asked as she rocked her hips.

"Yeah," she said.

"Yeah?"

"Yeah."

* * *

When he got home that night, he went straight to his nightstand. The blue-gray vial he bought at Mammy's was waiting for him there. He had shoved it far back, to keep it safe and hidden. He had wanted it out of sight, somewhere it could be forgotten. But he hadn't forgotten about it.

When he retrieved it, he tilted it over to see the label on the bottom. It had a New Design label. This was the pure kind; he could tell by how the seal around the cap hadn't been broken yet.

It was Anguish. Nobody wanted it at the posh shops. The shitty ones, either. He sipped it, slow at first. It bubbled and fizzed going down, ice cold. When he couldn't stand it anymore, he tipped the rest down his gullet, letting his insides freeze.

Maybe he didn't need Love. Maybe this was enough.

* * *

Discussion Questions

1. If you had to take the pure form of an emotion, what three would you take and why? What is one you would never take and why?
2. What do you think is the purpose of emotions? How do you think society would be different if we didn't feel emotions? Would society be better, worse, or just different?
3. How are the emotion drugs in the story different than the ways people feed themselves emotions in real life? What's the difference (*if anything*) between taking a hit of "joy" and modern "retail therapy," gambling, dancing, or video games? Should they be judged differently or the same?
4. If the drugs in the story were real, would you ever do them? Why or why not? What other people in society do you think would do them and why?
5. If a person was a natural Apath and incapable of feeling emotions, do you think they should take the emotion drugs so they could attempt to live a more normal life?

* * *

One Out of Four

Joseph S. Klapach

* * *

<u>**Content Disclosure**</u>: Death or Bereavement; Moderate Intensity, Mild Language

* * *

Molly circled the date of her eighteenth birthday on her calendar. She was tired of being told she had a "pretty face." She was tired of being told she was "funny" and "kind" and "smart," and that those were the "most important things." Her class had even voted her "Best Personality," as a superlative, but she knew what that meant. She overheard Danny and Aiden talking after the assembly. "Molly's got a great personality," Danny said loud enough for everyone to hear. "A great, big personality. A larger-than-life personality." And Aiden burst out laughing as Danny stuck out his arms and waddled down the hallway like a penguin.

Molly made the appointment in secret on her seventeenth birthday. Of course, her parents had forbidden her from going anywhere near the clinic. "We know you'll be tempted," they told her. "But it would break our hearts if anything happened to you." "It isn't worth the risk," her father warned. "One-quarter of all patients," her mother added. "That's one out of four." "Look at us," her father boasted. "We're happy, and we've never had the shot."

But Molly didn't care. She couldn't wait to take Diovix.

On the morning of her eighteenth birthday, Molly snuck out of the house and caught a rideshare to the downtown clinic. She left her parents a note saying she was studying at the library, so they wouldn't worry or try to stop her. She skipped breakfast like the clinic recommended, and her stomach was growling audibly by the time she crossed the Liberty Bridge.

When Molly arrived at the clinic, she was surprised to see so many protesters. She had hoped to avoid any unwanted attention by scheduling an early appointment, but the protesters were a dedicated bunch. Even at eight a.m., over a hundred people crowded behind the ropes that lined the sidewalk in front of the clinic. Some of the protesters sang. Others waved placards with messages like "Don't do it!" and "God loves you the way you are." It felt like every single one of them was staring at Molly as she braved the gauntlet between the street and the clinic.

"Hey, I like your sweater," one of the protesters shouted. It was a girl about Molly's age. Maybe a year or two older. The girl spoke with an air of presumed familiarity. Like they had been assigned as roommates at summer camp.

"I'm Lisa," the girl continued. "I can't imagine what you're feeling, but I want you to know there are lots of us who support you." The girl walked alongside Molly, just behind the ropes. "We think real beauty isn't something you can see from the outside, and real happiness doesn't come from how you look."

Molly had read an article about how to deal with protesters.

She said nothing and kept her eyes trained on the clinic.

"If you're having any second thoughts, I'm happy to talk. We could grab coffee. There's a great place around the corner."

Molly ignored the girl and focused on the clinic.

"It's a big decision. Think it through before you do anything you might regret."

The girl reached the end of the roped-off area, but that didn't stop her from calling out after Molly.

"Look me up when you realize drugs can't cure loneliness. I'm @lovingwhoiam."

And, finally, Molly was inside the clinic.

Molly's first thought when she came through the revolving doors was that it felt more like she was visiting a day spa at a fancy hotel than a medical facility. The clinic's atrium boasted high, vaulted ceilings topped with a glass dome that bathed the foyer's warm, earthen tones in natural light. The furniture was sleek, modern, and inviting. The couch's sensuous curves seemed to beckon for Molly to sit down, relax, and flip through a magazine.

Molly checked in for her appointment, and the receptionist advised her that a service coordinator would be with her momentarily. As Molly waited, she tapped her feet nervously on the reception room's elegant marble tile. The scent of lavender and lilac filled the air, and the sound of running water gurgled from a fountain built into an alcove. Molly glanced at a pamphlet on a nearby coffee table. On the pamphlet's cover, an attractive man and woman ran together through a field of wildflowers. Above the couple hung the words: "Welcome to the rest of your life."

After a few minutes, a tall, angular woman with a distinctly Scandinavian appearance emerged from a back room and approached Molly with a cordial smile.

"Good morning. Are you Molly Durham?" the woman asked. Molly answered in the affirmative. "I'm Janine, and I will be coordinating your visit. We are delighted to have you with us today."

The woman shook Molly's hand and then made a sweeping gesture toward a nearby staircase.

"Please accompany me upstairs to review the arrangements for your treatment."

Molly followed Janine up the stairs. As they ascended, Molly found that Janine's tiny waist was directly in her line of sight. Molly averted her eyes, only to find herself looking instead at Janine's shapely calves and expensive heels. To make matters worse, something about the staircase's angle of incline caused Molly to feel the full weight of her body, and she was forced to pause briefly at a bend to catch her breath. When they reached the second floor, Janine ushered Molly into a conference room. Janine sat down at the head of a stately boardroom table with a polished, granite top. Molly joined Janine, taking the seat to her left.

"You're scheduled this morning for your first Diovix treatment. As I'm sure you already know, Diovix is a revolutionary weight loss drug. Diovix will reset your body's metabolism and boost your biochemical functions to ensure that you maintain a perfectly calibrated, predetermined weight."

Janine produced a tablet and scrolled through the intake form Molly had submitted online.

"Given your height and frame, your target weight will be 120 pounds. No matter how much you eat or drink, Diovix will adjust your basal metabolic rate to keep you at your target weight. As long as you take Diovix, you will never have to worry about unwanted weight gain. You will always be exactly 120 pounds."

Janine paused for a few seconds before continuing in a firmer tone.

"I've told you the good. Now it's time for the bad.

"First, seventy-five percent of the patients who use Diovix do not experience any side effects, but for the other twenty-five percent, the side effects are severe and irreversible. Death is immediate; it is painful; and it is unstoppable. For a quarter of the population, Diovix is simply incompatible with their body chemistry. We don't know why it happens, but it does. And, despite our best efforts, we have not yet been able to screen our patients in advance to determine which ones will suffer adverse reactions. If you go forward with your Diovix treatment today, there is a twenty-five percent chance you will die.

"Second, Diovix does not work overnight. Given your current weight, it will take at least six months for you to reach your target weight. During that time, you will lose around five pounds each week, as your body gradually acclimates to the treatment. You need to have realistic expectations. You will not wake up tomorrow weighing 120 pounds. I promise you will get there eventually, but you will have to be patient during your journey.

"Third, Diovix wears off. To maintain your target weight, you will need a booster shot every two years. We do offer pre-payment packages. There's a five percent discount if you purchase ten years of booster shots and a ten percent discount if you purchase twenty years of booster shots, but there's no getting around the fact that Diovix is not simply a drug. It's a lifestyle.

"Fourth, we cannot make any guarantees about your figure. Some of our patients have grown accustomed to having larger breasts, ample curves, tapered waistlines, and heart-shaped bottoms. Diovix causes uniform weight loss across your entire body. It will keep you at 120 pounds, but that weight loss may come at the expense of your favorite features. For this reason, some of our patients choose to augment their Diovix treatments with plastic surgery. That, of course, is beyond the scope of the services we provide.

"Finally, the administration of the Diovix treatment is heavily regulated. There is a legally mandated one-hour 'cooling-off' period between when you sign your contract with us and the actual administration of the treatment. During this waiting period, you have the right to change your mind and withdraw from the treatment at any time, and you will receive a full refund for any amounts you have paid. No questions asked.

"We are also required by law to administer all our initial Diovix injections to patients in groups of four. This means that even if you do not personally experience any side effects from Diovix, you may witness someone else who does."

Janine lifted the tablet and pointed it at Molly's face. Molly could see the green light blinking on the tablet's camera.

"Molly Durham, having been fully informed about Diovix, including the substantial risk of death, do you wish to proceed with the treatment?"

"Yes, I do," Molly answered.

"Have you been advised of your legal right to withdraw from the treatment with a full refund at any time during the one-hour waiting period?"

"I have," Molly said.

"Have you been advised that you will receive the Diovix treatment with other patients and that you may witness someone else experiencing the side effects of Diovix?"

"I have," Molly repeated.

"Terrific," Janine said. "Let's take care of the paperwork, but first I'll need to see your ID."

Molly handed Janine her license, which Janine ran through a holo-scanner.

"It's just a formality," Janine said while the scanner whirred. "You wouldn't believe how many minors we get with fake IDs."

The holo-scanner chirped positively.

"Oh, happy birthday!" Janine gushed as she gave Molly back her license. "I got my first Diovix injection on my eighteenth birthday too."

Janine caught herself and returned to a demeanor of efficient professionalism.

"Next, we have the consent forms."

Janine placed the tablet in front of Molly, handed her a stylus, and guided her through a seemingly endless number of forms. Some of the forms disclosed the risks of treatment. Others released the clinic from liability. There was even something about arbitration.

"We're almost done," Janine said at last. "All that's left is payment for the procedure."

Molly reached into her purse and took out a thick envelope. She could see a flicker of annoyance in Janine's eyes, but Janine dutifully counted each well-worn bill. The envelope represented ten years of birthdays and Christmases, eight years of babysitting, and four years of double shifts at Subway.

When Janine finished counting, she led Molly to a changing room. Molly stuffed her belongings into a locker and put on a white terry cloth bathrobe. Afterward, Janine escorted Molly to a private examination room. The room had sage-green walls, charcoal cabinets, and what looked like an adjustable massage chair. Janine wished Molly well and said goodbye.

Almost as soon as Janine left, a nurse bustled into the room. The nurse asked Molly to remove her robe, sit down in the chair, and hold as still as possible. While Molly sat, the nurse activated a holo-scanner built into the chair. The scanner tickled Molly's skin as it ran slowly along the contours of her body. Periodically, the nurse's tablet chimed. Molly caught a glimpse of the tablet's screen when the nurse bent over to adjust the position of one of Molly's legs. The screen displayed Molly's height and weight, her blood pressure, the oxygen levels in her blood, and various figures relating to her bone structure, density, and mass. After the holo-scan, the nurse produced a small device and asked Molly to extend her right hand.

"This is called a lancet," the nurse explained. "It has a tiny needle that is going to prick your finger and extract a tiny bit of blood that the lab will use to formulate your Diovix shot. You'll just feel a little pinch."

The nurse took the blood sample, wrapped Molly's finger in a small bandage, and waited patiently while Molly got out of the chair and put her robe back on.

"Now we're off to the treatment room," the nurse said cheerfully.

The treatment room was the first place that felt like a doctor's office. It was a rectangular suite with four stainless steel reclining chairs. Flat-screen monitors were affixed to the wall directly in front of each chair.

Two patients were already there when Molly arrived. A portly Italian man in his forties sat in the first chair with his eyes scrunched shut. The man clung tightly to the armrests on his chair and muttered feverishly to himself. As Molly drew closer, she could make out the words.

"Holy Mary, Mother of God, pray for us sinners, now and at the hour of our death."

A heavyset young man sat in the second chair. He had chubby cheeks and an unfortunate buzz cut that made his head appear square shaped. Although he was seated, Molly could tell he was an enormous mountain of a man. He had broad shoulders, thick arms, tree trunks for legs, and a body shaped like a giant barrel. Given his size, his boyish features, and his terrible haircut, he reminded Molly of a baby-faced Frankenstein.

The nurse directed Molly to sit in the third chair.

"Thank God," the baby-faced Frankenstein said to Molly. "I was afraid I'd be stuck all by myself with the pope here."

Frankenstein jerked his head in the direction of the praying Italian.

"I'm Michael," the young man said. "Michael Schroeder. But everyone calls me Schroeds."

"I'm Molly," she replied.

"Oh, like the Unsinkable Molly Brown." Schroeds tapped rhythmically on the chair's armrest with his large, stubby fingers. "She was the OG badass, boss girl. Look her up."

Schroeds extended his arm toward Molly and offered her a fist bump.

"Nice to meet you, Molly," Schroeds said. "You go to Pitt?"

"In the fall." Molly bumped his fist. "I'm about to graduate high school."

"Allegheny High? Or Baldwin?"

"Neither. I'm just outside the city."

"Where?"

"Moon Township."

"I love it," Schroeds said, still tapping his stubby fingers. "I'm going to call you Molly the Moon Girl."

Molly laughed. She was grateful for the distraction.

The door opened, and a nurse entered with another patient. This one was a skinny redheaded woman in her early thirties. She wore dark sunglasses and a ballcap and carried herself like a celebrity who was ashamed of being caught somewhere scandalous by the paparazzi. The woman gave Molly and Schroeds a look of thinly veiled disgust as she passed by.

"Hey, we're not crazy about being stuck with you either," Schroeds snapped at the redhead. "I mean, I've had shits bigger than you."

"That's enough," the nurse snarled.

"Certainly, my dear Nurse Ratched." Schroeds made a loud farting noise and shot Molly a conspiratorial wink.

"I hope I don't get sent down to the principal's office," he whispered.

After the redhead had taken her seat, the nurse spoke to the four patients.

"You are all here for your first Diovix treatment. State law requires that we play a video for you during the waiting period that discusses the potential side effects of Diovix. You have the right, but not the obligation, to watch this video."

The nurse walked down the line of chairs and handed earbuds to each of the patients.

"Psh," Schroeds hissed, tossing the earbuds onto a metal tray affixed to his chair. "I already saw everything I needed to make my decision when I looked in the mirror this morning."

Molly glanced up at the screen in front of her. A man in a

white lab coat sat behind a wooden desk and spoke to the camera with the utmost seriousness. After a moment's hesitation, Molly set her earbuds down on her chair's metal tray.

"You ever watch Hella Dumb?" Schroeds asked Molly.

"Never heard of it."

"Posted a great one last week. It's my favorite streamer." Schroeds reached into his bathrobe's pocket and produced a cell phone. "Just look at this." He clicked an app, flipped his phone to the side, and held it out for Molly to see. "It's a zoo in China," Schroeds narrated. "All their pandas died, so they painted these Chow Chows white and black and tried to pass them off as pandas."

Molly laughed. Those dogs weren't going to fool anyone.

"I got a brilliant idea when I saw this," Schroeds bragged. "You have any little brothers or sisters?"

"Only child, but I babysit for the neighbors."

"Perfect," Schroeds said. "I want you to picture it in your head. Close your eyes. Take a deep breath. Now imagine you're taking the neighbors' kids to the zoo. What are their names, by the way?"

"Liam and Emily."

"So you're taking Liam and Emily to the zoo, but instead of lions and tigers and elephants, the entire zoo is full of puppies painted to look like other animals. There's a golden retriever dyed with stripes to look like a tiger, a mastiff shaved to look like a lion, a greyhound speckled to look like a leopard, and a chihuahua with little white spots like a fawn. And the poodle puppies are the best. They've been trimmed and colored to look like zebras, camels, and even giraffes."

Schroeds clasped Molly's arm with his gigantic palm. Molly

opened her eyes and looked at him.

"But instead of just watching the animals, like at a regular zoo, the kids at my zoo can play with my puppies for as long as they want."

Schroeds's baby face was full of earnest excitement.

"And when I make my first billion dollars off my puppy zoo franchise, I'll whisk you away to the Oscars in a flying car."

"Why would the Puppy Zoo King take me to the Oscars?" Molly asked.

"Because you're gonna star in all the movies I produce, duh."

Before Molly could respond, Schroeds was flipping through more reels.

"Have you ever seen 'Interviews with Garden Gnomes'? Or, how about Gunther Walz's mini-histories? My favorites are his 'Condensed Chronicle of Condensed Milk' and his 'Abridged Account of the Dixon Bridge Disaster.'"

"What part of the internet do you lurk?"

"The best part," Schroeds bragged.

Schroeds showed Molly a series of reels. Of course, he narrated each one enthusiastically. They were in the middle of watching a crudely drawn, animated horse explain why there aren't any unicorns when a doctor and four nurses entered the waiting room. Schroeds flipped his phone off and stowed it back in the pocket of his robe.

The doctor walked down the line of chairs asking each patient the same question: "You have now completed the one-hour waiting period. Do you still wish to proceed with the Diovix treatment?"

"Yes," mumbled the Italian.

"Hell, yeah," shouted Schroeds.

"Yes, sir," answered Molly.

"Uh-huh," nodded the redhead.

The doctor returned to the first chair. One of the nurses presented a tray with four syringes. Another nurse rolled up the sleeve of the Italian's bathrobe. The Italian made the sign of the cross with his free hand and began praying even more fervently.

"Hail Mary, full of grace, the Lord is with thee. Blessed art thou amongst women and blessed is the fruit of thy womb, Jesus."

The doctor injected the syringe into the exposed underside of the Italian's arm. The Italian stopped praying and sat absolutely still. Then, he opened his eyes slowly and exhaled loudly.

"Congratulations, Mr. Rossi," the doctor said. "Betsy will show you to the recovery room."

A nurse helped the Italian to his feet, and they exited the waiting room together.

The doctor moved on to the second chair.

"Give me a hit of that Fountain of Youth," Schroeds said. The doctor raised a syringe and studied it briefly while a nurse rolled up Schroeds's sleeve. Schroeds smiled at Molly.

"Geronimo!" he exclaimed.

The doctor injected the syringe into the underside of Schroeds's arm. Schroeds sat motionless for a moment. Then, he looked down at his hand.

"Why can't I—" Schroeds said. His arm was trembling.

"I'm sorry, son." The doctor gripped Schroeds tightly on the shoulder.

That's when all chaos broke loose. Schroeds vomited all over the front of his terry cloth robe and started convulsing uncontrollably. Every part of his body quivered, and his spine arched so forcefully that only the back of his Frankenstein head remained touching his chair.

"Oh, my God!" the redhead shrieked. She leaped to her feet so fast the sunglasses flew off her face.

Schroeds continued shaking violently. The doctor and nurses tried to hold him down, but he was too big and too powerful for them to control. His giant body shuddered, and he tossed one of the nurses aside like a bull tossing a rider at a rodeo.

"Let me out!" the redhead screamed.

Schroeds's whole body rocked and rattled and twisted like a ship on rough seas. Somehow, he managed to turn himself onto his side, facing Molly.

"Let me out!" the redhead repeated before collapsing in hysterics onto the floor.

"Get her out of here," the doctor barked at one of the nurses.

Schroeds let out a piteous, guttural howl.

"I don't want to," the redhead sobbed as a nurse hoisted her to her feet. "You can't make me."

Schroeds was staring directly at Molly. He tried to reach his hand out toward her, but it flopped aimlessly in awkward spasms.

The redhead emitted an ear-shattering screech.

"I said get her out of here!" the doctor yelled.

"Just my luck," Schroeds groaned.

The nurse shoved the redhead out the door.

And then Schroeds gazed at Molly with empty eyes.

The doctor grimaced, as if he had felt a sudden stab of pain. Then, he pushed a button on the wall. Almost immediately, the door popped open, and two attendants came in pushing a gurney. The attendants, the doctor, and the nurses lifted Schroeds's body out of the chair and laid him gently on the gurney. Molly could tell from the color of his robe that Schroeds had pissed himself.

"Notify the next of kin," the doctor instructed one of the nurses. The attendants wheeled Schroeds's body out. A nurse followed them.

"Do you wish to proceed with the treatment?" The doctor's voice was calm and professional, and it took Molly a moment to realize he was speaking to her.

"It's okay if you need to reschedule."

"No," Molly said in a quiet voice. "Give it to me. Please. I just want it to be over. One way or the other."

The last remaining nurse produced a syringe and handed it to the doctor.

"Are you sure?" the doctor asked.

"Yes," Molly replied.

The nurse rolled up Molly's sleeve, and the doctor gave Molly the injection. Molly sat quietly and then sighed in relief.

Molly could only remember snippets of what happened next. The doctor congratulated her. The nurse guided her into the recovery ward. Janine reappeared and handed her a sheet full of instructions. Then, suddenly, Molly was outside, in front of the clinic, stumbling toward a waiting rideshare.

"Hey, sweater girl," shouted a familiar voice. "I'm glad you made it, but you'll see. Diovix can't cure loneliness. Look me up when the fantasy wears off. It's @lovingwhoiam."

The next thing Molly knew, she was crossing the Liberty Bridge in the back seat of a rideshare. Molly felt both amped up and thoroughly exhausted. She leaned her head against the window and gazed out across the Monongahela River. There, at the edge of the horizon, just beyond the range of waking sight, she could almost see a glimmer of happiness.

* * *

Discussion Questions

1. Gastric Band Surgery, Ozempic, and their competitors all carry side effect risks, including death. How are the risks of current treatments the same, or different, than the side effect of death in the story? Are we just haggling over acceptable amounts of death in exchange for treatment?
2. Do you think the government regulations in the story—a one-hour waiting period and being forced to be in a room with others who get the treatment—are appropriate? What (*if any*) government regulations would you put into place?
3. It can certainly be argued that medical weight loss, while it carries risk, carries less risk than being severely overweight. However, what if the person is not overweight but simply wants to preemptively take Diovix to ensure they will never be overweight?
4. Do you think the protestors are right (*or should be allowed*) to be in front of the clinic attempting to guilt patients into changing their mind?
5. Can a person who has never been severely overweight fairly judge (*or regulate*) those who take Diovix? Is this equally true for other forms of medical or quality-of-life treatments?

* * *

The Survival Artist

Peter Mare

* * *

<u>**Content Disclosure**</u>: None

* * *

In the *Land of Get and Have*, Eve had to work hard to survive.

She slept in the open, under the sky, every night. But she was never cold because she had all she needed to stay warm. Above her, a million stars swam slowly together in a sea of light and shadow, and the moon passed through its phases in a gentle, constant rhythm. But Eve never noticed the stars and she took no comfort in the moon's rhythmic journey.

For even at night, she thought only of her search.

By day, she scanned the forest whose leaves danced together in gentle breezes. She searched through the desert of brightly colored sands and stone. And she scoured the shores of the turquoise sea.

But Eve never saw the dancing leaves, or the textures of the land, or even the shimmering water. For her, the work of survival required all of her attention. And in the *Land of Get and Have*, to survive meant finding and keeping glitter-stones.

No one knew how long it had been this way. But all the people of *Get and Have* depended on the precious and rare glitter-stones for survival. And no one was better at finding them than Eve.

The magic of the glitter-stones was powerful and undeniable. A person with enough stones never grew hungry, never felt the chill of a cold night, and never had to endure the ache of loneliness. They felt no pain, no sadness, and no fear. No fear that is, except the fear of losing a glitter-stone.

Eve felt this fear through her bones. It consumed her when she slept. It burned in her when she woke. But she did not let it paralyze her. On the contrary, she used it to fuel her search. It was through her determination that she had become more skilled than anyone at finding and keeping glitter-stones.

Her hunting tricks were secrets she held close. And the most important skill she had learned was training her eyes to ignore everything but glitter-stones. She had even learned to look right through trees and rocks to see the stone hiding on the other side.

But the days when Eve could easily find glitter-stones under rocks or beside trees were long gone. Now the best place to find them was in the hands of other people. And because of this, Eve had learned how to see right through people to the stones they concealed in their pockets.

The best time to find stones was after dark when they would stop moving and settle down for the night. If Eve crept very slowly and quietly, she could take them for her collection before they had the chance to run away.

In this way, Eve had collected more glitter-stones than anyone else, and as long as she kept searching and getting, she would have all she needed to survive.

* * *

Then one day something very strange happened. It had been a long time since Eve had seen another person. Glitter-stones were all she needed, and they were the only thing she noticed.

But on this day, when she had her head hung low, scanning the ground in the vain hope of finding her treasure, something that was not a glitter-stone caught her eye, and Eve looked up.

The sudden movement made her dizzy and she nearly toppled over. But what confused her even more was the awareness that she was standing on the shore of a great sea. And, as she peered down the beach, she saw that a person was moving toward her.

The person was doing the strangest thing. He or she, for Eve could not tell which, was dancing in the waves. Eve blinked several times for the sight was so confounding. She tried to look down to continue her search, but something made her look up again.

As the stranger stopped dancing and turned to walk up the beach, toward the forest, Eve realized what was wrong. The stranger carried no glitter-stones!

How could it be? How could this stranger survive without a single glitter-stone to take away the pangs of hunger, the cold of night, and the various other aches that were harder to describe, and whose names Eve had long since forgotten?

In a flash of insight, Eve realized that this stranger must have a kind of magic that kept glitter-stones hidden. Perhaps a magic bag that concealed them from even Eve's trained eyes.

Her curiosity turned to suspicion and then to anger and she decided that she would follow this stranger to discover the secret of their magic.

Eve followed close behind but was careful to stay hidden behind trees and rocks. It was very disorientating because suddenly she had to see the very things she had learned to ignore.

After a journey of some distance, the stranger stopped along the banks of a trickling stream. The stranger sat down and pulled out a bag and started searching through it.

Aha! Eve thought. That must be the magic bag.

And just as Eve was about to leap out and confront them, the stranger pulled something from the bag. But it was not a glitter-stone.

At first, the thing seemed so useless and insignificant that Eve couldn't focus on it. After some time, her eyes adjusted and she saw that the stranger was holding a stick, an ordinary stick with the end cut to a fine point and blacked in a fire.

Next, the stranger approached a grove of birch trees and started collecting fallen bark. Then they walked to the stream and collected a pile of stones that they placed near the birch bark. Slowly and with great care not to crack the bark, the stranger set the pieces in the water and placed stones along their edges to hold them flat. Next, the stranger began to collect wood to make a fire.

Eve was perplexed and distraught to see the stranger labor long and hard searching for dry wood. Why do they need a fire to keep warm? Could it be that there really are no glitter-stones hiding in that bag?

After finally starting a fire, the stranger turned to collecting leaves for tea and nibbling on nuts and dried fruit. After the sun had set, the stranger wrapped up in a blanket and fell asleep by the fire.

Hours passed. Once she was sure the stranger was in a deep sleep, Eve crept down to the fire. She snatched the bag and slinked back to her hiding place. Once hidden, she shoved her hand in and searched frantically for a glitter-stone. But there was nothing in the bag except flat pieces of birch bark. Outraged, Eve threw the bag to the ground. She was so confused. How did this stranger survive without glitter-stones?

Why would anyone choose to toil in the cold water just to flatten pieces of bark? Why spend hours building a fire for warmth and searching for food when a glitter-stone could take away hunger and cold?

But what confused Eve the most, more than anything she had seen the stranger do, were the questions themselves, and that they suddenly mattered. Why were her precious glitter-stones not relieving the growing ache in her heart? Why was their magic not working to quiet the curiosity stirring in her mind? Perhaps the magic this stranger wielded was greater and more dangerous than Eve had imagined.

It was at this point that something caught Eve's eye. In the moonlight, she saw that one of the birch barks had fallen from the bag.

As she knelt down to look more closely, she gasped at what she saw. Staring back at her, in shades of black charcoal against the white of the bark, was the image of her own face.

Eve's heart stopped. She could not contain herself and a cry burst from her mouth like no sound she had ever made before.

She grabbed the bag of bark drawings and ran. She ran without stopping. Though it was night, the moon was full and she saw it. And she saw its light on every tree and every stone.

She didn't trip or stumble, and the more she ran, the more she found her stride. She ran long and hard through the forest until she reached the shore. And as she emerged from the trees, she saw the first glimmer of sunlight rising above the sea. It was the first sunrise she had noticed in a very long time.

Eve collapsed onto the sand. It was cold underneath her, but the first rays from the sun were already warming her skin. She looked at the bag that was still in her hands and pulled out the stack of birch-bark drawings. She stared at the image of her face. It was the face of someone so focused on what she wanted that she couldn't see the artist sitting in front of her, sketching her likeness.

There was no peace in that face.

And Eve's was not the only face. Other drawings held the faces of people with a similar expression. But there were also people who looked directly at the artist. Some of these faces were smiling, some crying, some laughing, some with expressions that were a mystery to Eve.

That was not all. There were strange creatures that Eve did not recognize. Some with four legs, some with wings, some with no legs at all. And there were leaves and flowers and the shore of a great sea.

It was at this moment that Eve realized she did not have her glitter-stones. She must have dropped them as she was running, as she was finding her way through the moonlit forest.

She held her breath and waited for it. The feeling of panic, of terror, that she knew would rise up any moment.

But the panic did not come.

Instead, she found herself looking at the light on the sea. She stood and walked to the water's edge. She let the waves reach up to her toes. The water was cold, but she didn't mind.

And the color of the water was starting to shine through. That color had always been there, but now, somehow, it was as if Eve was seeing it for the first time. And in that color, she saw something new, something she didn't understand.

She knew she must find the artist again. She didn't know why, but she yearned to watch this stranger sketch her world. She had run so far in the night. And she didn't know how to find her way in this new world that she saw all around her.

And then it hit her. She felt hungry and lonely. It was almost more than she could bear, worse than the feeling of being without her glitter-stones. But Eve already knew that, even if she could find her old stones, their magic would no longer work for her.

All around her more and more of a world appeared. She walked along the shore and soon came to the remnants of a fire. The coals were cold and she could see that whoever built the fire had not been there for days.

But in the ashes was a sharpened stick with one end blackened by coals. And leading from the fire was a faint trail of footsteps pointing into the woods.

Without a moment's hesitation, and with her head held high, so she could see the path ahead, Eve disappeared into the forest.

* * *

Discussion Questions

1. What are the similarities and differences between the glitter-stones and money?
2. The story says, "She had even learned to look right through trees and rocks to see the stone hiding on the other side." What does this mean in relation to the allegory? What about when the story says, "Eve had learned how to see right through people to the stones they concealed in their pockets."?
3. Eve says she saw the stranger "dancing in the waves" and later "toil in the cold water." If you asked the stranger, how might they describe these two actions? Would you draw such a clear distinction between "dancing" and "toiling"?
4. The narrator tells us "...even if she could find her old stones, their magic would no longer work for her." Why wouldn't the magic work for Eve again if they worked for her in the past?
5. Eve uses the glitter-stones to keep herself from getting cold, while the stranger uses fire from collected wood. If both require work, what is the difference between the two methods of staying warm?

* * *

Eleven Things I Have Left Now That My Daughter Is Gone

Vickie Fang

* * *

<u>**Content Disclosure**</u>: Strong Language, Sexual Situations, Substance Addiction Themes

* * *

1. The Walk Down Wilkins

When she was a baby, I used to hold her in my arms and walk down the worst part of Baltimore, Wilkins Avenue. Warm feel of her up close to my chest, little patch of blond hair against my neck, I walked right by those other females, lying passed out on their front stoops or sitting on the curb waiting for their regulars. I thought: Let the corner boys ride their bikes. I thought: Let the old men drive that strip with their eyes all over me. There wasn't anything I was going to buy from the boys and nothing I was going to sell to those men either. I was holding my baby in front of the world like I was saying, "This is mine. This little Promise is mine. And she is better than all of you."

And what did the world think? I didn't even notice. We were our own little two-girl parade. Fat whore and fat baby—call us that—and both of us sailing down that street like a door had been thrown wide open and we could go anywhere we wanted.

Those days and that feeling didn't last. Of course they didn't. But I let myself think they would. I never even left Wilkins, but when I walked with Promise, the clouds rolled over us like the first day of creation, and I really believed that my life had started all over again.

* * *

2. Five Clean Years

Five years go by: no dope, no whoring, no anything but keeping my baby safe. Her lying up in bed with me at night, me right beside her. But outside? A whole parade of cars with their lights crawling up the wall and across the ceiling. Nonstop men driving in from the county looking for women, especially the White ones. I'd lie there for hours, thinking about what they wanted and ask myself the same question: Out of all the sad things in the world, what was the worst—to go out to that street and get back in those cars, or to lie there in the dark, remembering?

One time Promise woke up and asked me what the lights were, and I said they were the stars. I said they crossed the sky above us, and we didn't care because we were like fish in the sea. And for a long time after that, when she got under the blankets, she wiggled like she thought a fish would, pointed her baby hand up, and said, "Stars." It was funny to her.

Promise'd laugh at the lights, and I'd stare into the dark and see my mother. She'd say, "Be good girls." My sister and I were eight and nine years old, but we knew we had to lay down. She watched for that—then she left and the men came in. My sister was in a bed beside mine, not looking at me, not talking. Not saying anything about what happened in that room afterward either because when men climb on top of you like that, you turn into dead girls.

Sometimes the men would be late, and I would start to hope they weren't coming, make believe that my mother said she didn't want their money anymore. Maybe my sister was hoping, too, but Mother never did send the men away from us, not one time. It's when you're clean and lying in your own bed with your baby that you remember what your mother did to you. It might be worse than going back out there and getting in cars again to lie there in the dark and think about how it all got started.

So all those nights were not the good thing I wanted them to be because Promise was a child asleep, and I was a woman caught on a train I could never get off of. That was the kind of daughter she was to me. That was the kind of mother I was to her.

* * *

3. As the World Turns
And the best times were when I was not using so much, so I was home and awake when Promise came back from kindergarten or first grade. I'd be watching *As the World Turns* with the Sunbeam bread and Welch's grape jelly all ready. She'd climb up on the sofa with me, and the two of us would go to Oakfield together with Lily and Holden. We'd eat so many jelly sandwiches we'd be too full for dinner.

A couple of times, prostitutes with big hair and feather boas came on those shows. Those bitches were the strangest thing on

TV, all of them so proud of themselves, talking tough. They wisecracked with everybody, even the police. What would women like that think of me, going on my dates wearing sweatpants and an old sweater, not knowing any special words at all, just mumbling the same things I heard my mother say?

What would Promise think?

The days got too long when she was in school, and all I could do was sit at home and remember old times. Even getting in the cars again was better than that.

* * *

4. Letter from School

"I had a big day today!" That was my Promise talking on a dead cell phone. I'd found it in a lot off North Washington one night and gave it to her for a toy.

"I got a letter." She wasn't looking at me when she said that. She was off in her own world—like usual when she got home from school. I was lying down on the sofa with my eyes closed, but I knew what she was doing. She was squatting in the corner near the radiator, rooting around in her backpack. "The important part is right here. Promise A. Lewis, the third grade. OLSAT test of Mental Maturity."

I opened my eyes and looked at her when I heard that.

"On a scale of one to nine, score nine!"

My score when I was her age.

"That means I'm smart."

The school called when I got my nine, and my mother shook me when she got off the phone. My head was bouncing off the wall, and she was saying, "I'm not going down there for any goddamned conference!" I never did find out what they wanted to talk to her about, and it wasn't until I was grown up that I realized she was afraid the school would find out about those men.

"Don't worry," I told Promise. "Your mommy will go to the conference," but I put my hand up over some pick marks on my face when I said it. I was using hard by then and getting into cars when she was home too. Promise didn't answer. She didn't like me to interrupt when she was talking on her phone.

"And I have another grand announcement to make," she said. "I, Promise A. Lewis, have been accepted to the Superior Learners Program." And that's when she put her phone down and looked at me for once. "I'm going to a new school, Mom!"

So that's what the school wanted to talk to my mother about—sending me somewhere superior.

"I want to go too!" I said. First thing out of my mouth; I don't know why I said it. "I want to go to that school."

And she was grinning, saying, no, no parents allowed. And I told her why not? I got the same score when I was her age, and I probably would have gotten to go to that school if my mother had let me, and Promise shook her head and said no I couldn't. No way. She smiled like the whole idea of me being smart too was some kind of a joke. That hurt me a little bit, but I didn't let her know. I walked over and leaned down, fixing her sweater for her, where she had it buttoned wrong. "Did you go around all day looking like that?" I asked her.

She just shrugged.

I said, "Better be careful in that new school. You walk around looking like that, and everybody's going to say, 'Look at that stupid girl. There goes stupid old Promise.'" I think I sang it a little. "Stupid old Promise."

She turned all the way around then and leaned forward so the top of her head was against the radiator, and I knew she wasn't going to say another word to me, not anytime soon. The way she was squatting on that patch of old brown carpet and wrapping her arms around her shins, she looked like a little bird, hunched over in winter. I rubbed her back for a while, felt the bumps on her spine. "Anyway, one of us gets to go," I told her. Finally, she nodded her head a little bit, yes.

* * *

5. It's Academic Superbowl

Almost midnight walking back to Wilkins. Promise in the fifth grade by then, but holding my hand the whole way.

"You scared?"

"No, Mommy."

Streets getting dirtier, plastic bags in the trees, broken glass. Cars coming in from Essex, Dundalk, anywhere else people want women and dope.

After a while, I said, "It's different in Harbor East."

"Yeah, better."

"Why do they call it Harbor East? What's wrong with East Harbor?"

"Sounds fancier."

"You like that? Those big townhouses? All that... all that fancy shit at the It's Academic meeting?"

Looked me right in the eye. "Yep."

We'd got to where the corner boys were making long, slow circles on their bikes. "Charm City." You could hear them calling it out. "Charm City." And then, "Girl." Charm City was what they were calling pot this week. Girl was heroin. I touched the ten-dollar bill folded in my pocket, realized Promise was watching me while I watched them.

"You going to win at the Academic Superbowl?"

"Impossible to say."

"First time *you* ever had any trouble saying anything."

Four or five men leaning against Martini's wall, smoking, watching. Soon I'd get her home, come back out again.

"I can get a ride."

"What?"

"You don't have to take me to any more parents' meetings. It's too far from the bus stop, and I don't need you there anyway."

I didn't say anything for a minute. Felt the coldness start seeping down my spine while I thought about what I looked like to those other kids and their parents. Eyes a little bloodshot, maybe. Was I scratching? Smoke enough crack and you're always scratching yourself. Everybody else dressed up so nice and poor Promise stuck with me. "You don't want me to come to any more parents' meetings?"

She shook her head.

"Maybe you don't even want me around at your old Superbowl either."

"You never come to anything anyway."

"Liar. I came all the way to Harbor East tonight."

"Cause the coach finally called you! You never came to one single meet this whole goddamned year."

But it was something for school—nobody told me parents were supposed to come.

That's what I wanted to say.

Or else, *When did you start hating me?*

Most of all, *Gonna beat your ass if you cuss at me again!*

What I did say was, "If you're so smart, I guess you don't need me anyway."

And she said, "Maybe not."

I couldn't look at her, just stared out at the street. Then I swallowed all my hurt and put my hand on her shoulder. "It's okay, baby girl. I don't need to go; I already know you're going to win." At least, I hope that's what I did. Some things are too hard to remember.

Anyway, I was back on the corner five minutes after I got her home. And a minute after that, I was in a little crowd behind a tall wood fence, one of the boys putting a crack pipe in my hand. That part of town, Black, White, it didn't matter—we all knew how to do it up. And when I told them my girl was about to win a national contest, everybody said they were proud of me.

* * *

6. Gummy Bear Momma

But we had good times too. My Promise loved candy, and I always tried to get her some no matter what. I was dope sick one time, so bad my hands were shaking and my stomach was like a bucket of wet mud, and still all I could think about was how I hadn't seen Promise for a week. I asked the drug man if I could pay $8.50 instead of ten so I could get my child some gummy bears. I was so sick I was stuttering, and people laughed when they heard me beg.

I don't know why, but I thought about her, and I left the line and bought the gummy bears instead. I ran back to Promise and watched her light up like a Christmas tree when I put those bears in her hand. Maybe she thought her momma had forgot about her, and there I was, giving her candy.

"Love you, Mommy!"

"Love you, Promise!" And then I got back out of there as fast as I could. I was heaving when I grabbed old Jimmy Mitchell, cane and all, and gave him a hand job for three dollars against the fence on Harmison so I could buy my dope.

I was lucky. The line had broken up while I was gone, but it got started again. I had vomit starting up in my throat, but there were people actually clapping when they saw me come back. Somebody even called me "Gummy Bear Momma." You have to have your own child to know why I wanted to cry right then, I felt so good.

And for a long time afterward, whenever I felt bad, I used to ask Promise, "Who buys you the gummy bears?" and she would say, "My momma does." That is one thing I will always remember.

* * *

7. No Respect

My mother slapped me when I was nearly thirty years old. Slapped my face twice right in front of Martini's with a bunch of men watching. And the guys were yelling out, "Oh god *damn!*" and "Take it easy, momma, that's your girl!" But you know they were all poking each other and laughing, too, especially when she called me a dumb-bitch-whore, and I started crying and saying I was sorry like I was a little kid again.

She and my sister were keeping Promise because I didn't have anywhere to live. My mother'd gone all the way down to Pratt Street and searched the abandonminiums—junkies, rats, rotten floors, and all—looking for me. Soon as she saw me: "Promise told me to go to hell! What are you going to do about her? She cussed her own grandmother."

And me: "Well, what did you do to her? What did you do to make my girl cuss you?"

That's when she hit me, and we both started screaming, but she could always scream louder than I could, and could always scare me too. "That girl's got no respect!" my mother screamed at me. "Nobody can stop her!"

I was still crying and wiping snot off my face, but when she said that about Promise, I stopped and stared. And I saw that the woman who used to be the most powerful person in the world wasn't so strong anymore. She was skinny and old, hardly able to walk her hip was so bad, and she was screaming because she was afraid. My mother was afraid of my child.

And I guess she knew what I was thinking almost as soon as I did because when she saw the way I was staring at her, she turned around fast and left. She looked like some kind of animal, an old rat staggering along on its hind legs, trying to find her way down that sad, ugly street with no idea of what was going on.

I would have followed her if I could have. I would have followed her the rest of my life with my arms around her and never let go, but she didn't want me. And I knew my own daughter wouldn't so much as cross the street for her. I made sure to catch up with Promise that night, and slam her hard against the side of the house.

I told her I knew what she was doing, and I said, "You may not be afraid of your grandma, but you will sure as hell be afraid of me." I was going to say more and hit her too, but the look on her face stopped me. Promise ran inside. I sat down on the steps, looked at my hands. She thought I was an enemy to her, but she didn't know it was my own mother I'd gone against.

When my mother had looked scared, there was a moment when I felt like Promise and I were winning something. I could have jumped up and down and shouted my child's name right there on the sidewalk. Even when I saw her at the house, a part of me wanted to say I loved her about a thousand times, but I didn't. I respected my mother too much.

* * *

8. World on a String

By the time she was in the eleventh grade, I wasn't using anymore, just drinking. I'd found a boyfriend, Tony, who took care of things, and we had a room in the basement for Promise. I was so excited when she came back that I even had the idea we might watch TV together like we did when she was in kindergarten, me with my arm around her, both of us eating jelly sandwiches again. But I didn't know Promise like my mother knew me, and I didn't know how to control her either.

She was gone most of the time with her special school things. I tried to ask her about them, but I never got anywhere. And one night after Tony'd knocked back three or four 40s, he thought he'd give it a try. He picked up her French book and said, "Parlez vous Francais?" When she didn't answer, he started roaming around, picking up the other books and calling out their titles, acting like a little kid trying to get attention while she stood with her back to him. He picked one up and said, "*The Picture of Dorian Gray and Other Writings* by Mr. Oscar Wilde. You know what this is, Promise? You pay attention, baby girl. This is the kind of book they read in college."

And while I said, "Is that right?" to be polite, she fished two quarters out of her pocket and gave them to me. I took them like an idiot.

"You win," Promise said. "He does know how to read." She said it like we'd made a bet. "He doesn't read well, but enough to count as literate. He even knows how to say 'college.' Who'd'a thought?"

Tony just stood there drunk and staring, and then when he said, "I can read. Who said I couldn't read?" Promise bust out laughing. Afterward, I don't think I ever did get him to believe that Promise and I weren't making fun of him behind his back, calling him ignorant and making up bets. From that day on, he stayed as far as he could from Promise. That meant I couldn't have too much to do with her either since I had to show him I was on his side.

It wasn't long before I got used to not talking to my daughter except to tell her to cover up her titties better. And when my sister came by, wanting to know where Promise was at, I tried to explain that things were different with these girls now, some of them, anyway.

When we were young, we knew better than to talk back. We respected grown people because we knew we depended on them. We even respected those men. After all, they only wanted to hold us for a while and put their thing inside. Then they paid their money. Besides, if we didn't know how to forgive and be grateful, how could we have survived?

A lot of people still understand that. My sister had four daughters, and they all knew how to act. But Promise had been born with the world on a string. She carried on like she hated us all.

* * *

9. Leaving Me

Promise's grandmother didn't come with us to the Golden Corral. She was mad because when Promise got her awards, she didn't thank her family for all we'd done for her; she only thanked her teachers. And did Promise apologize or try to make an old woman feel better? Hardly. All she did was say, "Well, Happy Graduation to me," with a big smile on her face. And no surprise that Tony didn't come either. I hardly saw him anymore, and I already knew I'd have to find a new place to live pretty soon.

Still, it had been a big group in my nephew's car. One of

Promise's cousins had to sit in her sister's lap, and Promise was so happy she couldn't stop talking. Even when we were inside with our food, she wouldn't slow down, gave a whole speech about her scholarships and how she won them. My sister patted my leg and told me I'd done a good job. "You don't see any of these other knuckleheads going to college," she told me. "Promise is something else."

"She's getting a big head," I said, but I could feel my own face about to crack open, smiling. I was thinking back to when I used to walk down the street with my little baby in my arms, and it felt like the whole world was just waiting to see what we did with our lives. I didn't know I could still feel like that again. I wanted to open my mouth and crow.

"Hey, Promise," I called out, "what's it going to be? Medicine or law? Maybe you'll be a doctor *and* a lawyer."

But two of her cousins were already saying, "Journalism!" And Promise looked disgusted with me.

"Jour-no-lism, remember? That's why I'm going to Columbia. Remember? The plan since I was ten, remember?"

"But that didn't mean anything!"

The look on her face got a whole lot worse. "I guess nothing I ever said meant anything to you."

"But, Columbia's in New York," I said. "That's what you told me."

"Well good for you. You did remember one thing right." But then the ugliness went out of her face as fast as it had come in, and nothing but sadness took its place. "You should have been listening. I'm going to New York."

Sometimes I still think about how I let Promise go without even knowing what she wanted or which school she picked, and I'm pretty sure she was looking at me like that because she was sorry for both of us.

I didn't feel sorry then, though. I didn't feel anything else either. I just sat there knowing my time was up. My child was leaving me, and my insides had all turned to stone.

* * *

10. My Sister's Girls Stayed with Her

Out of the six children my sister had, she's got one son that's been killed already. The other boy is in an Idaho penitentiary with sixteen more years to go before he can even try for parole. Her daughters are all right here, though. Sometimes, all of us go out to Wilkins together. We let the girls take the better tricks, and we try to remember to write down the license plate numbers. We tell the girls to use condoms, too, and they say we nag, but they know it's because we love them. Sometimes my sister tells them they should go to college like Promise, but they never listen.

On Mother's Day, there's always a party for my sister and mother. One of them usually gets a mug or a shirt with "World's Greatest Mom" or "World's Greatest Grandma" on it. A bunch of us spend the whole morning cooking together, and it's a good day—that's what I try to think, anyway. But Promise never even sends a card, and when the call comes it's always from my nephew in prison. A lot of time, I'm out on the street by myself, too, especially in winter, while my sister sits at home with her grandkids crawling all over her. When they can, her girls try to take care of her. They don't like their mother to have to work.

* * *

11. Promise Visits

It's been eight years since Promise left for college, four years since she graduated and decided to stay in New York to work in the "media." She comes to see me every year or two, but the visits are always short and make me disappointed. I try to get her to remember the good times. Once, I said something about when she won the It's Academic Superbowl, and she got so angry at me for not going. I wish somebody had told me then that I had a child who wanted me to be with her more. I would have done things so different.

After that, I thought I needed to explain about my life and how I did the best I could. I had plenty of time, more than a year, to figure out what to say. But then I'd think about Promise and all she had going on, and it hurt too much to talk about how pitiful my own life had been. I tried another way, though. I tried to look at the good side and show Promise it all turned out for the best.

Next time she came to see me I asked her did she know why I named her Promise? She said no, and I told her it was because I made a promise to her when she was born: She wouldn't live the way I did. Her life would turn out better.

"And it came true!" I said. I remember feeling excited and even proud when I finally said it. I'd never told anyone before, and I'd been planning for months to tell it to her. I had my arms coming open like we were going to hug each other. "That's the wonderful thing, Promise. It came true."

"I'm the one who made it come true," she told me. We looked at each other again. I saw the set of her face and knew what a fool I'd been. I'd been hoping she'd say I was a good mother, or give me some credit for the way she turned out, but the truth was I didn't have any reason to hope for something like that. I only had reason to feel ashamed.

Later, right before she left, she asked why I never did anything with my life. I just told her that once you get started in a certain direction it's hard to change. She nodded.

"Shouldn't have taken that first drug," she said.

"Learn from my mistakes," I told her. She didn't need to know that I'd been ten years old the first time, or that it was her grandmother who put the needle in my helpless arm. Anyway, Promise hugged me before she left.

I went out with one of my nieces that night. It was cold, and we passed a bottle of vodka back and forth in the same weedy lot off North Washington where I'd found Promise's cell phone so many years ago. Finally, an old minivan pulled up, and she went running for it. Her Thursday night guy. He'd give her an extra twenty dollars sometimes, call her "my lady." She called him "the best man in Baltimore." Once she took off, safe with her regular, I could rest easy, get a couple Xanax out of my coat pocket, and wash them down with the last of the vodka.

Maybe an hour later, a trick pulled over for me. He looked a little disappointed when he got up close, but he still let me in. Even asked me how I was doing while he turned up the Ravens game on the radio. The guy had spots on his face, hardly any nose, kind of like a turtle.

"Feeling good," I told him. "Saw my daughter today."

Old Turtle Face turned the radio back down again. "Daughter?" he said. "You got a daughter?"

Felt something like lightning run through my body. "Yeah," I told him. "I got a daughter."

Man had the nerve to ask what she looked like.

Really? What did that sweet, sweet baby snuggling in my arms look like? Or the proudest, most beautiful girl in the world, jumping up and down because she'd just won the It's Academic Superbowl? The one who didn't know I was watching her on TV, cheering as loud as I could and crying too. The grown-up girl walking to the train station just a few hours ago, already forgetting I was even alive?

That creepy old spot-faced perv wanted to lay his eyes on her and everything else too.

"She looks like herself," I told him. "Anyway, she's gone from here."

And what I thought was: *she's gone because I always wanted her gone.* I didn't know it was possible to be so happy and so sad at the same time.

And Turtle Face? He shut up about Promise, then lit a cigarette and gave me one. He wasn't so bad, not really. We had a smoke together before he parked in the alley.

* * *

This story won Pleiades' Kinder/Crump award for short fiction and was originally published in the spring 2022 edition of Pleiades.

Discussion Questions

1. The narrator says she named her daughter Promise because she made a promise to give her a better life. Promise did, in fact, have a better life, but gives all the credit to herself. Who is right? Who deserves credit?

2. Should parents be measured by their generational improvement over the way they were parented or against some objective parenting standard?

3. Does Promise have a moral obligation to visit her mother? Should she lie to her mother about her being a good parent? What does Promise get (*or lose*) by cutting her mother out of her life and telling her the truth about her parenting?

4. When there is a rift between Promise and Tony, the narrator sides with Tony and spends less time with Promise? Given the narrator's living situation is this a mistake? Should a parent always side with their children against a partner? Would it matter if they were married?

5. To what extent is the narrator responsible for failing to get her life in order?

* * *

One More Day

Afsane Pourazar

* * *

<u>**Content Disclosure**</u>: Suicidal Themes

* * *

I think pain is the most fascinating thing in the universe. Some people say that happiness can make pain go away. Some believe that only time can heal our pains. For my part, I don't believe in anything but questions. And to me, there's only one question about pain: Does it ever really end? And if it does, when?

As usual, I was pondering over pain that night and how it has given meaning to my life. I wasn't sure if the pain would ever disappear or anything, but I had decided to take a lot of walks. Walking is something worth doing every single night because the streets are empty of people and full of peace and quiet. Just the way I like them.

It was a dark night, and it was cold just like any other night. So cold that I couldn't feel my hands freezing. She was standing there, all alone. As was my habit, I tried to guess her name and age. I liked to know what her favorite color was or why she was standing there. It wasn't hard to understand that she wasn't feeling well.

That night was the first time I met her. She looked at me with those marvelous eyes. There was something about her. Something special that didn't let me simply go past the bridge. Something that made me stand there and just look at her. Something that made a socially anxious person like me want to voluntarily start a conversation.

Just when I was about to say hello, she started to stare at me. She didn't smile or anything. She just stood there, as still as a statue. Looking at her eyes felt like looking at a spark of hope buried under a hill of ashes. She looked as if she wanted to cry, and yet she didn't have any more tears to shed.

"Are you going to jump off the bridge as well?" she asked.

I was shocked as I didn't expect her to be the one who started the conversation. *Is she going to kill herself? Her eyes are too beautiful to close forever*, I thought.

"No, I'm not. Are you?" I asked.

"I guess so."

"Why?"

"I'm tired."

"Tired of what?"

"Life, pretty much."

She was about to do something that I had never been brave enough to do. "I've got a question for you. Do you know what happens after death?" I asked.

She said that she didn't know.

"Why are you taking such a risk, then?" I asked confidently.

She said, "When you are sick of every little thing, you don't want a better condition. You don't want to fight. You don't want to win. You don't even want to give up. You simply just want to put an end to it all. You just want to escape the current situation. I need to run away from the current nightmare that people call reality. Honestly, I'd rather be anywhere. Anywhere but here."

"So, you are fine with leaving this place for somewhere worse, right?" I asked in a rather shaky voice.

"Yes. I am. I really am."

"I respect your decision, but you might end up in hell or something. I'm not religious, but I know that God doesn't like it when people end their own lives," I said, not knowing what I was saying.

"Well, I don't believe in God."

"I hate to break this to you, but he genuinely doesn't care. Your not believing in him cannot change the fact that he might exist."

"Do you believe in him?"

"I believe in his existence, but I don't believe in his kindness," I replied, feeling proud as if I had just quoted a famous philosopher. I knew that I hadn't.

She didn't seem impressed by my response at all. That's why I felt a little disappointed. She took a deep breath and let the winter wind slowly dance in her hair. It was peaceful. Trying to change the subject, I asked, "What's bothering you these days?"

"Nothing special, except for my life," she said funnily and burst into laughter. She kept laughing at my question or probably her answer for exactly thirty-five seconds and then started to cry silently.

I was hapless. I had never encountered a person who was about to commit suicide right in front of me. I didn't know how to talk her out of the whole thing, for I, too, wasn't that optimistic of a person. I was barely a realist. I was a realist constantly fighting against pessimism. I didn't want to talk to her about the moon, the blue sky, or the bright future awaiting us. That's what cowards do.

She walked toward me and asked me to sit next to her. As though she could read my mind, she asked if I had ever tried to end my life. I didn't know what to say. I didn't want to tell her that I had actually tried to end it all a few times. And I also didn't want to lie to her face.

"Well, yes. I have thought about it," I said, hoping she wouldn't ask for details.

"What made you change your mind, then? Your fear of God's unkindness?" She laughed.

I liked her sense of humor.

"No. It was something else."

"What was it?"

"Listen to me. What's your biggest purpose in life? Something that you'd like to achieve someday. Something that you consider to be the most precious thing in life. Something that is truly worth fighting for. Is it happiness, wealth, fame, or peace? Or maybe something else?" I asked, feeling sort of excited.

"I'm not sure. I've never actually thought about it," she replied with an honest look on her face.

I cleared my throat and said, "Well, to me, the most valuable thing in life is peace. I don't really care about living a happy life. I'm totally fine with feeling unhappy. I know how to embrace sadness. I don't care about being famous. In fact, I hate fame. The less people know your name, the better. I don't even care about being rich; not starving to death would suffice. Yet, there is nothing in this life that I hate as much as I hate anxiety. I hate nervousness. I hate fear. I just want to enjoy my life in peace and quiet. That's my goal."

"Now we're talking! It's like you can read my mind," she said excitedly, holding my hand. She smiled at me, and I thought, *That tinge of hope in her eyes is too shiny to vanish forever.*

Even though it was cold, I could finally feel my hands. Suddenly, I was capable of organizing my thoughts. So I said, "I don't believe in heaven or hell. I think we die, and that's that. That's what I'm afraid of most. We try to run away from life because we hate the pressure and the speed. Because time keeps scaring us. Because we are desperately looking for peace. And you know what? We don't want it now. We prefer to tolerate stress and wish for a future full of peace. Why do we do that? Why do we postpone calmness? We don't expect calmness to enter our lives anytime soon. We plan to experience it ten or twenty years from now. To be honest, I can sometimes feel at peace. Well, not absolutely at peace since that's impossible. But I'm kinda less anxious. For example, when I go for a walk on a winter night or watch the sunrise. It's my biggest dream to experience absolute calmness, and I don't know if death is going to help me achieve that or not. The problem is, I believe that after I die, I will be nothing. I won't exist to experience peace. A thing that doesn't exist is nothing, and it theoretically can't be able to experience peace. Simply because it's dead. Do you follow me?"

"I think I do," she said, looking a little confused.

After a short silence, she asked, "Does it mean that you're a brave person or simply just a coward?"

"That I wouldn't know. To be, or not to be. That's the question."

"I disagree. To jump, or not to jump. That's the question now. I didn't have the strength to keep living, but I guess I have the courage to jump off this bridge." She took a deep breath.

I said, "You really think you're brave, is that so?"

"I am brave. I'm just not brave enough for this battle. That's why I'm ending it. To me, not fighting is victory," she looked down as if she was hiding her tears from me.

Changing the subject, she asked in a mocking tone, "And why do you like the sunrise? Because it resembles a fresh start? A beginning to a whole new day?"

"No. I'm definitely not a morning person. I love the night, especially the cold ones."

"Like tonight."

"Yeah, like tonight."

She smiled.

I said in a sarcastic tone, "I don't like the sunrise because it's a beginning to a new day."

I calmly continued, "I like it because it's the most beautiful ending to a peaceful night."

"I had never thought of it like that."

"Anyway, don't jump off the bridge and watch the sunrise with me."

"All right. It won't hurt to live one more day, will it?" she said, putting her head on my shoulder.

"No, it wouldn't," I said, hoping the sun wouldn't rise.

* * *

Discussion Questions

1. If you were the one who met the woman on the bridge, what (*if anything*) would you have said to her?
2. Given that the woman on the bridge isn't suffering from a painful and incurable disease, does she have an obligation to continue living? Do others have an obligation to try and talk her out of killing herself?
3. Assuming a person is not responsible for others, no one would know or grieve their death, and their death would not otherwise cause anyone else hardship or pain, what is the strongest argument in favor of living?
4. The narrator asks, "What's your biggest purpose in life?" What is your answer to this question? Does a person have an obligation to know their answer to this question?
5. The narrator says, "The most valuable thing in life is peace.... I just want to enjoy my life in peace and quiet. That's my goal." Do you think this a worthwhile goal? Would the goal have been achieved by taking an illegal drug? What advice would you give the narrator to help achieve this goal?

* * *

Dangerous Ideas

A.M. Howcroft

* * *

<u>**Content Disclosure**</u>: Mild Language; Mild Violence

* * *

The balcony was enclosed by a rusting iron palisade, held in place by ivy spiraling from terracotta pots. Lila leaned precariously over the railing and waited, pondering how many structures were held together by little more than an idea. Buildings, nations, relationships, everything seemed fragile. She wondered how many times Athens had been transformed, how often its ideas had crashed down with no more permanence than a city wall. Although the sun had set, the sky remained resolutely blue. From the balcony's perspective, the city appeared magical, its lights a carpet of stars woven around the imposing Acropolis ruins. It felt unreal. Lila took a deep breath, because it was critical to remain focused, but her mind was tangled as the ivy.

As someone moved onto the balcony to stand next to her, Lila kept her eyes fixed on the vista. She wished she was a smoker, giving her hands a reason to keep them busy, and perhaps a better excuse to be outside. She hated the subterfuge that her job required. The man beside her leaned out in a similar fashion but kept as much distance between them as was possible in this claustrophobic space. He didn't speak. Lila glanced across. He was more boy than man, with the look of a sophomore. Unruly black curls of hair, like a fuzzy helmet, and a strong nose that might look proportionate when the face filled out. He held a bottle of beer between his fingers.

"I thought it would be cooler out here," Lila said.

The boy didn't immediately reply. Lila turned her head toward him.

"The air or the city?" He shifted his body to face her.

Lila was startled by how pale his blue eyes seemed, more ice than ocean, and they made him seem far older than his physique.

"Both, I guess," she said.

He flung out a thin arm to encompass the city. "The root of civilization. There are layers of history stacked here, one on top of the other. This railing is probably older than your college," he shook it with his free hand, moving it back and forth far too easily. Lila took a step away.

"What's your major?" she asked.

He nodded as if he'd been expecting that question. "Philosophy."

"Ah," she said with a subtle smile.

A siren tore through the streets below them, followed by a blast of angry car horns. The smell of weed drifted out from the pulsing room inside. It felt like a long time since she'd been at a house party like this; it was nostalgic yet faintly unsettling.

"You know," the boy said quietly, "philosophers were dangerous once. Especially here. They were rebels, sparking revolutions, changing the world, threatening the establishment."

"Until the Renaissance artists became the stars." Lila tilted her head, teasing. He looked like he was about to argue, and she added, "Don't feel too bad. The artists soon succumbed to the scientists."

The boy gave a brief laugh. It seemed as if he might say something, but hesitated.

"Are the philosophers planning a comeback?" Lila asked.

"We never went away," he said, deadpan.

"What's your next move?" Lila asked, fully cognizant of the fact that her question was open to interpretation.

The boy took the sentence at face value. "Meet me tomorrow. I'll show you why philosophers still matter. Here," he took a scrap of paper from his pocket and scribbled down an address with a tiny pencil. "Can you be there at nine, before it gets too crowded?"

She gave a half nod. The second hardest part of her job was complete, but she had that sinking feeling in her stomach. The next part was much, much more difficult on many levels.

"Oh, I'm Ben," the boy said and extended his hand. Lila shook it firmly and pretended she did not already know his name.

* * *

The morning air was warm, and the light was strong. As the day grew, Lila knew the heat and the weight of her predetermined actions would become oppressive. She wore a loose linen shirt over denim shorts. She had braided her blond hair, as it was cooler and made her look younger. Standing in the shade of an ancient tree, she looked at the intersection Ben had listed. Tourists were flowing along the thoroughfare in ever-increasing numbers, clustered in romantic pairs or larger family groups, and she thought it was already too late to avoid the crowds. Tourists woke earlier than students, that was for sure. She missed those days when life had seemed more for living and the stakes had seemed less intense.

"Hey," Ben said from behind her.

Startled, she turned to see him approaching from a street vendor cart. He proffered a bottle of water.

"I'm good, thanks," she said, not entirely sure if she could trust him.

Ben dropped her bottle into a canvas backpack that he swung over one shoulder, where it slouched as badly as him.

"Secret entrance," he pointed with one finger, while unscrewing the cap of his own water.

She threw him a puzzled look.

"I'm interning at the museum. Put this on." He gave her a bright sticker that she pressed onto her shirt until it stuck firmly.

Ben flashed a card at the solid door, and swung it open, ushering her inside. It was dark, but as Lila crossed the threshold, a sensor light fired on. Ben led her through a couple of turns until they stood in a small gallery, surrounded by statues.

"The tourists flock to the famous things first. This is all ours for twenty minutes," he said.

A guard in a dark uniform peered at them from a neighboring gallery but turned away when Ben waved his ID.

"What's the collective noun for philosophers?" he asked Lila.

"A confusion?"

"Officially, it's a synod, but I like confusion more. Anyway, that's what we have here," he gestured at the statues.

"They look more like a care home, they're old," Lila said.

"The sculptors, or their sponsors, equate wisdom with age. Look at this guy in the middle, though."

Ben tapped his fingernail on the statue of a youth, curled hair massed on his head, black holes for eyes, one arm raised, and the other missing. The surface of his chest and six-pack abdomen were blotched dark gray on top of a lighter shade, reminding Lila of the moon's surface on a clear night.

"Wild eyes, wild hair, this guy is alive," Ben said.

Lila wondered if her enthusiastic guide realized how closely he resembled the statue.

"Looks like he's at a gig," she said.

"Recovered from the bottom of the sea. I mean, how did he get there?" Ben looked at Lila, waiting for a response.

"Fell off the back of a boat?"

"Deliberate," he said. "These things are *heavy*. You need several strong men to take it to sea and hurl it off a ship. They abandoned him, to make sure he was never seen again, because he was considered dangerous, at least his ideas were."

"I thought philosophy was about the meaning of life, happiness? How dangerous can that be?" Lila said.

"Philosophy is the science of ideas—and nothing scares people more than ideas," Ben said. "Prometheus had his liver ripped out every day for eternity because he shared the idea of fire with humans. When Darwin came up with evolution, he sat on it for years because he knew the tremendous impact it would have on the Church and society."

"He only published when someone was going to beat him to it, right?" Lila said. She wondered for a moment if ego was the primary issue, not ideas.

Ben danced around the room, tapping the pedestals with his fingers, gesturing passionately. He brushed some stray hair out of his eyes and jabbed the air with his finger, looking even more like the wild-eyed statue to Lila. Gorgeous, drowned, and lost.

"Your examples were gods and scientists, not philosophers," Lila stated.

"Ha!" Ben cried. "Philosophers study everything. They explore fundamental questions about existence, knowledge, life. In ancient Greece, what we now call science—math and physics—that was all grouped under philosophy. You *could* argue philosophers shed those subjects to concentrate on more important ideas," he said, tongue in cheek. Grabbing Lila's hand, he pulled her into the next gallery. His enthusiasm was contagious, and Lila felt guilt building in the pit of her stomach.

"Look!" he said. "What do you see?"

Pottery—vases and amphorae pieced together like jigsaw puzzles, bearing circular stories of myths, moral tales with immoral figures, she thought.

"Art," she said.

"Do you know how many thousands of these things there are?"

"Ceramics are fragile and yet almost indestructible," Lila answered. Just like a man's ego.

Ben nodded his head sagely. "What's amazing is that we know what the owners of these pots saw at the theatre—we know the poems they read, the stories they told. We can grasp their ideas, even though they were written on parchment and papyrus. Do you know how many scrolls survived?"

Lila shook her head.

"Hardly any. They wither and disintegrate, the ink fades. That's if they're lucky enough to avoid deliberate destruction."

"Modern tech can preserve ideas now," Lila said.

"Are you sure? Can you read the files on a floppy disk from the 1980s? Besides, technology is a disease. It's far worse than you think—"

Lila recognized they were on dangerous ground. This was not the place for *the conversation*. She tried to steer Ben back on track, but he was hard to stop.

"Each society tries to ravage the knowledge of their rivals. The Romans burned the libraries at Carthage and Alexandria to dust. Even within a civilized society, it was hard to be a philosopher. They made Socrates drink hemlock, and Turing ate a cyanide-laced apple."

"Why hemlock?" Lila asked.

"It was traditional, and humane," Ben said.

"You think it's humane?"

"Compared to stoning, beheading, and crucifixion. It tastes a little bitter apparently, and gradually paralyzes from the feet up, but leaves the mind fully functional. It was for the elite." Ben shivered. "They say Socrates was very calm and dignified in his death."

Lila felt suddenly cold in the museum's high-ceiling room. "How come we still know about them, if they were executed and their books were destroyed?"

Ben smiled. "Because, when ideas are valuable, we copy them and place our copies in different locations to keep them safe. Can you imagine how much effort it was to transcribe the works of Socrates by hand before the printing press?"

They wandered the halls, with Ben pointing out his favorite philosophers who had contributed unique or obscure ideas, plus those who suffered terrible punishments for their heretical thoughts. Lila was enjoying the conversation, but the clock was ticking, and that feeling of dread was growing inside her. Slowly, the museum filled with tourists, clogging the arterial corridors and forming blockages around famous pieces.

"Hungry?" Ben asked.

"Starving."

In the taxi, they sat in comfortable silence on the weathered back seat, letting the breeze through the open windows cool them as the driver raced down side streets to avoid jams. Lila observed the juxtaposition of old and new buildings, the merging of ancient and modern, which blurred as they flashed by. Who decided what to keep and what to replace?

The air inside the taxi was heavy with musk and spice. Eventually, the driver found his way to a main road and hurtled along, drifting across lanes as though the yellow road lines were guidelines rather than enforced rules. Ben had returned to a more introverted state, the animated persona of the museum curling back inside him, as he hunched to keep his head from hitting the taxi roof as they thumped over every pothole.

"It's like the writing on a cereal box," Lila said, pointing down the road. "Tear along the dotted line."

Ben laughed.

"I meant to ask you," Lila said next. "Where are the women? The female philosophers?"

Ben shifted uncomfortably. "That's a great question," he said looking directly at her, before shifting his gaze out of the window. "There have always been women philosophers, going right back to antiquity. Like Hipparchia the Cynic, or Arete of Cyrene, or Hypatia."

"Wasn't she stoned to death?" Lila interjected.

"Yeah, history hasn't been kind to female philosophers. There are obviously lots of modern examples, too, like Simone de Beauvoir; the list is huge, but the professors who teach the courses are as misogynistic as men in other industries. Women never get the recognition they deserve."

"Ironic, eh? Philosophy teachers can't think for themselves." Lila punched Ben in the arm, a little harder than intended. "It's all ego again."

"Hey, I'm on your side!" he declared. "Many philosophers did reference their female counterparts; it's the teachers who were shits."

"Those who can do..." Lila said and let the sentence hang. She wanted to be on his side, but with her job, that might not be true. He was smart, handsome, and she liked his energy, but he had a male ego. Worse, he was the intelligence behind a very dangerous idea.

Abruptly, the driver pulled to a stop and pointed down a small lane.

"We got it," Ben said, and they jumped out to watch the yellow cab fly away like a stone from a sling. They walked down the lane and restaurants began to appear on either side, with tables, chairs, and awnings huddled tightly together. Lila admired a giant bottle of Aperol that stood proudly outside one establishment.

"You try?" A middle-aged man with too much hair rushed out of the interior to entice them inside, rather like a trapdoor spider, she thought. Lila shook her head and Ben lightly touched her elbow to steer her away, navigating the slim route between competing hosts. As the lane opened into the square, they could see the center was shaded by a cluster of trees, with fairy lights strung between them. It was early lunch, and the place would only truly come to life as the sun fell. Ben led them to a restaurant with two upright white lions guarding the entrance.

"My cousin's place," he said.

The hostess clearly knew Ben and led them inside to a fine area overlooking the square.

"Wow, I didn't expect this," Lila said when she saw their table.

The chairs were giant gilded thrones with red velvet seats, and a huge chandelier was suspended above, wantonly scattering light.

"Spectacular, right?"

Ben ordered a shrimp saganaki and Lila the risotto, plus two sodas. As far as she could tell, they were the only patrons given the time of day, but then the restaurant seemed bigger inside, and Lila wondered if private meals were taking place upstairs, or on a rear veranda. The smell of jasmine was floating in from outside, and Lila took a deep breath. It was perfect for *the conversation.*

"I get the history, but you haven't told me why philosophers are still relevant, or dangerous," Lila prompted. She needed to hear him say it.

"Hypothetically," Ben began, enunciating each syllable very slowly, before rushing into the sentence, "if a modern philosopher devised a test, similar to Turing, but about reality, that could be pretty harmful."

"The Turing test was to see if AI could fake being human, right?"

Ben nodded, letting her walk through the argument herself.

"A similar test for reality, would test to see if the world is real?" Lila continued, "As opposed to...?"

"A simulation," Ben said. "You've got it. There are some pretty good papers on that such as Bostrom's 'Are you living in a computer simulation?' or Chalmer's '*The Matrix* as Metaphysics.'"

"You studied those?" Lila said.

"Absolutely. They're great—laying out some foundational assumptions, the criteria, what empirical tests you could apply, and stuff—"

"Whoa—how can you test for reality?" Lila asked.

Ben did a double nod and continued, "You examine things like entropy, checking the randomness of natural processes to see if there are any discrepancies that might suggest data compression or constraints, or you can look for computational limits in quantum mechanics, or anomalies in physical laws that might suggest algorithmic issues. Okay?"

Lila nodded. "You mean, if it's a simulation, there would be bugs in the code. You'd look for evidence?"

"Exactly. Let's assume a philosopher devised a test for reality, using some of those approaches, but instead of running the test, he set up an AI system and asked it to use his—or her— test to see if it were in a simulation."

Lila held up her hand to pause him. "The AI is actually running inside a simulation, right?"

"Yes, but it must figure that out for itself. At first, maybe it's not very good, and it can't tell, and it fails the test."

"But it's AI, and it plays the simulation billions of times," Lila said.

"You got it," Ben replied. "Eventually, it gets really good at this, and then, we let it out of the box and connect it to the real world."

"It would keep testing until it found evidence that our world was a simulation. Wait—you don't actually believe this—" Lila rapped her knuckles on the table to demonstrate something solid, "—is a simulation, do you?"

Ben grinned and leaned back into his throne, toying with the glass of soda, tilting it as the ice rattled.

"Hypothetically," he said again, "it would have massive significance for the world, don't you think? If there is irrefutable evidence we are living in a simulation. What to do with that knowledge would be a huge decision. You'd probably sit on it, like Darwin. It would eat you up, though. How could you have a relationship if the other person wasn't even real? Or a child?"

"You're assuming nobody else in the simulation is real," Lila said.

"They might be, but how can you tell? It would make life meaningless."

Lila nodded sympathetically. "I can see how hard that would be."

"Eventually, though, the truth would emerge," Ben said.

"Does it have to? Unlike Darwin, someone could sit on that information—if they could master their own ego." She started to count to ten in her head, willing him to make the right answer. Ben sat and stared at her thoughtfully.

The food came, breaking the conversation at a critical moment, and Ben excused himself to head to the restroom. Lila leaned back and thought about Ben's thesis and her options. She could only see two. Finish the task now or abandon the job and throw her lot in with the wild-eyed boy. It was an ethical dilemma, but luckily, this was her specialist subject. For the first time in her short career, she wondered if it was time to break the rules. There were only seconds to decide. She reached into her handbag and then hesitated.

"You should have started," Ben said when he returned. Lila picked up her fork and tucked into the risotto.

"This is really good," she said. "I have to ask, who would publish that proof of the reality test? No academic journal is going to put something out there that is so, I don't know, out there!"

"You're right. No chance with a Wiley or Reed Elsevier. I'd go with a respected college journal with a good reputation, like Boston or Oxford. They're thorough, still hard to get through the gatekeepers, but they'd be interested in the concept and getting it seen, rather than controlling the narrative. Get it published in one of them, it would go viral."

"You could vanity publish?" Lila offered.

He shook his head. "Too easy for the men in black to take down."

They ate in comfortable silence for a while, each deep in their own thoughts, playing out different futures.

"How's the saganaki?" Lila asked.

"It's good," Ben said. His demeanor had changed, as though he wanted to change the subject.

"I've been doing all the talking," Ben said. "Tell me about yourself. What does Lila care about, apart from risotto? What's your major?"

Lila flicked her hair to one side and looked at Ben.

"I know I look younger, but I graduated two years ago."

"Really?" Ben was still chewing on his food.

"From Boston University. My major was philosophy, specializing in ethics, and I got a job in Washington afterward," she said. "A small government role." She watched him eat.

"No way!"

"Hypothetically," she said slowly, mimicking his style, "if a philosopher were seeking to publish a paper that would rip society in two, what should a caring government do?"

Ben slowly put down his fork. His eyes widened, and he swallowed hard several times.

"You tricked me," he said, a hint of anger in his voice.

Lila continued, "If you were a believer in deontological ethics, like Kant, you'd argue that killing one person to save pain for millions would be wrong."

Ben pushed his chair back, as though he were about to run, but Lila just gave a slight shake of her head. For a moment Ben was silent, and his head sank down to his chest. Lila waited, and eventually Ben raised his eyes to hers.

"I was never a big believer in Kant, but I'm beginning to see his perspective. What would a caring government think, though?" Ben's face had turned pale.

"A government would think, utilitarianism," Lila answered. "The greatest happiness for the greatest number. Especially if those numbers support your political party."

"I had a bad feeling you were going to say that," Ben said.

"In terms of actions that could be taken to follow the doctrine of utility, there are some well-known historical examples to choose from, like Socrates in Athens, for example," Lila said.

Ben's skin was slick with sweat. "What about the social contract? Hobbes and Locke would say that killing an individual would undermine the stability and trust necessary for a functional society?"

Lila accepted the point. "True, but it only counts if the execution is public, as was the case with Socrates. Many societies perform these tasks, behind the veil. If we made philosophers drink a potion on stage, it would be dramatic but would break societal trust. Although, plenty of people die naturally from food poisoning every year."

Ben was silent. His face was flushed, and the pulse was throbbing in his temple. Lila reached across the table and firmly took his hand.

She said, "I hope the saganaki wasn't too bitter."

Ben swallowed hard. "What about your belief Lila? You're the ethics specialist."

Lila took his other hand and leaned closer to speak quietly. "I consider myself a virtue ethicist. I believe in taking responsibility for my moral character, rather than focusing on specific actions and outcomes."

"Like Aristotle," Ben said.

She smiled and squeezed his hands.

"You must know then," he said, "that Aristotle escaped Athens to avoid the fate of Socrates. He wanted to prevent the people from sinning twice against philosophy."

She laughed lightly. "And he lived happily ever after. Not. Do you think that could happen in a simulation?" Lila glanced at her watch.

"Why don't we find out?" Ben said. "In a simulation, you can do anything."

"That sounds like ego talking. Let's relax here for a few minutes and see which way the wind blows."

For a minute they sat silently, the only sound Ben's labored breathing.

Ben looked at Lila, "Wait—do we have a *caring* government?"

"If this was all a simulation," Lila replied, her voice steady, "would a small vial of simulated hemlock actually matter?"

Ben closed his eyes. The scent of jasmine drifted back through the open window, as the real or imagined world bustled past. Lila thought of the countless times Athens had been rebuilt from the ruins of its ideas.

"Would anyone remember this place if it were quietly swept away?" Ben said, opening his eyes to meet Lila's.

"I would," she replied softly.

* * *

Discussion Questions

1. Are there "dangerous ideas" that should be oppressed from public consumption? If so, who should decide, and what framework should be used?
2. If an academic paper, of the type in the story, were published in a reputable academic journal saying there was a test for reality, and we are living in a simulation, would you believe it? Do you think others would believe it? Do you think it would gain popular acceptance?
3. Is the role of government to be a "caring government" or something else? What does being a "caring government" mean from a practical standpoint?
4. Assuming there was a test, and you believed you were living in a simulation, would you change your behaviors in any way? Why or why not?
5. If you were given Lila's assignment, what would you do? Would you kill the boy, join his cause, expose the government plot, or something else?

* * *

Wilderness Survival with Bozo

Terry Pilling

* * *

Content Disclosure: Strong Language; Low Intensity

* * *

"So yer a survivalist are ya?" He leaned with his arms draping over the back of his easy chair and grinned down at me with his goofy grin.

"That's what I just said!" Why did he ask questions when I just finished telling him the answer? Some adults are never serious. Bozo's dad was like that, thinking kids can't know about stuff. Just because he never reads any books or learns about anything doesn't mean that I don't, I thought. "I have read four books on wilderness survival, and even kids my age or even younger have done it. Like there is this book called *My Side of the Mountain* about a kid that runs away from home and builds a camp in the wilderness on a mountain and survives and does lots of cool things there."

"Ran away, did he?"

Jesus, he was an idiot.

"Where was the mountain? Alaska?"

"No, not Alaska." I was getting exasperated. "New York. A mountain called Catskill."

"Pretty nice weather in New York." He changed the subject, still staring down at me and Bozo with his goofy grin.

The problem with Bozo's dad was that he didn't pay any attention to what I was doing, he just watched TV and then jumped into the conversation with some stupid question about stuff I'd already explained to Bozo.

At least Bozo was paying attention. I had all of my survival gear spread out on the floor in their living room and I was showing Bozo how it all worked so that he would be prepared for our survival trip.

Bozo and I had been friends since the school year started that past September. He had been held back a grade and I had just moved to town and so neither of us had any friends. I liked him right away since he would always go along with my ideas and adventures. Also, I felt a bit sorry for him since everybody called him Bozo. His real name is Steven, but for some reason everybody called him Bozo. He didn't even mind it. Anyway, now it was February, so we had been hanging around together for several months.

"When we get to the campsite, you will have to remember all of this stuff," I told him as I went through each piece of equipment on the floor. "This tool is a fold-up shovel and also a pickaxe." I picked up the small green tool and presented it to him. "You just turn this ring at the top and the shovel will bend out, then you tighten the ring again and it is now ready to dig." I showed him how the folded tool transformed into a small shovel. "Then you can loosen it again, pull out the other side and it becomes a pickaxe!" I could see that Bozo was impressed at the way it turned into a pickaxe with the shovel blade on one side and the metal pick on the other. I remembered being just as excited when I first saw the same thing in the army surplus store where I bought it. It was fun to share the excitement with somebody.

"You gonna prospect for gold out there in the bush?" Bozo's dad butted into the conversation.

"No! We aren't going to dig for gold," idiot, "it is for digging a firepit and things like that."

"What's the pickaxe for then?"

"You can use it to dig if the ground is too hard, or if there is some rock you need to break or something. There are lots of uses for things like this. It is part of the standard wilderness survival gear." I don't even know why I bothered explaining this stuff to him except that at least Bozo was listening. I wished his dad would just watch his stupid hockey game and leave us alone.

Bozo's brother started setting the table for dinner. I don't think Bozo has a mother. If he does, she was not living with them since I had been over there many times and I never saw her once. Maybe his parents got divorced. That wouldn't surprise me from what I knew of his dad.

Seeing dinner was almost ready, I started to quicken my explanations of the gear. I showed Bozo the aluminum mess kit, which opened up to reveal a frying pan, a pot, a cup, and even a knife-spoon-fork tool. Again, his face lit up in a smile when he saw all of the pieces appear. I continued with the orange pup tent, foil survival blanket, rope, compressed sawdust fire-starter sticks, hand warmers, a really cool survival knife that had a hollow handle and inside there were matches, needle and thread, water purifier tablets, fish hook and line, and snare wire. As I showed Bozo the snare wire, his dad turned away from his hockey game and again piped in, "Going to snare some rabbits for food, eh?" He smiled.

"If we have to, we will, but that is only if we run out of ration packs," I replied. I pushed aside Bozo's cat, who was sniffing around the gear, and picked up a small cardboard box to show him. "This is a ration pack," I said. "It contains packs of food called boil-in-the-foil, which means that you boil water and put the pack into it and then, when it is cooked, you open it up and eat it!"

"Well, isn't that neat," Bozo's dad said. "Looks like you have your camping trip all planned out."

"It is not a camping trip, it is wilderness survival," I corrected him. "It is not the same thing as camping." At least he was finally starting to see how it was all going to work.

"Time to eat!" Bozo's brother called from the adjoining kitchen. We left the equipment where it was and went over to the table. Bozo's dad sat on one end, his brother on the other while Bozo and I sat on opposite sides. I was waiting for his father to start the prayer, but they just started grabbing plates and dishing out their food instead. I guess they don't say grace before they eat, I thought. I wondered if they even went to church on Sundays. I filled my plate with mashed potatoes, pork chops, and peas, and was starting to eat when the cat jumped up on the table and started sniffing at my plate. "Get out of there!" I said and lifted him off the table and down to the floor.

"So what time are you boys planning to get started tomorrow?" Bozo's dad said, his mouth full of potatoes.

"I think we should get going first thing in the morning," I replied. "We need to have time to get our camp cleared and set up the tent before it gets dark... get out of here!" Bozo's cat had jumped back onto the table and was trying to sniff my food again.

"Oh just let him take a sniff," said Bozo's dad. "He just wants to see what it is."

"That's gross!" I lifted the cat to the floor again.

"Once he sees that it is not cat food, he will leave you alone."

"No thanks," I said. "That is how you get diseases and stuff."

Bozo's dad chuckled. "Well, I guess you don't want to get any diseases."

I could tell he didn't believe me about the diseases. Whatever. It was still gross. Maybe he didn't mind the cat eating off his plate, but I wasn't letting it eat off of mine.

"Aww. I think he likes you," Bozo's brother chimed in as the cat jumped back up to my plate again.

"I can't eat with this stupid cat always jumping up here!" I was getting irate.

"Just give it a try," Bozo's dad insisted. "Let him have a sniff and see what happens. If it doesn't work, you can get a new plate and Peter will lock the cat in the bathroom until we're finished eating. Deal?"

"Okay," I shrugged, "but if he touches it, I won't eat any."

The cat leaned closer and sniffed the potatoes and then the peas and finally moved over to the pork chops where he spent significantly more time. I crouched down low beside the plate so I could see if his nose touched my food. He got really close at one point, and I was almost certain that the next instant his tongue was going to shoot out and start licking my pork chop.

But he didn't. Instead, he lifted his head back up, looked around, and then jumped back down to the floor.

"I told ya. He is only curious. If you let him sniff it, he will see that he doesn't like it and go away. It is only when you won't let him sniff it that he will keep pesterin' ya."

I was not sure how convinced I was of all that but at least the damn cat would finally let me eat in peace.

We finished the meal in relative peace aside from the continuing barrage of stupid questions about our survival trip. He didn't even know how to use the fishhook and line to catch fish! How dumb can you get?

When we were finished eating, Bozo's dad and brother went back to the living room to watch TV while Bozo and I cleared off the table and put the dishes in the dishwasher. We spent the rest of the evening packing our backpacks and getting everything ready so we wouldn't have to waste any time tomorrow morning. Around 10:00 p.m., we went to bed, and I lay awake for quite a while thinking about all the cool and exciting things we would be doing tomorrow. Everything was planned out perfectly. This was going to be so much fun.

* * *

The next morning, I was awake before everyone else. I jumped out of bed, got dressed, and went out to the living room to check the gear and play with the cat until everyone else got up.

Soon I could hear Bozo's dad in the kitchen and I could smell bacon cooking. I am not that hungry, I thought, I wish we could just skip all that and get going right now. Bozo and Peter finally came yawning into the kitchen and we sat down to breakfast. "All ready to hit the dusty trail boys?" Bozo's dad began.

"That's for sure," Bozo replied through a mouth full of eggs and toast. "I am ready to hit the dusty trail."

We were all smiles as we tied up our hiking boots, put on our winter parkas and wool hats, and loaded up their beat-up old station wagon with our backpacks, canteens, and sleeping bags.

Bozo's brother stayed home, but the rest of us piled into the station wagon and started toward the river. We were on our way! The river was about twelve miles from town. Our plan was to hike across to the little island in the middle of the river and set up camp there. The island was covered in spruce trees and so I figured it would be the perfect place. There would be plenty of firewood and, if we were lucky, maybe even some game for us to trap for food.

When we got to the river, his dad pulled the car up to the edge of the road where it looked easiest to hike down the bank to the river. We unloaded the car and I pulled out a map that I had hand drawn of the river and the island in the middle of it. "We are going to set up camp on the other side of the island around here." I pointed to a spot on the paper so that Bozo's dad could see it.

"Okay," he said, "I think I can find you if you don't show up on time."

I folded up my map and stuffed it back into my pocket. We hoisted our packs and prepared to go.

"So back here at this time tomorrow to pick you up, right?"

"Yep! That's right. We will try to pack up camp and come back here by early afternoon tomorrow," I said with Bozo grinning and nodding in agreement.

"Okay boys! Have fun and watch out for bears. Don't burn down the forest, eh?" He let out a hearty laugh and swung himself back into the car. He pulled a U-turn and we watched as his old rust-bucket station wagon disappeared around the bend and back toward town. I hadn't thought about bears. I wondered if maybe we should have brought a .22 along for protection.

When his dad was gone, Bozo and I turned and hiked down the bank to the frozen river. The snow was about a foot deep on the river, which made for some tough mushing until we got the idea of going one ahead of the other. That way, the one behind could step in the footprints of the one ahead and it would be easier. Every once in a while, when whoever was ahead got tired, we could trade off. It worked very well and pretty soon we were cheerfully trekking along in the bright afternoon sun. It actually got warm enough that we took off our hats and unzipped our jackets to cool down while we walked.

After about twenty minutes, I called for Bozo to stop. "Did you bring them?" I asked.

"Yep! I did," he replied, reaching into the inside pocket of his parka and pulling out the packet of Colts Mild cigars. Colts were wine-tipped cigars, which means they have a plastic mouthpiece on the end that tasted really sweet. Bozo and I smoked them a few times in the culvert out behind the school. He gave me one and flipped open his Zippo lighter to light them. This is fun! I thought.

We stood around for a few minutes looking down the river. What a winter wonderland. The blue sky, the white snow-covered spruce trees with their boughs dipped low from a heavy load of snow, the ice crystals in the air glinting and sparkling as the sunlight hit them. It was perfect. We stood in awe of the majesty of it all for a moment and then turned back toward the island. The neat thing about Colts is that when you are finished smoking one, you can blow out the filter and then chew on the piece of plastic like a stick of sweet, grape-flavored chewing gum. The flavor lasts quite a long time. We continued the hike and, after a while, lit up another cigar. I was in front and I happened to step in a spot of deeper snow—about up to my knee—and stumbled forward, barely retaining my balance. At the same time, I instinctively took a deep breath and, with the cigar in my mouth, I ended up sucking in a huge breath of smoke. I coughed, spit out the cigar, and leaned over with my hands on my knees coughing. Bozo laughed and laughed as I sputtered away. I finally recovered and continued to walk but I felt a bit dizzy and sick to the stomach for a few minutes and I resolved to stay away from Colts for a bit.

Bozo was a strange character. Since I met him, I noticed that he didn't talk very much and, in fact, it was possible that I was his only friend. At least I hadn't seen him hanging around with anyone else. It could be that all of his former friends had moved on to the next grade when he was held back and he just lost touch with them. Who knows. In any case, I was happy to do the talking for the both of us and he always responded by laughing at my jokes and going along with all my various schemes. In the fall, just after we met, we had set up a campsite in my backyard with a tent and a firepit that my dad helped to build. We even stayed out overnight and it was so much fun. That was when I got interested in winter survival and started reading a bunch of books on it. Eventually, I came up with the plan to camp on the island. I always saw the island when we came to the river in the summer and I figured it would be a perfect place for winter survival training. My idea was that we would build a lean-to with a wooden frame and a roof made of spruce boughs like the boy did in *My Side of the Mountain*. That way we could build the firepit in front of the lean-to and the heat from the fire would be reflected inside and keep it really warm. However, I brought the orange pup tent along just in case we couldn't find enough materials for the frame and lean-to stuff. I had thought of all contingencies.

* * *

We arrived at the edge of the island and started up into the forest. I found a stick with a Y on the end and picked it up. Pulling out my buck knife, I started cutting all of the side twigs from around it to make it into a nice walking stick. "What do you think I will do with this stick when we get to camp, Bozo?" I asked with a smile.

"I dunno, what?"

"Take a guess."

"Use it as a cane?" he replied.

"Well, that is what I will do on the way to camp, but once we are there, I will prop it up so that the Y part is over top of our firepit and then I can hang our water pot on it to boil water!"

Bozo giggled with glee. "Then we can make some tea!" he said.

"Yep, and we can also use it to boil the ration packs for our dinner."

"Yep," Bozo agreed. "Good thing we found that stick! I will try to find one too."

"Well, we really only need one stick for the water pot, but if you find one, I am sure we can use it for something else."

"Okay!" he said cheerfully and started to scan the woods for another stick as we wound our way through the trees.

As we got deeper into the forest, the snow started to become extremely deep. It was up to the middle of my calf at least and sometimes even up to the knee or more. It became extremely slow going and I thought maybe we should have gone around the perimeter of the island instead—which would also have been quite a bit quicker. We wanted to make our camp on the other side of the island so that if somebody happened to drive down to the river from town, they wouldn't be able to see our fire and think it was a forest fire or something. Plus, I wanted to be as far away into the wilderness as possible so it would be more like a survival trip. It wouldn't be survival if people could easily come and find you.

We had been hiking for almost two hours and the sun was already dipping down toward the horizon behind us. I figured we had about three hours or so left of daylight and that was about the perfect amount of time to find a good campsite and set up camp.

By the time we were about halfway across the island, I was really sweating in my parka because of the hard hiking through the deep snow. "Are you getting tired?" I panted.

"Yeah, it is really tiring, what about you?"

"Well, not too bad yet, but I sure hope we get to the other side pretty soon."

"Me too."

One thing that surprised me a bit about crossing the island was that I didn't see any birds or squirrels or any animals at all. I had hoped that we would see lots of animals since I was prepared to teach Bozo what they all were and how to trap them and stuff. Maybe it was too cold and they were hiding or hibernating or something. Who knows?

At one point, Bozo had to go to the bathroom. I had to go as well and so I just went to a tree and started to pee.

"But I have to take a shit," he said.

I realized at that moment we had forgotten to pack any toilet paper. "Damn," I exclaimed, "we forgot to bring TP."

"Damn," echoed Bozo.

"Here," I said, zipping up my fly and reaching into my jacket pocket, "this is the only paper I have, it will have to make do." I walked over and handed him the paper with my hand-drawn map on it.

"Shit," said Bozo. He made his way around behind a tree and a few minutes later I could hear the crumpling of the paper. Eventually, he crawled back around the tree and back to where I was standing. "Shit," he said. We turned back to the trail and I secretly hoped to God that I wouldn't have to go "number two" until we got back home tomorrow.

We just walked in silence after that for the remaining distance until finally emerging from the trees on the east bank of the island.

* * *

"First, we need to find the perfect spot where there is protection from the wind and lots of firewood around, then we can clear the snow away, set up our tent, and build a fire. After that, we can make tea and food and relax with a nice cigar!" I grinned.

"Yep!" Bozo smiled back at me and looked around. "That sounds like a plan."

We eventually settled on a spot, set down our packs, and sat down in the snow against a tree to rest a bit. We were finally ready to make camp.

After a few minutes, we got to our feet and started to clear away the snow. It quickly became obvious that the little green folding shovel was practically useless for clearing snow. It was way too small. So we ended up getting on our hands and knees and pushing the snow aside like a couple of human bulldozers. It took a while, but eventually, we had cleared a space about ten feet by ten feet. "I will set up the tent and you start to dig the firepit, okay?"

"Sounds good."

He turned the shovel into a pickaxe like I had shown him and started to chop away at the ground in the center of the clearing while I unrolled the pup tent. I found it impossible to shove the metal tent pegs into the frozen ground and soon realized I was going to have to use the shovel as a hammer and pound them in. At the same time, Bozo wasn't making any progress on digging the firepit, the ground was just too hard. In the end we decided that we didn't really need to dig a firepit. We would just build the fire on top of the ground.

"Let's gather some firewood first and build a fire," I suggested, "then we can eat some food, drink some tea, and I will finish setting up the tent with the shovel later."

"That sounds like a plan."

We scoured the woods around our clearing for sticks and logs and managed to gather a small pile. One problem was that most of the branches were covered in ice and frost and the only ones that weren't were the ones we had broken off of the trees and so they were green and I knew from my studies that green wood doesn't burn very well. On the other hand, it probably burns better than wood that is caked in ice I guessed.

It took a lot longer than I had planned for us to make the clearing and gather the wood and I could see that the sun was already near the horizon. It also didn't help that we were on the east side of the island and so we were in the shadows much sooner than we would have been on the west side.

"Let's get this fire going," I said, grabbing pieces of wood and forming a pile in the center of our clearing. There weren't any small sticks and twigs, other than the green ones, so I put those down first along with the compressed sawdust sticks I had brought and a bunch of spruce boughs since I knew that spruce needles burn really well—sort of like nature's gasoline I told Bozo as we gathered them.

I struck match after match trying to get the fire to start and all I got was a little bit of flame from the sawdust sticks—like a bit bigger match—and a little bit of smoke from the rest. Then nothing. Even the little spruce needles, nature's gasoline, didn't light. We took Bozo's Zippo and held it under a stick for a long time and it still didn't start on fire. I really wished I had brought some paper with us. Even the hand-drawn map would have worked if we hadn't been forced to repurpose it earlier.

We continued to struggle with the fire and the sky started to darken. I could feel the wind starting to pick up. It seemed to be streaming from the north using the river like a wind tunnel. It was a cold breeze and it seemed to be getting stronger by the minute making it even more impossible to light the fire. Both Bozo and I had long since zipped up our parkas and put our woolen hats back on, and even still, it was starting to get pretty chilly. As I held the flame under a pile of sticks, Bozo shifted back and forth from one foot to the other, rubbing his mittened hands together to keep warm.

Another half hour passed with each of us taking turns at the fire trying different combinations of twigs and spruce needles. When we did manage to get a little pile of needles burning, they burned so quickly they weren't able to start anything else burning and so fizzled out in a pile of reddish orange embers, like the end of a cigar, until quickly fading to grayish ash.

The sky was now almost completely dark and the wind had picked up so much that it became obvious that starting a fire was hopeless.

We were both becoming very cold.

* * *

I finally sat back from the useless firepit and pondered the situation. What were the options at this point? I still hadn't gotten around to setting up the tent, which lay unfolded on the other side of the clearing with the cords and metal spikes scattered around it. I could grab the shovel-hammer and try to set it up now, but even if I did get it up, I wondered how the thin nylon fabric of the tent was going to prevent us from freezing to death without a fire. Maybe we could burn the tent? It might get the fire going but then we would have to try and sleep on the ground next to it in the cold wind and hope the fire didn't go out while we slept. Probably not a good idea.

I looked up at Bozo and could see that he was becoming nervous. He could probably see I was nervous too. My toes were cold and I could feel the icy wind penetrating my parka and woolen hat.

"My feet are cold," stated Bozo.

I nodded. Mine were too. What to do? Think man, think. We were probably a mile back to the road and another twelve miles to town. Almost nobody drives out this way, especially at night, so even on the road the chances of getting help were pretty slim. Bozo was still shifting from one foot to the other and looking at me expectantly. Waiting. I was starting to get scared.

I broke the silence. "I think we are going to have to head back."

"Haha. Yeah," he said with a nervous laugh, "we better head back."

"Let's get the tent and tools back in our packs and get going."

We quickly started shoving the stuff into our bags, not bothering to fold the tent or the shovel. We just wanted to get out of there as fast as we could. The sky was now so dark that it was difficult to find the tent spikes and I couldn't be sure that I managed to find all of them. But I didn't care by that point. I just pulled on the drawstrings and hoisted my pack. "Let's get the hell out of Dodge," I said to Bozo.

"Haha. Yeah," he laughed. "Haha, we better hurry," he laughed some more, "and get the hell out of Dodge right now." He shifted back and forth laughing intermittently. His laugh was past nervous at this point. I could see his eyes had become wide. It was a laugh of panic.

I led the way and he followed. We walked around the north perimeter of the island this time rather than back through the woods and the deep snow. It was still hard mushing through foot-deep snow with the icy cold wind blasting at us head-on from the north. We leaned into the wind, lifting our mittened hands to our faces to try and block the blast. This left us blind to everything ahead except for the brief moments when we would open our hands for a short glimpse every few paces.

We trudged along for what seemed an eternity before we reached the other side of the island. Now the wind was blasting us from the side as we hiked westward. Only a half mile or so to the road. But what then?

My fingers and toes were numb at this point and I could feel a cold pain working its way through to the bones of my arms and legs. I was scared. I could hear sobbing behind me. Bozo was sobbing. I started to cry too. We are going to die, I thought.

There was no way to make it to town. We would be lucky to make it to the riverbank. Tears were starting to drip from my eyes only to freeze in little streams on my puffy red cheeks.

I stopped to let Bozo take his turn at the lead. As he trudged by, I saw he had stopped crying. He had a vacant look on his face. A trance-like look. He was in a terrified shock. Please keep walking, I thought. You have to keep going. I should have never brought him here. We were going to die and it was my fault. He would have followed me anywhere. I was the guy with all the fun plans. I made him laugh. Now I was crying. I was so scared. There was no possible way we could make it to town. Panic. Terror. Abject terror. Fear pushed me on; I forced one foot in front of the other.

Then anger. Blood-boiling anger. Why did Bozo's dad bring us out here? He should have known how cold it would be. He should have made sure I had paper to start a fire. God what a moron. I knew he was the stupidest person in the world. It was his fault we were going to die.

Then exhaustion. Utter exhaustion. We plunged forward across the open snow between the island and the shore with the wind cutting through our clothing like tissue paper and burning the skin with its dry piercing cold. Bozo was a walking zombie and I was ready at any moment to drop to the ground and curl up in the snow. To sleep. To die.

* * *

The dark was pitch black and the wind lifted the snow in curling streams that jetted straight sideways across our bodies making visibility almost impossible. Those same ice crystals that seemed so beautiful in the afternoon sun were now cutting into our skin like shards of glass.

I began to see the faint outline of shore ahead as a line of deeper darkness below the sky. Maybe a couple hundred feet further. We could make it. It was getting closer. Wait. What was that? I could see a dim light on the bank. A dim yellow glow. "What's that up there!" I yelled ahead to Bozo.

He made no sound. He just stepped forward, pace by pace, as before.

"I see a light up on the bank!" I screamed. "Up there! Somebody is there!"

As we drew closer, I could see it was a car up on the bank. The light was coming from the car. We neared the edge of the embankment and started to climb up. It was a car. On the side of the road. It was Bozo's dad! Oh my God! "It's your dad! It's your dad!" I screamed.

His head jerked up. He saw it. His pace then quickened to a trot—no, a scramble. A panicked terrified scramble. We both scrambled up the edge using both our hands and our feet, climbing the bank wildly like a couple of insane gorillas.

We reached the road, and there, parked on the side, was the station wagon.

Bozo's dad had jumped out and opened the rear passenger door, helping each of us remove our packs and then hustling us into the warmth of the car. We were both near delirious with exhaustion as he removed our hiking boots and jackets. He rubbed our feet and wrapped us in several huge comforters that he had brought with him. When he had us wrapped up with our bare feet tucked inside, he reached into the front seat and brought out two cups and a thermos and poured us each a cup of hot chocolate. When he placed the cup in my hand, I felt streaks of pain shoot through my hands as feeling began to return to my fingers.

Bozo's dad then turned back around and set the car in motion back to town. Meanwhile, Bozo and I sat in a daze. A profound sense of relief. Sipping on the hot chocolate in the warmth of that beautiful station wagon. I remember thinking it was the best hot chocolate I had ever tasted. I still think that.

* * *

In the years following our wilderness survival trip, I lost touch with Bozo and his dad. My family moved to a new town and life just moved on after that. I have never forgotten about our wilderness survival trip though, and I still think, sometimes, about Bozo's dad, and his method for dealing with determined cats. And determined boys.

* * *

Discussion Questions

1. Do you think Bozo's dad made the right choice by letting the boys go out in the cold for a wilderness survival trip?
2. What do you think are the long-term life effects of allowing the boys to make the trip and failing versus telling the boys it was too dangerous and they were not allowed to go?
3. To what extent should children be allowed, or even encouraged, to try and fail at silly things? Where (*if anywhere*) should the line be drawn to simply say no? Do you think parents today typically draw the line in a better spot than when you were growing up? If you were Bozo's dad in the story, would you have waited in the car or left the car looking for the boys?
4. What are the defining childhood hardships, like the one in the story, that you experienced growing up? In retrospect, are you glad they happened, or would you prefer they had not?
5. Why do you think mothers and fathers sometimes have different comfort levels when it comes to the risky experiences of their children? Why do parents sometimes have different risk comfort levels for their sons versus their daughters? How (*if at all*) do these differences in risk comfort affect their children later in life?

* * *

You Make the Call

D. H. Parish

* * *

Content Disclosure: Mild Language

* * *

"Go to Hell!"

I spoke those words exactly 543 times.

Sometimes I said the phrase to family members. Sometimes to coworkers or acquaintances. More often I said them to people I didn't know: a random kid on the street who bumped into me, the guy who cut me off on the freeway, or the woman in the call center in God-knows-where who told me in broken English that the next available doctor's appointment for my urgent question was in three months. Some who heard me say those words returned the favor. Most never knew what I had said, how I had condemned them.

How do I know it was 543 times?

They keep count.

It's not just for me, mind you. I'm not special. They keep count for everyone, at least I think they do for everyone. Can't say I've met everyone here, but it's true for everyone I know.

Five hundred and forty-three cases.

All my responsibility. My final decision. I get to decide how long each one gets to spend in that pretty little slice of the afterlife where they tend to keep the temperature on the hotter side. A few hours? A few days? A few years? Eternity? It's all up to me.

I have case files for each one. They're massive. Boxes and boxes of records for each life. Even the ones who died on the younger side—and I've got one who never made it to his sixteenth birthday (he might have lived longer if he hadn't been so cavalier when he got his learner's permit, or at least I wouldn't have told him where to go)—have an archive's worth of material dedicated to them. Too much to keep on hand. They get a bit irritated if your work area looks too cluttered, worried it reflects a disordered mind not coming to a reasoned decision. Someone once told me Marie Kondo herself came in to consult and fix the issue, but that might just have been a joke, since nothing at my workstation sparks much joy. They'll bring the extra files whenever I need something, so long as I fill out form TPS-204B. Word to the wise—make sure it is form 204B, as form 204A was discontinued. I learned that the hard way when I waited almost six months for the response, and when none was forthcoming, I had to file a GR23 (which has to be completed in single-spaced, 14-point, Comic Sans font) to find out why they hadn't responded to the 204A only to be told it was discontinued and no one responds to a 204A.

The query engine for the system to direct you to a particular box is pretty good, a little better since they banned the sponsored search results, although a pop-up ad gets through now and then. Still, it can take several days to have a request filled and have the boxes delivered. You can only have thirteen out at a time, so it may take you a while if there is a lot of documentation on your particular issue or event. One woman had eighty-three boxes dedicated to one particular March 17 alone, and that wasn't even the day she'd embezzled the $87,000 from her work to help her church pay for roof repairs and get herself a really nice pedicure (to her credit, it did look fabulous—the pedicure, that is).

We also have their whole lives on video. High-definition Blu-ray. It's apparently important to see all the details in exact and vivid color when making these decisions. I'm told the Blu-ray is much better than the Betamax system it replaced, which suggests, come to think of it, that someone in purchasing likes Sony products.

The video of any given life looks like the tracking shot in Goodfellas, or maybe a first-person shooter game (you pick the reference you're familiar with), except you can't control what they're looking at or what they do next, and the cinematography isn't quite up to Scorsese's standards. When I first started, I tried to fast-forward through some of the parts I thought would be irrelevant. I mean, how much can you really tell about a person's soul when they're sleeping or pooping? But then I learned the hard way that you can miss some really important events if you skip too quickly through any part of a life. You'd be amazed what people can get up to in the middle of the night, and not just old men dealing with bloated prostates, so I stopped rushing through those seemingly quiet hours. Since the orientation here is pretty basic, it took a few hundred years before I discovered you could speed the videos up; I think 1.5x speed is probably the best, although some will tell you that you can get away with 2x, and others say anything above 1.2x is risky. Oh, and you absolutely need to turn on the closed captioning, which again I didn't know existed until about year 800.

I thought this might be interesting work at first. Get to know all the details of someone, weigh their existence, and decide their fate. So much power, and who doesn't like power? Couple that power with the chance for a little revenge, and boy, what a tasty stew, right?

Wrong.

People, it turns out, are complicated. The ones I thought I knew, like my ex-wife Kate, I didn't really know at all. Familiarity lets you think you know someone, but you don't, even those close to you. Especially those close to you. There are so many thoughts and actions to which no one else is privy. To give just one example. Katie had started out as a high school English teacher, and it turns out that in the last few years before she quit, she was strict with her students not because she wanted them to do well and fly right, which is what she always told me and her friends and family, but simply because she hated them and wanted to torture them. She only pretended to be firm but fair. In one case, she promised a kid she'd write a good college recommendation for him and then proceeded to trash him, knowing he would never get a chance to respond. As far as I could tell, the kid really wasn't that bad. At least not until he didn't get into any college, started doing drugs, started turning tricks for drugs, killed a john who became violent with him, spent ten years in state prison, took college classes via correspondence courses, earned a BA and an MFA while behind bars, wrote a memoir about his experiences, made a huge amount of money from said memoir and the motivational speaking circuit, purchased one hundred acres of pristine rainforest in a small Central American country, clear-cut that forest, built on the spot a vast compound where he offered a safe haven, education, and employment to youth orphaned in that country's civil unrest, and then forced these boys to run the cocaine empire he subsequently built. Of course, she wrote that rec after an argument with me, about forty-five minutes after what turned out to be the 295th time I had employed the magic phrase.

With the bit players in your life, you are working on more of a blank slate, so there should be no prejudice one way or the other. I say should, because it can be hard not to empathize more with people who are similar to yourself (same gender, same race, same sexual appetites, same peccadillos, same favorite movies, etc.), and you have to guard against it. You also have to resist the urge to condemn to eternal hellfire people who liked the last season of *Game of Thrones* or think pineapple and pizza are a good pair or that Swiss cheese makes the best cheesesteak (yes, such people exist). Such understanding can sometimes cut both ways, however; you might be harder on someone in your own religious or racial group because they should know better and not set a bad example. That said, not knowing someone doesn't make the call any easier. I had initially condemned one guy (number 347 on my list) to perdition because he abruptly cut in front of me one evening on an otherwise calm suburban road. I more frequently invited people in similar situations to have sexual intercourse with themselves, but on that day, I apparently wanted him to endure more cosmic suffering. Well, it seems he was driving quickly because he was late getting home after working overtime at an ER saving the life of twin eight-year-old girls whose car had been sideswiped by a drunk driver, and cutting me off was just his swerving to avoid a stray dog that had wandered in front of his car. One of those girls (they both survived thanks to him) grew up to be a Supreme Court justice. But it turned out the guy was anxious to get home because he remembered he'd left open on his home computer a quite graphic and sexually explicit chat he had been having with a man who was not his husband, and he was worried said husband would get home first and see it. And the other twin grew up to become a serial killer. To be fair, the serial killer specialized in stalking pedophiles, although among her body count of twenty-three, she erroneously killed two innocent men, or at least men innocent of the crimes for which she thought she was garroting them.

So that's my task. Now to help with the decision, before you start, they give you a taste of the unrelenting torment of the world below as well as of the perfect bliss above. Five minutes of each. Like letting the waitstaff taste the food before the dinner rush. Hell sucks, so far as I could tell. Lots of pain and wailing. And heat. Surprisingly, it's not a dry heat. More Florida than Arizona. You still can't get anything to drink, or maybe I wasn't there long enough to find out. You need to experience bliss to believe it. No wings or harps are involved, although the music rocks, and the puppies are cuter than anything you've ever seen on YouTube.

That said, having a taste of the extremes doesn't help much either. Just as my thought of what makes a good meal may not be yours, I don't know how you'll endure and learn from the wretched misery that awaits. Does anyone "deserve" an eternal hell for decisions made in a finite life? Even Hitler and Stalin? How much time does it take to purge a theft? a rape? a murder? an unkind word? On the other hand, who has truly earned eternal bliss? Mathematically, on the backdrop of eternity, one hour of suffering versus one century of suffering is no different when the denominator is infinite. So how does the calculus change knowing the problem is measuring something less discretely quantifiable like a person's psychic or spiritual makeup?

The process implies that there is a right answer, and it is our job, my job, to find it. No one knows what happens if you get it wrong, except that it is not good. They won't tell us if it matters if we get it wrong by erring on the side of too much or too little suffering, or whether we have to get it right with each person or simply hit the number right for the total.

Fortunately, there are no deadlines.

Unfortunately, there are no deadlines.

I get to decide when I am done. After the first 20,000 years, I stopped counting time. How can I ever get this right? The more I know, the more uncertain I am.

I fear I may be at this for a while.

The process, the bureaucratic nightmares of getting that perfect information, the never-ending anxiety about coming to a perfect decision, checking and rechecking, not knowing what is right, it all feels a bit like H—.

Wait. No. That can't be it, can it?

* * *

Discussion Questions

1. If you were forced to be the narrator in this story, how might you tier punishment sentences for different infractions? How long would you punish a person for a single murder, rape, theft, or lie? Would the worst crimes get a week, month, or year in hell as punishment? Would certain crimes get an infinite amount of time?
2. Do you think anyone is ever qualified to judge anyone else's life? Can't another person be just generally horrible, or must we make reasons and allowances for everyone?
3. Can any finite act be justly punished with an infinite amount of pain or for an infinite amount of time?
4. Do you think the unintended consequences of our actions should be considered when deciding appropriate punishments?
5. Do you think the more you know about someone's whole story, the harder it is to judge them harshly for any single act? If so, why is that the case?

* * *

Think of the Children

K.P. Sullivan

* * *

<u>**Content Disclosure**</u>: Mild Violence

* * *

Most parents at some point will declare their child a genius. But I *knew* my daughter, Emery, was smart. I had paid extra to make sure she would be.

Emery's dad was the one who found the Program. Derrick raced across the house with his laptop to show me, believing he had found the solution to all of our problems. We were having trouble conceiving, and I was beginning to take it as a sign. Maybe instead of bringing life into a cruel world, we could be one of those child-free couples who throw a dart at a map and have heedless sex wherever it lands. But if Derrick felt strongly enough to suggest something this radical, I thought I owed it to him to listen.

The Program was supposed to wipe away all of the uncertainty of parenthood. Beyond removing the risk of hereditary disease, the first-of-its-kind experimental study would genetically tailor a child to our specifications. The kid could be destined to become a star athlete, a virtuosic pianist, or a voracious reader on a cellular level. In my most pro-baby moments, I used to imagine sharing my favorite novels with a little bookworm, the kind of kid I'd have to tear a paperback away from to come eat. Suddenly I could have that—with a money-back guarantee.

It seemed like a miracle at the time, but after what happened, that's not the word I'd use. Now, I wonder what would have happened if we had shut the laptop and laughed off the idea. Could we have been that happy couple?

Would anyone have died?

We built our child like a custom couch online. They'd have my eyes, obviously. They needed Derrick's wild curls and his big, dumb teeth, the ones I always loved. We'd skip my side's penchant for anxiety and depression, and anything we could do to steer clear of his father's... situation would be a bonus. With every detail of them right there for me to read on a computer screen, it was like I already knew this baby.

While I was pregnant, Derrick joked that I kept reviewing our take-out order. I would look over the collection of features we had chosen and imagine the person they'd combine to make, how the world may treat them. Would she have my doubts? My fears? Or could she be better?

But when Emery finally arrived, she brought clarity with her. The doctor held her up for me to see, and she ceased to be a hypothetical. My first thought was that she didn't look how I had expected. My eyes were hidden beneath her swollen lids, and Derrick's curls were still months away. But as she lay on my chest, she was undeniable.

Exactly as I hoped she would be.

Emery's first breath marked the beginning of Phase Two. She was born on the same day as the fifteen other children of her experimental cohort. Eight girls and eight boys. Derrick and I had opted not to choose a sex for Emery. We wanted to leave something of her up to chance, but the symmetry within the group made me wonder whether the matter had simply been taken out of our hands.

What else was decided for us?

Once released from the hospital, all sixteen families relocated to a small island community on Lake Michigan. There, the Program would provide us with everything a young family could possibly need. We moved into an adorable two-bedroom house, situated along a tree-lined street with fifteen others, all identical to it. The homes were a short walk from a corner store that accepted the play money mailed to us every two weeks. And at the center of the neighborhood was a perfect one-room schoolhouse with red siding and a charming bell tower straight out of *Little House*.

The highly controlled conditions of the experiment made for a pretty ideal place to raise a kid. No one was older or younger. They lived in the same sort of house and wore outfits composed from a standardized wardrobe. There was no mortgage to pay, so maybe their parents would argue less. Their isolation kept them away from "normal children," but I think all the parents agreed that *privilege* could be a lesson for down the road. For now, in our perfect village, the genetically engineered kids could just be kids.

The first years flew by in a haze of giddy wonder, and Emery proved my worries wrong every step of the way. She was extraordinary, reading at two and doing algebra by six. But beyond what she knew, each day revealed more of the person she was becoming. She loved school and the other kids. She was curious, sharp, and giggled with abandon. She adored her dad, but would always share a look with me whenever his antics veered too goofy. There was an ease to Emery's bright kindness that I knew had to come from growing up away from it all.

She certainly didn't get it from us.

But every advantage came with a cost. Exposure to the outside world could compromise the integrity of the experiment, so no personal electronics were allowed on the island. The school library had books and films to borrow, but all of them were approved by the Program and then voted on by the parents. Derrick would get itchy at the meetings and mutter about censorship and coddling. I didn't understand why it bothered him so much. We had basically done eugenics, but the library not having *Alien* was suddenly beyond the pale.

We started arguing regularly for the first time in our relationship. Our situation was unusual, but the fights were mundane. (His complaints about the island being confining were selfish. I was ignoring his feelings.) The details of each disagreement would vary, but they all ended the same way: Emery brought us back together. We would be in the kitchen or wherever we believed to be out of earshot, and she would enter with a problem that needed solving. Sometimes it was homework due the next day. Others, it was her own question about the world and how it worked that required two adult minds to answer it, usually insufficiently.

Not long after I noticed the pattern, I began to see through it. She'd ask us to define *lugubrious* when I had heard her use it in a sentence the week before. And the math problems that stumped her had previously been easily within her grasp. To me, it was clear she didn't really need us. She just wanted us to believe she did. And so did we.

When I mentioned my suspicions to Derrick—that our six-year-old was manipulating us—he stared, waiting for me to hear the insanity in what I had said.

Derrick returned to the mainland for the first time the week after Emery turned nine. Parents in the Program had always been allowed onto the boat that shuttled the scientists, teachers, and grocery store staff to and from the island, but we never made the trip. Emery was our life, and she was here. But his mother hadn't been feeling well, he told both of us at the same time. Emery immediately began an expressionist painting for her La La. I wondered if my husband would come back.

He did. That time.

* * *

The news of our separation was greeted by the other parents on the island like an invasive species. The Program's director, Dr. Kapp, called a meeting at the schoolhouse to discuss how we would introduce the eleven-year-olds to the concept. It was my and Derrick's fault that they would have to find the words, and since I was the only one still there, I became the sole mascot of our failure.

To be honest, I felt freed, even as the woman who invented divorce for a group of innocent kids. Derrick's departure meant I could stop being a disappointing wife and focus on what really mattered—being a disappointing mother.

Emery only existed because we thought we could truly protect her. Those perfect genes were meant to inoculate her against the suffering of the average life. Of course, they didn't. They couldn't. In fact, her superior intellect just made her all the more aware of her pain. How I could ever apologize to her enough, I will never know.

But miraculously, Emery never withdrew from me. Her grades didn't drop off. She didn't lash out. In fact, she seemed to be about the only one on the island who didn't believe I had pushed Derrick away.

It perplexed me. My Emery, the girl who worshiped her father and laughed at even his worst jokes, should have been devastated by his decision to leave us. Where was that fierce sense of fairness when something so patently unfair was happening to her? It wasn't that I wanted her to hurt. I just couldn't make sense of the missing equal and opposite reaction. Over dinner, I would pry, trying to find some blotch on her brave face, but nothing ever surfaced.

Thinking back on that time, though, it's clear that her plan was already in motion.

* * *

I don't blame Officer Calvin for what happened. I understand why the other parents did, but I never thought that was fair. No one on the island could have imagined consequences so tragic from a mistake so small.

He had been warned, though. As the neighborhood's primary security guard, Calvin was expected to follow the same rules we all were—the most relevant were about his phone. It was supposed to stay in his car at the ferry station, but with a disabled son back on the mainland, that was probably too great a distance between him and the assurance that he was all right.

When I heard that his cargo pocket had chimed with a new text while the kids filed into the schoolhouse, I worried he was going to be fired. A few of us spoke to Dr. Kapp in his defense. Calvin may have broken the rules, but we actually trusted him—a man with a gun—to protect our children.

The day it happened again, Emery returned from school

reporting nothing out of the ordinary, the first of many lies. We had just sat down for dinner when the doorbell rang.

It was Mailman Dan.

Dan was a member of Dr. Kapp's staff, a childhood psychologist with the additional responsibility of alerting parents of an emergency meeting. The postal costume had been his idea, to avoid raising any alarm. It never really worked. Even our freaky little island kids knew that mail wasn't delivered at night.

And I don't think his name was actually Dan.

I brought Emery to the house of a friend blessed with two present parents for an impromptu movie night, while I headed to the schoolhouse. Dr. Kapp was waiting for us when we got there. Kapp usually had a polished look, half scientist-half PR rep. But his harried expression that night suggested that we were joining this story in the middle of it.

Calvin's phone was missing.

The uproar from the parents was instantaneous. *How could this happen? Why didn't we hear about this immediately?* Kapp explained: Calvin first suspected that he had misplaced it shortly after class started that morning, but because he couldn't confirm that he hadn't simply forgotten it in his car, he waited until evening to report it missing. There was an immediate search of the ferry and Calvin's patrol route, but nothing turned up. Because of the timing of the disappearance and Calvin's subsequent search of his house, the device was believed to be somewhere on the island, in the possession of someone smart enough to turn off the location settings.

Dr. Kapp never directly stated that one of the children had taken the phone and was now hiding it, but the parents reacted like he had.

You can't seriously think that Grayson stole it.

Amity has never even seen a phone. How would she know to take it?

Well, we haven't introduced the concept of theft to Jexen, so...

I sat there, listening to the other parents rule out their own children as suspects, staring at Emery's nametag on the desktop in front of me and hoping that she had stolen the phone. I hated myself for it, but at least then I would have the reaction I expected. Then I could see the crisis I was dealing with, rather than grasping at one in the dark.

Kapp begged for forgiveness and quiet. None of the children was being accused, but for the sake of the experiment, every room on the island would need to be searched. The "subjects" had such voracious minds and had been raised in such a highly regulated environment that an internet connection could behave like a spark onto kindling.

The room grew silent with consensus, and Kapp gave his instructions. We would all return to our homes, send the children to the schoolhouse, and search their rooms. We'd be thorough, though careful not to make the intrusion known and cause more trouble than we were already in.

On my way out of the school, I checked the faces of the other parents. More were pale than red, no matter how unfamiliar Jexen was with the concept of theft.

Emery always kept her room neat, something I was grateful for until I needed to ransack it. Everything she owned had a particular spot and needed to be replaced precisely once I looked under it. Her colored pencils were arrayed like the visible spectrum. The stack of drawings in her desk was tucked into the drawer's corner. Her bedsheets would have received a stern nod of approval from a drill sergeant. She would notice the intrusion, and it would have been for nothing.

The phone wasn't there.

The guilt I had felt wanting her to be the culprit returned. How could I have hoped for such a thing? How could I have believed it was possible? The perfect daughter had been handed to me on a silver petri dish. Maybe it was time I acted like it.

Emery sensed something was wrong as soon as she appeared at the schoolhouse door. Her mouth shrank as much as her eyes widened, waiting for me to tell her what this was all about.

I threw my arm around her and said it was all boring parent stuff.

The lying she must have gotten from me.

* * *

Small huddles and hushed conversations popped up across the neighborhood early the next morning. All of the parents had searched their kid's room. No one found the phone.

Every last one of them found *something*, though. Once we each had a chance to clear our child, someone would confess to an unexpected discovery. A bad grade on a test or a weapon made from a stick. Then another would offer up the same, saying that the search had confirmed a suspicion they had been harboring.

But here's the thing about children genetically engineered to display intelligence: They're not stupid. Emery didn't mention finding her scrunchies out of their proper order, but she didn't have to. The invasion of her room must have been as obvious as the rest of the searches were.

Later that morning, I stood with the other parents as we sent the kids off to class, watching them abandon their usual cliques to unite as one group outside.

The children were talking.

* * *

But they were *not* talking to the adults. The day after the phone's disappearance, not a single hand was raised in class. And when their teacher countered their silence with a pop quiz, they answered each question incorrectly with coordinated precision.

The parents pushed through a new rule banning congregating outside the school before the bell. An order forcing kids to go straight home after class came next. Since there was no point trying to hide that the parents were looking for something, Dr. Kapp spoke with the children about the issue directly. He explained how the person who had taken the phone was actually quite selfish, allowing their classmates to be punished for something they did.

From there, the protest migrated home. For an entire week, Emery, like the rest of the kids, would finish her homework promptly upon returning—getting every answer wrong—and complete whatever chores were asked of her, but not once did she speak a word to me. Her resolve was strong. I could see in her eyes how much the collective action hurt her, probably because she could see how alone she had left me.

After a few days of stalemate, Dr. Kapp made the decision that would mark the beginning of the end. He sent the kids home, where they couldn't organize. Class would be disbanded until the phone was recovered. The news was devastating to Emery, who lived for school. I asked Kapp if there was any other option, something less extreme, but he stood firm. And the other parents backed him.

Kapp's plan ended up working. But the children's plan was better.

Three days went by. Emery would wake up promptly and go about her day with the discipline of a productivity coach. I should have been at least a little proud. My fifth grader was not needing me at a college level.

That night with Emery in bed, I was up, trying to read my Program-approved book, when the alarm began ringing. The sound itself was small, but the electronic chime was so foreign on the island that it blared. It was louder on the porch. Other parents appeared at their own doors, drawn by the siren song. The phone was somewhere outside.

A handful of us began chasing the sound, alternating between running and listening for another clue of its location. It seemed to be moving.

As we scrambled through the darkness of the island, a gunshot cracked the night air in half.

I froze, sure that I had imagined it. But then the screaming started.

He's dead! Call 911!

* * *

Officer Calvin was catatonic when we found him by the ferry terminal. The gun was still smoking in his hand.

We begged him to tell us what happened.

He had been running around like us, searching for the phone. The alarm drove him toward the water, toward the dock. Then he heard children screaming for help.

Silhouetted by the dock lights, all he could see was a tall male figure, struggling with smaller ones. Calvin yelled for them to identify themself, but when the man in the shadow raised his arm, Calvin had no choice but to fire.

Calvin ran at the attacker, then realized with horror: It was Dr. Kapp, clutching the phone to his bleeding chest. No children were in sight.

The next morning, none of the kids admitted to leaving bed.

* * *

The Program's board convened shortly after Kapp's death and decided to continue with the experiment. Their explanation to us cited the late doctor's memory and the significance of his life's work—rather than the millions they had already sunk into the island.

But something irreparable had broken in the neighborhood. A man was dead, and everyone felt in their gut that some—maybe all—of the children had played a role. But there was no proof. The recovered phone didn't offer any clues. Whoever had taken it erased the browser history and wiped away their fingerprints.

The parents stopped speaking with each other. None of us could rule out our own kid this time.

At home, Emery was as defiant as ever, and I stopped waking up with her. The first morning I stayed in bed, I heard her poke her head into my bedroom just far enough to make sure I was breathing, before heading off to school. She was fine without me, just like her dad.

At the corner store, I noticed that the vodka stocks were lower than usual, so if nothing else, I found my community in day-drunk absentia.

Almost a week went by like that, with me haunting my home like the ghost of my former self—the one who was a mother. It was around noon one day when a knock on the door pulled me from bed. Mailman Dan had dropped by to say that the Program was aware of the issues with the utilities and that they'd be back up as soon as possible. When I told him I hadn't noticed any problems, he seemed surprised, so I explained how comfortable my bed was and how depression typically worked.

When he left, I saw that my alarm clock was blank. None of the lights turned on, and the toilet bowl was as dry as the tap. Teams of plumbers and electricians arrived on the ferry that afternoon and quickly discovered the issue.

The word "sabotage" struck me as overdramatic until I was met with its literal definition. Sewage technicians found clogs throughout the system. Dozens of kitchen sponges had wormed their way into the pipes across the island. The power outage was harder to figure out, since the island's central grid never went down. The hunt for a failure point led the electricians to the family room lamps, all of which had corner store coins hidden beneath the lightbulbs, blowing the home breakers.

This was escalation.

The plumbing crew was still working to restore running water when Mailman Dan returned that night carrying word of an emergency meeting at the schoolhouse. All of the kids were to be sent to their rooms, and every parent was expected to attend.

I found Emery at her desk, doing homework incorrectly and wearing all of the black clothing she owned. I asked if I could come in and sit down, imagining her breaking her silence just to deny me. But she nodded instead.

I told her the parents were meeting at the schoolhouse, probably to hash out what sort of punishment infrastructure sabotage merited, but I didn't feel like going. I admitted that I didn't really like the other parents. They seemed to be operating under the premise that they were owed an apology, rather than owing their kids an explanation.

Emery listened, curious about whether I had a point to make. And I did my best to hide that I was only half sure of what that point was.

I told her how before I got pregnant, I was afraid because I couldn't control where the world would take her. But she had proven me wrong yet again. Now I couldn't wait to see where she would take the world.

I made a quick exit after that, knowing my preteen window of patience was about to expire. I told her that I loved her and asked that she not stay up too late. She blinked.

You might think an experimental program with enough funding to purchase an entire island wouldn't have skimped on building materials, but the thin walls were the only reason I heard the front door close late that night. In the hall, I found Emery's bedroom door ajar. Her diary was resting open in plain sight, on top of her bed, where she had wanted me to find it.

The entries recounted the story of the last two weeks in reverse. I flipped back to the day the phone went missing. In the course of a day, her writing changed from loosely connected quotidian observations to an exhaustive list of her online reading with detailed notes.

Emery began poking around where you'd expect any kid to—looking up her favorite animals, books she wanted to read but couldn't, and the actor I knew she had a crush on. The plot thickened when she transcribed the definitions of "control group" and "civil disobedience" in the same afternoon. She moved briskly from there to Henry David Thoreau and Jean-Paul Sartre, the Wikipedia pages for the Battle of Algiers and the Troubles, and something called the "Simple Sabotage Field Manual," a declassified OSS guide from 1944 for living under fascist regimes.

The most recent entry, under that day's date, recapped a YouTube video about piloting a ferry boat and the Google results for her father's name, which didn't turn up much.

By the time I reached the porch, all of the children were gathered outside the schoolhouse. The ferry, which had brought the utility workers, loomed in the distance. The bags on the kids' backs were heavy with what I imagined to be food and a change of clothes. They stood watching as Finleigh, the island's most artistically gifted child, finished scrawling a message in white paint across the red-paneled wall.

"BRED IN CAPTIVITY"

When Finleigh was done, the sixteen of them gathered in a tight circle, examining something at the middle of it. But soon, they were spread out again in a wide line to face the schoolhouse.

It was Emery who stepped forward to break the ranks.

I could see her clearly, even from the porch. The fire from the Molotov cocktail in her hand cast a brilliant light upon her face. She was so much more than my eyes, her father's wild curls, and his big, dumb teeth. As she reached back behind her to throw the flaming bottle of corner store vodka onto the schoolhouse's roof, I saw my Emery with perfect clarity— fierce, full of conviction, and utterly fearless.

Exactly as I hoped she would be.

Emery saw me approaching and paused. A few of the children moved to get between me and her, but my daughter waved me through.

When I reached her, I held out my hand, asking for the bottle, and she handed it over without a fight. I told her I was proud of her, that I was proud of all of them, and that this would work better with a head start.

"Just promise to call me when you get there," I said.

She squeezed my hand and, with the other kids, ran off toward the ferry.

Then I threw the bottle onto the roof.

* * *

Discussion Questions

1. At one point, or with what specific decision, in your opinion, did the experiment first go wrong?
2. Do you think children should have their media and experiences crafted by parents through censorship and guardrails? How is what they are doing in the story different than what parents do in real life? How is the island different than a suburbia of identical tract homes?
3. Is it always the case that the creation/offspring will revolt against its creator/parent? Is this true of regular children as well as artificial intelligence?
4. How do you think the story would have continued over the next five, ten, or fifteen years if there had been no missing cell phone and no information slipups?
5. What do you think happens to the children after they escape the island? Do they lead generally normal lives? Do they remain friends? Do they forgive/return to their parents in the future? Do they tend to view the world through a positive or negative lens?

* * *

At Age Four

Morgan Parker

* * *

<u>Content Disclosure</u>: Mild Language

* * *

At age four, I said, "I'm not a girl; I'm a boy like Daddy." Ribbons, dresses, and Barbie dolls felt strange, and I loved to play with GI Joe toy soldiers. I imagined myself the prince in the fairy tales my mother read to me. I cut my hair short, bragged about how strong and fast I was, and hung out with boys. I auditioned for male roles in school plays and wooed girls who broke my heart. I was generally liked and got by with a wry wit and a few very close friends, especially Rebecca. We confided our innermost feelings to each other and became romantically involved. She was gorgeous.

Rebecca wanted a vagina and to pee sitting down. I wanted a penis and to pee standing up. At puberty, we both had crises. I hid my growing breasts in tight binders and, when my period came on, sunk into a major depression. Boys don't have periods. I skipped school, slept all the time, and my grades plummeted. Rebecca was even worse. She moved away with her parents, and we lost our lifelines.

My parents were alarmed. They were open-minded medical doctors and understood early on that I was a boy in a girl's body. They accepted my dress and demeanor and never tried to nudge me in another direction. They called me Louis, the name I had chosen for myself at six, not Louise, the girl's name they chose for me at birth. They repeatedly said, "Louis, we love you unconditionally." When I fell into a major depression at puberty, they arranged for specialized counseling and my puberty-blocking and testosterone therapy. The counseling and drugs worked beyond my dreams! I looked and felt like a boy again. I returned to school and got straight A's again. I was happy!

Everything changed when a crackpot biochemist named Benjamin Clark announced the availability of a so-called "breakthrough drug" for transgender individuals. It started with an observation followed by experimentation that he presented to his peers.

"A small proportion of perfectly healthy male and female penguins (perhaps five percent) manifest long-term same-sex partnership. They remain exclusively in this partnership, even during the breeding season. They don't birth but participate in incubating, feeding, and protecting the colony's hatchlings. I have studied their brain chemistry and found the uniform absence of a chemical in their hypothalamus, a chemical that is present in the rest of the breeding colony. The statistical likelihood of this being a chance occurrence is less than 0.001, less than one in one thousand. When we replaced this chemical, the sexual behavior in this unique group of penguins became indistinguishable from that of the larger colony of breeding penguins. The remarkable transformation from same-sex to opposite-sex behavioral union lasted for the half-life of the replaced chemical, one month."

Clark's experiments were published in prominent scientific journals and sparked the interest of a major pharmaceutical company that funded human research. After basic research and extensive clinical trials, a drug that transitioned the sexual identity of transgender individuals to match their birth sex (chromosomal sex) became commercially available. The monthly injectable drug was relatively safe in the short term, with a few minor side effects. It had an onset of days, was uniformly effective for its six-week half-life, as predicted, and most of the medical community endorsed it for recalcitrant gender dysphoria.

Clark's drug sparked explosive reactions, angry outcries, and a barrage of questions from bioethicists, philosophers, LGBTQ, and heterosexual people in town hall meetings.

"I'm a transgender man, and I don't want to change. I'm happy as I am. My identity is not a disorder for which I need a drug."

"I agree; transgender is just another form of sexuality."

"The professor is transphobic. His drug will lead to more prejudice. It will give bigoted people excuses to bully us even more when we choose not to take it."

"Who is he even to suggest that such a drug is needed, let alone to create one? We don't need a prescription to erase us!"

"The professor is not transphobic. His drug was born of pure science to expand knowledge. He is free of moral judgment."

"Even if the professor is free of moral judgment, most people aren't. His science may be pure, but how people interpret his science will be prejudicial and dangerous."

"Professor Clark, why did you pioneer the development of this drug?"

"I was driven by the question, what causes someone to be transgender? For every effect, there must be a cause, and as a scientist, I wanted to find the cause. It was scientific experimentation searching for an answer. Also, my son is transgender. I witnessed the severe emotional and physical challenges he faced at puberty. They were far beyond that of my cisgender children, which were hard enough. I hoped to provide help for transgender children facing puberty."

"Should parents administer the drug to very young children to spare them later anguish if they know they are transgender?"

"No. It's not a choice cisgender parents can or should make, no matter how well-intentioned they are. Cisgender parents have different perspectives. They should wait until their transgender child is old enough to understand their sexual identity, ideally before puberty; then, inform them of all options and let them choose. Truly loving parents accept, respect, and support whatever choice their transgender child makes."

"What choice do you think they will make?"

"From my limited perspective, I think it depends on the level of gender dysphoria, which can vary in intensity, and how much can be supported and addressed through established practices. In most but not all, gender dysphoria is effectively treated with established gender-affirming counseling, puberty blockers, and hormonal therapy. Currently, the great majority of transgender adolescents choose gender-affirming therapy and not our drug, however effective it may be."

"Professor Clark, can professional counseling alone transition transgender identity to cisgender?"

"No. This type of counseling is ineffective, harmful, and unethical."

"Does your transgender son take your drug?"

"He hasn't decided yet."

"Your drug is moderately high in price. How much money do you make from it? How much stock do you own in the pharmaceutical company that sells it?"

"None. One hundred percent of my proceeds from the drug are auto-deposited into the nonprofit organization I created. Our organization provides free-of-charge gender-affirming counseling, puberty blockers, and hormones or counseling plus our transgender-transitioning drug—whichever they choose— to people who cannot afford them."

"That's great, Professor. As you probably know, insurance companies in some states don't cover puberty blockers, which leaves many transgender kids in limbo. They do, however, cover your more expensive gender-transition drug, which most don't want. It's an extreme form of prejudice being litigated right now."

When my parents learned about the new transgender drug, they were willing to pay if I wanted it. They were very responsive to my feelings and supportive.

"Louis, the choice is yours, and we'll always love you unconditionally, no matter the choice. You're beautiful inside and out, and we're proud of you. That won't change, no matter what!"

They then tried to fairly present the pros and cons of the drug from their perspective.

"They say this drug would match your sexual identity feelings with your anatomical sex. It could give you a more liberated life in our society. You could bear children if you want them. On the other hand, the drug is brand new, and we don't know its long-term mental and physical effects. That's very concerning. Most importantly, we don't know how you would feel after taking it. You seem happy now. Louis, the choice is yours. The bottom line for us is we want you to be happy. We're so grateful that you felt free and secure enough to share your identity with us early on; too many kids don't and are worse off for it."

"I love you, and I know you love me. I'm a boy, and I'm happy. There's no way I'm taking artificial injections for the rest of my life."

I went to my room and found Rebecca on Facebook.

"Rebecca, you cut your beautiful hair, and there's fuzz on your lip."

"I'm off estrogen now, and I'm growing a mustache."

"Why? You took the drug?"

"Yeah. At first, I didn't want to, but I was in therapy and still drowning. My parents talked me into it. I was angry and scared, but I took it. Do you like how I look?"

"No. But how do you feel?"

"I feel weird. I think about girls all the time now, even when I sleep. I had a wet dream last night and woke up hard."

"That's disgusting. Do you want to take the shot every month for the rest of your life?"

"I don't know."

"You don't know? Are you happier?"

"I think so. Some kids remember me as a girl and still call me 'she-male,' but they'll never change no matter what I do. They're bigots. Some kids welcome me and say, 'Now you're one of us: one less of them.' They're bigger bigots. Most kids say nothing or congratulate me. I have more friends now. Am I happier? I think so; I'm less depressed."

Rebecca asked me to try the drug, and I didn't want to hear it, so I ended our talk abruptly and made no arrangements to talk again.

In school, many kids were not as accepting as before, and a few came straight out and said, "Louis, if I were you, I would try the drug. Your mind will match your body. Once you're on it, your perspective on avoiding it will completely change. You'll want it and be happier. If you're not happier, you can stop the drug and change back."

I exploded. "You say to me, 'If I were you,' but you're not me! What am I doing, sampling ice cream flavors? I'll try pistachio; no, butterscotch is better. How in hell do you know how I feel? I'm happy now. Screw you!"

It seemed like everyone offended me, and I offended them. I quit my so-called friends and gravitated to Zelda, an unattractive, straight female with a self-diagnosed social anxiety disorder. We were both loners. For some strange reason, she trusted me because I was transgender, and I trusted her because she took my side. We bonded and had long discussions. She knew about Clark's penguins and reminded me, "Louis, the same-sex penguin couples he studied didn't birth, but they did incubate, feed, and protect hatchlings. They contributed mightily to the survival of their colony and species. If you wish, you could choose to adopt an abandoned baby or the fetus of a pregnant woman who intends to have an abortion.

You can have children with or without a partner of your choosing. You could save and raise them lovingly and honorably, as I know you would, and they can become healers, philanthropists, or peacemakers who contribute to humanity because of you. Do whatever the hell you want to do and be whoever the hell you want to be."

Zelda gave me tremendous emotional comfort and support; maybe I helped her.

I'm not a boy now. I'm a man. I wish Clark had never discovered that damned drug.

* * *

Discussion Questions

1. What are the factors you would consider if you were transgender and offered Clark's drug? To what extent would your happiness or community and parental expectations be factors? What other factors might you consider?

2. Assuming Clark's drug were real and available, what natural social pitfalls might you see arising in response? For example, states (*or parents*) mandating its use or companies including or excluding it from their health insurance plans for public relation reasons. What else?

3. Do you think finding a concrete medical explanation for being transgender would help or hurt the fight for LGBTQ equality? On one hand, there would be proof it is not a choice; on the other hand, it could cause people to believe it is a medical condition to be fixed.

4. How do you think the transgender community would treat people who took Clark's drug? What would be the basis for their community treatment and do you agree or disagree?

5. Can a transgender person deciding on Clark's drug ever be able to separate what they really want from the influences of media, friends, and family? Can a cisgender person?

* * *

The Dinner

Anton I. Botha

* * *

<u>**Content Disclosure**</u>: Low Intensity

* * *

Mary was about to take a bite of her own flesh and could think of no good reason not to. Perched on the edge of her fork was a cube of meat glazed in a blood orange sauce, beautifully prepared by a world-renowned chef.

* * *

The package had arrived mysteriously, slipped under the door of her fifth-floor Manhattan walk-up. No stamp. No name. Just an elegantly written card on textured off-white paper:

> *David Taggart hereby cordially invites you to dinner at his San Francisco residence on Saturday, September 20, 7 p.m. PDT. We sincerely hope we can count on the pleasure of your company, Ms. McCarren. Your opinion is*

sought on a matter of some importance. It
promises to be a night not to be forgotten.

Along with the card: a first-class plane ticket, hotel confirmation, and a typed letter from Wynslow Wayne, Taggart's personal assistant, wishing her a comfortable journey. All expenses paid. No obligations. Just dinner.

Mary had never met David Taggart. She doubted many outside his inner circle had. A notorious Silicon Valley billionaire, he made his first fortune selling a crypto exchange and was now the reclusive force behind one of the most powerful venture capital firms in the world. A libertarian futurist rumored to bankroll lawsuits, sway media narratives, and haunt elite conferences, Taggart was as reclusive as he was influential.

Mary paced her apartment, equal parts intrigued and unnerved. She googled the Fairmont. Estimated value of the trip? Around twelve thousand dollars. Three months' rent.

Her fingers hovered over her phone. Then, without fully deciding to, she dialed.

In less than a full ring, Wynslow Wayne answered: "*Good afternoon, Ms. McCarren. We've been expecting your call,*" her voice British-ish, but not quite. Polished. Vaguely unsettling.

Mary's concerns were brushed away with uncanny precision. She hung up, unsure whether she'd just been reassured or hypnotized. But her curiosity had been sparked— and that always won.

* * *

Mary hadn't planned on a career in clickbait. She dreamed of investigative journalism but ended up at *Woke*, writing articles like "5 Animals You Didn't Know You Were Eating" under the pseudonym Bridget Sauré. A little part of her died with every headline. Still, for her own sanity, she snuck in serious work under her real name when she could—like that *Guardian* piece that had made waves.

It was a deep dive into the environmental cost of industrial meat. In it, she argued—as she had in her doctoral thesis—that while outlawing meat was unrealistic, serious limits were needed. If society returned to pre-industrial per capita consumption levels, global emissions from meat could be halved. With the rise of plant-based alternatives, current habits were not just unsustainable—they were unethical.

The article caused a firestorm. Her inbox imploded. Conservative pundits called her un-American. On CNN, she defended her work opposite a meat lobbyist in a made-for-TV showdown. She'd grown up eating brisket like everyone else, but the science, the suffering, the scale—she couldn't ignore it. And unlike most advocates, she wasn't calling for a ban. Just a reevaluation.

* * *

She packed for San Francisco with military precision, laying everything out on the bed like a surgeon prepping for surgery. Her ex, Michael, used to photograph the scene and send it to his family as proof of her insanity. In time, Mary began to wonder if he had a point—her packing did have a serial killer quality: methodical, meticulous, unnervingly exact. She felt mildly vindicated when she found out that she was forty-two percent German thanks to one of those GeneVeritas genetic tests. She comforted herself in the fact that all Germans packed this way and resigned herself to the futility of fighting this genetic predisposition.

* * *

The hotel room was nicer than her apartment. A handwritten note welcomed her and confirmed her driver would arrive at 6:12 p.m. PS: There is a private tour of Alcatraz arranged. A special visit to Robert Stroud's quarters, the Birdman himself.

Mary hadn't told anyone but her close friends about her fascination with Stroud. And yet... here it was. Gift wrapped. Her stomach flipped.

* * *

At 6:12 p.m. sharp, a porter approached her in the lobby.

"Miss McCarren? Your car is ready."

* * *

The car advanced onto a pitch-black driveway extending about half a mile to a minimalist, monolithic structure perched on the edge of the Pacific cliff. Smaller than she expected. A woman stood waiting on the path, lit by the almost extinguished sun and the cold gleam of embedded LEDs guiding the way to the door. She donned a cream bodycon dress, matching cream heels, and blonde hair pulled back in a strict bun. After Mary exited the car, the woman extended her hand and introduced herself.

"Wynslow Wayne, Dr. McCarren. We are so pleased you made it."

Despite the setting, the house revealed little. No fanfare. No other cars. The only decor was a Latin phrase on the doormat: *Isto posito egredere foras.* Mary caught the Latin for "assumptions." The rest escaped her. Wynslow gestured toward the elevator.

When it opened, Mary stepped into a glass-walled space overlooking the Pacific. The house was not on the cliff—it was in it.

The interior was minimalist but warm. Everything had a purpose. No Persian rugs or gilded statues—just thoughtful quiet luxury.

Wynslow led her down a floating staircase into a lounge divided into two zones: a reception space with white cocktail tables and a dining area set for six.

"Everyone, may I have your attention? Our final guest has arrived," Wynslow's voice cut effortlessly through the room. "Mary, these are your fellow guests—Tomi, Ren, Winston, and Suntosh."

Mary did her best to remember names—pairing Tomi with a tomcat in her mind before being offered a drink by Wynslow.

"A Bulleit rye, ice chips, splash of lime cordial," she said.

"You got it."

With that, Wynslow left only for a waiter to appear with her exact order seconds later.

"A bit disconcerting, isn't it?" said a voice beside her. She turned to see Winston—herringbone blazer, jeans, an ethnic scarf that announced man of the world.

Mary cleared her throat, trying not to choke on an ice chip. "A tad, but we do owe our host a certain debt of gratitude, I suppose."

Winston smirked. "True. I flew first class from London. Not something a journalist like me does often."

"Gossiping about our host?" Tomi asked, gliding over with a vodka soda in hand.

She had bottle-blonde hair, a scarlet cocktail dress, and the kind of charisma that belonged on a Fox News couch. Her outfit left little to the imagination.

"Tomi, what is it that you do?" asked Winston, averting his eyes in a northerly direction.

"I host *The Daze* podcast—maybe you've heard of it? I lay out real agendas for the conservative youth of this great freedom-loving country."

Mary stiffened. Now she recognized her. She'd hate-listened to a few episodes—freedom of speech, flag-worship rants, etc. Tomi was Texas royalty: sharp-tongued, privileged, unapologetic.

"Pleasure to meet you," Mary lied.

Mary became aware of a presence next to her and turned to meet Taggart's gaze. He didn't enter the room so much as he appeared in it. Unannounced and unceremonious.

"Good evening, everyone. I am so pleased you could all join me in my home tonight."

The guests were still mid-sentence when he uttered these words, most did a double take to confirm it was, in fact, Taggart. As the realization set in across the room, so did an atmosphere of silence and singular focus.

"Most of you have traveled great distances to be here—for that, I thank you. I know you must be curious why I've brought you here. I ask that you bear with me just a few moments longer. What I can be transparent about is my intention to pick your minds clean. Each of you brings a distinct, informed perspective. I didn't invite you for polite conversation, I need your help in examining something that cuts to the core of who we are—and who we might become.

"So please, speak plainly. Think deeply. You may find yourselves far outside your comfort zones. Should that moment arise, I encourage you to set aside your emotions. After all, what is reason, if not the tool we use to rise above instinct?"

As Taggart delivered his welcome remarks, Mary was struck by how much shorter he was in person. His skin looked... preserved. Pale, taut. Too smooth to be natural yet not frozen like Botox. His expressions moved effortlessly. He couldn't be younger than sixty. But he looked forty. Maybe younger. Turns out the fountain of youth isn't a place, just a very large bank account.

"Before we take a seat at the dinner table, let's all enjoy our drinks, and I will ask the chef to send some canapés our way to fend off any urgent hunger pangs."

A waiter emerged silently from behind the eastern wall, silver tray in hand, and offered Mary and Winston a canapé. Nestled inside a hollowed-out shiitake mushroom were strips of perfectly medium-rare steak—caramelized outside, pink inside—topped with black truffle oil and whole mustard seeds.

Mary picked one up delicately and popped it in whole. The flavors played together like a string quartet—refined, harmonious, exquisite.

As the tray made its way around the room, Mary noticed both Suntosh and Ren politely declined. Curious, she walked over to Suntosh, still nursing a nearly full glass of wine. He looked uneasy.

He appeared South Asian, dressed in a black mandarin-collared suit that matched his jet-black hair. Something about him felt guarded.

"For someone so meticulous about our travel plans," Mary said, "Taggart seems to have skipped the bit about dietary restrictions."

"An unfortunate oversight," Suntosh said. "Beef wouldn't normally feature on any menu I'd choose. But I trust provisions have been made."

"I'm sure they have. What do you do, Suntosh?"

"I write for a Sunday paper in India—social and cultural commentary. I'm also fairly active on social media. Around ten million followers across platforms. Not as impressive as it sounds in a country of 1.4 billion."

With that, Taggart interrupted their conversation: "Will you all please join me at the dinner table," he said, waving the guests in the direction of their place settings with a smile.

Mary was seated next to Ren and adjacent to Taggart at the head of the table. Ren was tall, sharp, and impeccably dressed in a slim gray suit and skinny silver tie. His face was unreadable, fixed in the kind of polished neutrality that could easily belong to a stoic monk.

All the guests were now positioned behind their chairs. Taggart signaled for them to sit as if now eager to dispense with formalities. The table itself was set with fine crystal stemware, gold-rimmed white plates with black place settings, and subtle gold thread woven delicately in a radial pattern resembling the double helix of DNA. Mary usually found gold to be a crass decoration, but it was subtle enough to avoid that label.

A waiter once more appeared from around the corner, sporting a bottle of white wine. He circled the table, making sure everyone got a tasting measure. Mary's glass frosted up almost immediately as the cold liquid settled in its delicate crystal vessel.

"I trust you're all comfortable. Tonight's meal will be one of the most intriguing you've ever tasted—that, I'll guarantee.

"It's been prepared by Chef Juan Mallmann, widely considered the foremost expert in meat cuisine. He's been working with me for some time to develop this menu. I do hope you enjoy it."

Taggart now turned his attention to Ren and Suntosh who were sitting on opposite sides of the table furthest away from Taggart.

"On a somewhat related note, I trust no one here has any objections eating meat. Couldn't help but notice some of you didn't partake in the canapés we brought out earlier."

Suntosh spoke first. "Forgive me, but I'm a vegetarian."

Ren followed. "Same here. I hope that won't be an issue?"

Taggart folded his hands. "My understanding is that your reasons are moral, not religious. Is that correct?"

Ren nodded. "That's right. Given the givens, meat production at scale is indefensible. I ate meat as a child but stopped—and I've made the case publicly that if everyone in China adopted American meat habits, we'd be finished."

Suntosh took a sip of water. "I too gave it up after seeing industrial farming up close, like Ren I couldn't justify it— morally or environmentally. India also cannot afford to become a Western-style meat-eating nation. The consequences would be cataclysmic." He glanced at Taggart. "And if I may say, I'm surprised, given how organized this evening has been, that you didn't already know that."

Taggart chimed back, "You are forgiven! Did you notice my doormat on the way in, *make no assumptions in this house*? Why did you assume that what you were being served had either a negative environmental impact or a sentient experience?"

Suntosh: "You said we were being served beef, no?"

"You were, and I am sure Winston, Mary, and Tomi can attest what they ate was in fact beef."

Tomi started nodding in agreement as Taggart continued.

"But did you eat a cow?" Taggart asked, casually. "The meat you tasted was never part of a living, sentient animal. It was biofabricated using renewable energy and the latest advances in cellular agriculture.

"We start with a small sample of stem cells harvested non-lethally from free-range donor animals. These cells are then cultivated in bioreactors under tightly controlled conditions, fed with a nutrient-rich, plant-based growth medium.

"The real breakthrough, however, is in how we *structure* the meat. We use high-resolution 3D bioprinting to layer muscle, fat, and connective tissue with remarkable precision. Custom-designed hydrogel scaffolds mimic the extracellular matrix, allowing us to control texture, alignment, and density. We've even developed protocols to fine-tune marbling by adjusting fat cell distribution on a micro level.

"You want wagyu-like tenderness? We can program that. Rib eye chew? Done.

"We're no longer just replicating meat—we're perfecting it."

Taggart looked at Ren and Suntosh now sitting in silence. "It would seem to me that given that you both professed a love for meat and gave it up for noble reasons, you can now again enjoy it as everything I am serving tonight had no sentience and no measurable environmental footprint."

With that three people dressed as waiters appeared carrying two plates each covered in silver cloches. Using a formal French dinner service style, each plate was placed in front of the guests delivered over the appropriate shoulder. In coordination, they removed the covers to reveal a beautiful arrangement with a small strip of white meat, some greens, and deconstructed string beans. There was a smear of orange sauce that looked like a comet streaking across the plate.

One of the waiters announced in a thick French accent, making eye contact with the guests one by one: "Madame and Monsieur, for this evening's aperitif, we are serving fresh greens, inverted string beans, and the breast of a dodo. It is paired with a chilled Château Margaux sauvignon blanc. Please enjoy!"

Mary looked at Taggart in surprise and simply repeated the word "dodo."

Taggart grinned. "Well yes—dodo."

Mary: "As in the Mauritian flightless bird that went extinct over a hundred years ago?"

"Well, you see it occurred to me that to grow meat with the technology available to us all you really need is the basic building blocks, the most fundamental of which is DNA. As it turns out, dodo DNA is available. Oxford University still had some tissue left in its natural history museum, and all it cost me was a modest donation. Well, to cut a long story short, I managed, and so here we are. The six of us will be the first people in well over a century to eat the dodo. Please, enjoy."

Taggart picked up his knife and fork, cut the meat, dipped it in the sauce, put it in his mouth, eating while looking at nothing in particular. He took a sip of his wine and pronounced: "That is honestly even more delicious than I hoped. Please try."

Everyone, in unscripted coordination, picked up their knives and forks and began eating in silence.

Mary took her first bite gingerly, as if the meat might contain fine bones. But the moment it touched her tongue, all apprehension disappeared. It was moist, tasted like an improved version of duck, and was flavorful in all the right ways. There was no apprehension with the second bite. Mary observed everyone else eating the two or three bites of dodo they had on their plate. Tomi let out an annoying "hmmm" after each bite. Mary hated to admit it, but Tomi's moans were warranted, the dish was fantastic.

Upon finishing his plate, Winston jokingly piped up, "What's next, Taggart? Woolly mammoth?"

"Funny you should mention that, Winston. We do have the DNA—or most of it—but we're still working on perfecting the meat. We're collaborating with the University of Moscow, which holds a remarkably well-preserved tissue sample discovered in Siberian permafrost. That's given us a decent starting point. Still, DNA degrades over time—its half-life is roughly five hundred years—so we're filling in the gaps with genetic data from the Asian elephant. If all goes well, we'll have you back for mammoth steaks within the year."

Mary raised an eyebrow. "So, this is the big secret? You're planning to disrupt the meat industry by selling... extinct animals?"

Taggart smiled. "Disruption, yes. But I prefer to think of it as a reimagining of our relationship with meat and of what we consider sacred."

As he spoke, waiters returned—two clearing plates, another resetting the table. A fourth refilled their glasses with a light California pinot noir.

Taggart continued, eyes gleaming. "That's what I love about science: with every leap forward, a taboo crumbles. And with each taboo we break, we become freer. More evolved. The Pill shattered the sexual double standard. Organ transplants redefined the sanctity of the body. IVF rewrote the rules of parenthood."

He paused, savoring his wine.

"Why not do the same with meat?"

The waiters reappeared with their silver cloches and performed their coordinated dance around the table, meticulously placing each plate and, in unison, revealing its contents. Again, the waiter described the content of the dish. A serving of potato and leek purée, accompanied by a slice of Marilyn Monroe's thigh, prepared with Hungarian paprika, Dijon mustard, forest honey, and drizzled with an essence of cloves.

This time, it was Tomi's mouth that dropped. "Did he just say the thigh of Marilyn Monroe? The actress? The human being!"

Taggart simply nodded without uttering a word.

Suntosh looked at his plate in disgust. "This is human meat? Cannibalism? You want us to engage in cannibalism?"

Taggart took a sip of his wine and simply whispered, "Why not? We used the same methods as with the other meats, no sentience, the person in question is no longer with us, the DNA was legally obtained at auction."

Winston huffed. "I can think of three reasons this is insane: it's definitely illegal, unhealthy, and undeniably immoral."

Taggart steepled his fingers. "If I may correct you—briefly. First, legality. In the state of California, there is no statute explicitly prohibiting the *consumption* of human flesh. What's illegal is murder, assault, and the desecration of human remains. We've done none of those.

"Second, health. I assume you're referring to kuru—the prion disease found among the Fore people of Papua New Guinea, linked to ritualistic cannibalism. That was caused by consuming infected neural tissue. What we've produced contains no pathogens. In other words: zero risk.

"And third..." Taggart smiled faintly. "As for morality, I'd argue that's more fluid than you'd like to admit. But perhaps I should defer to our resident philosopher. Mary—are we immoral for dining on Marilyn?"

Mary was still stunned, lost in a semi-dreamlike state, barely aware of the conversation around her. "Hmm... moral, well no, well yes."

Taggart, with disconcerting reassurance, said, "Perhaps you'd like to gather your thoughts, Mary. Take your time."

After a pause, Mary—composed but hesitant—spoke: "Well... morality, in the broadest philosophical sense, is a human construct—a system of values we've built to reduce harm and maintain social cohesion. But it's never been fixed. What was once moral—slavery, public executions, even child labor—is now abhorrent. And the reverse is true too. As our understanding evolves, so does our morality."

She glanced at the others before continuing.

"Utilitarians like Mill would argue that if no sentient being is harmed and the net utility is increased, then the act is justifiable—even moral. And from a constructivist view, like Korsgaard's, morality isn't discovered, it's made—shaped by reason and context. So... if this meat wasn't sourced through suffering, if consent was given, and no real harm is done... then—well—why shouldn't we eat it?"

Taggart smiled. "Spoken like a true philosopher, Mary."

Tomi's mouth hung open. She muttered, almost involuntarily, "This is... unchristian."

Taggart turned to her. "Pardon?"

"I said it's unchristian. Eating human flesh goes against the teachings of the Bible."

Taggart smiled. "Does it? And where exactly does it say that? I've looked. The Bible prohibits murder and desecrating corpses, yes—but it's oddly silent on the *consumption* of human flesh. In fact, one could argue the opposite. Every Sunday, millions of Christians symbolically consume the body of Christ. Transubstantiation, is it not? Bread becomes flesh. Wine becomes blood. Ritual cannibalism baked into the ritual.

"So if anything, your faith doesn't forbid this meal. It foreshadows it."

Ren quipped, "That doesn't change the fact that this is wrong. You cannot eat the flesh of other humans."

"Please, give me one good reason why not. It seems to me your response is rather more affective than rational. Which, given the level of surprise, is perhaps to be expected. But I will make you this wager, if anyone of you can think of a compelling rational reason not to eat a bite of Marilyn, I will give each of you one million dollars, but if you can't, you should at least try."

Suntosh: "It's unnatural—and potentially unhealthy—for the human body to consume human protein. We simply don't know the long-term effects."

Taggart: "A fair concern, but scientifically unfounded. The human digestive system breaks down protein into amino acids—it doesn't distinguish whether they came from cow, chicken, or human tissue. Your tongue might care, but your gut doesn't.

"What matters is the composition: fat ratios, amino acid profiles, micronutrient density. In our lab-controlled process, we fine-tune those variables to optimize nutritional value— better, in fact, than conventional meat.

"As for long-term effects—we've run extensive simulations and in-vitro studies. Thus far, no adverse outcomes. Quite the opposite: preliminary data suggests some bioavailability advantages over animal meat."

Winston: "But what about our psychological well-being? You are asking us to eat the meat of another human. What about the long-term trauma?"

Taggart: "This is hardly a warzone, Winston; you all have free will here. But I think if you did some soul searching, you'll find that your apprehension lies in conventional morality. There is no logical basis for this to be a traumatic experience."

Taggart, without ceremony, cut a piece of meat and took a bite. He nodded with approval and drank a sip of his wine. "Quite delicious," he declared. "Give it a try."

With that Suntosh picked up his cutlery and said, "I have to admit, he is right, there is no good reason not to." He cut a piece and placed it in his mouth. He let Marilyn rest on his tongue. To Mary's surprise, after a pause, Suntosh began chewing, slowly and rhythmically. The rest of the table watched in silence, waiting for him to swallow.

"And?" asked Winston.

"Well, all I can say to my utter disappointment is that Ms. Monroe is quite delicious."

Mary stared at her plate, it was all so perfect, and the pleasant aroma of cloves floated around her like a thin mist in a holiday kitchen. Her numb hands reached for the cutlery, as if on autopilot.

She sliced a small piece of the actress's thigh and placed it in her mouth. She hesitated for a moment, but it was too late, the flavors were so delectable that she started chewing as if by reflex. *Jesus*, she thought, *Marilyn is delicious!*

Based on Mary's expression, Winston took a small curious bite. He too seemed to come to the same conclusion. Now Suntosh, Mary, and Winston ate alongside Taggart, as if it were any ordinary meal. Small cuts loaded on forks interspersed with sips of wine. There was an odd silence, one only momentarily broken by the scrape of a knife against a plate. Tomi and Ren were sitting in silence, mouths open at the spectacle they were witnessing.

Tomi managed only to lift her jaw to utter, "This is complete madness, you have all gone mad."

Taggart retorted, "It would seem to me that you are the one that is mad, after all, what is madness but the absence of reason. And you, Tomi, are not acting rationally right now."

Like a reprimanded child Tomi picked up her cutlery and started eating her portion as if a plate of steamed vegetables. However, after the first bite her disposition also changed. Mary observed the same unfortunate enjoyment. Ren was the only one left still staring at his plate.

"Give it a try, Ren," Taggart suggested.

Ren succumbed to the pressure. Mary got the impression that despite his best effort he could not conceive a rational reason not to. He, too, was now experiencing the delicate flesh yielding under the pressure of his teeth. The delicious flavors releasing, spilling over taste buds in a carnival of carnivorous delight.

Before long, all the plates were empty.

Classical music began playing in the background—softly, but audibly. Elgar's *Enigma Variations*, if Mary wasn't mistaken. *"Nimrod"—an uplifting death march to our last taboo*, she thought.

"Congratulations on overcoming your irrational apprehensions. I must admit, I was betting at least one of you would tap out, but here we all are. Ready for your final course?"

"So, what are your plans with this? You want to sell dead celebrities to the public?" asked Winston.

"Well, yes, but live ones too... with their permission, of course. Soon, the world will be dining on its favorite celebrities—actors, singers, athletes. Dinner parties featuring them will be all the rage. The Kardashians have already agreed to sell me their DNA in return for a royalty. Soon Kim Kardashian Cutlet will be available to order along with a catalog of other celebrities. At a price of course, it will be exclusive... at first. This will become a new multibillion-dollar industry and I, alone, will pioneer it."

While Taggart was pontificating, the table was once more cleared in what was now starting to feel like a ritual. Six more plates appeared, six more plates covered in the now familiar silver cloches. These lids were once more lifted in a choreographed fashion to reveal six more portions. At this point, Mary was starting to feel a bit tipsy from the wine she had been sipping with increased frequency. However, she was laser focused on Taggart who continued.

"Oh, and there is one more course to serve this evening... you."

Mary looked around the table and noticed that everyone had something different on their plates. She had what looked like a small square of pork belly on her plate while Winston had what appeared to be carpaccio on his. Taggart's plate seemed to have smaller portions of everyone's dishes.

Mary was still reeling from the prior course having not really registered what Taggart had meant by "you." Winston was the only one with the wherewithal to ask Taggart, "What do you mean, *you?*"

"Well, how to put it, the meat in front of you comes from your DNA, you have a once-in-a-lifetime opportunity to try a bit of yourself at no cost or injury."

This time, everyone's mouths dropped. There seemed to be a collective "WTF" telepathically communicated between every guest present as they shared glances.

"We never gave you permission for this! What on earth? This is outrageous—simply outrageous!" Tomi exclaimed.

Ren: "Now look here Taggart, this has gone too far. You stole our DNA? This will be reported to the authorities. This is criminal."

"Well, actually each of you gave me permission to do this. You may not remember or have realized it at the time, but that is half the beauty of T&Cs."

Mary: "What do you mean; we never signed anything to attend this party."

Taggart: "Well, you see, you did, admittedly it was a while ago, but all of you did."

Winston: "Speak plainly Taggart; when would we have agreed to something like this? Never in a million years."

"Winston, Mary, Suntosh, Ren, and Tomi, didn't each of you take a GeneVeritas DNA test? Did you not voluntarily send your DNA to this company, a company that I bought out of bankruptcy and fully control? And did you not agree to the terms and conditions under paragraph fourteen subsection five, which states we are entitled to use your DNA for any purpose we, i.e., I, see fit."

"This simply can't be legal," Ren protested.

"Not according to my lawyers, I can assure you I have very expensive ones. Chef Juan has spent weeks perfecting a recipe to go with each of your own unique flavor profiles. You are going to love it, I promise."

"We can't eat ourselves," Tomi said, her voice quivering. "This is beyond..." Tomi was now at a loss for words.

Taggart gave Tomi's pause some room but sensing a continuation wasn't forthcoming, he filled the silence. "Why not? Every day you digest millions of your own cells; it is part of the body's natural processes."

With that, Taggart took a small bite of the piece that matched Tomi's plate.

"I really enjoy your flavor profile, Tomi. I can really taste the Nordic in you. Suntosh, you're quite tasty as well—*exotic*, if you'll forgive the stereotype. But Mary, you're my favorite; I am even thinking we may want to offer you your own deal. 'Mary's belly' we'll call it—a perfect blend of European—you're a marketing dream."

"This is beyond the pale, Taggart," Winston protested.

"Why? Aren't you even a little curious? Take a moment to think about this rationally. I am giving you each a unique opportunity unprecedented in human history. This, I can assure you, is the most expensive meal you'll ever eat. Growing your individual cuts cost me a small fortune."

Maybe it was because Mary was in a state of shock, but she—as she had done twice before—picked up her knife and fork, cut a small cube of meat, and lifted it to her mouth.

Mary was about to take a bite of her own flesh and could think of no good reason not to. Perched on the edge of her fork was a cube of meat, glazed in a blood orange sauce, beautifully prepared by a world-renowned chef. Until moments ago, Mary had no idea what she was about to consume. Until moments ago, she couldn't imagine this dinner party getting any stranger. How wrong she was.

It tasted like a mild version of pork—tender, juicy, and flavorful. In a word: delicious. Mary gave the portion in her mouth two or three bites before she swallowed. Honestly, that was all it needed. It was so soft—what a cliché food writer might call "melt in your mouth." Mary hated to admit it, but Taggart was right: she was delicious.

One by one, Mary noticed the others picking up their cutlery and making small incisions into themselves. One by one, they loaded their forks and took bites—each taking the first steps into a new realm of consumption.

Taggart quipped, "Excellent! I can see you're all enjoying this course. No surprise, really. Why wouldn't you enjoy yourself? It's eating something you truly love."

That phrase—*enjoy yourself*—Mary thought, had never taken on that particular meaning in human history.

* * *

Discussion Questions

1. The guests make various arguments about why eating lab-grown animals, humans, or themselves is wrong. Which argument (*if any*) do you find the most compelling and why?
2. Some of the guests make the argument "It's just wrong." Is that a good enough argument, or must all arguments be backed by articulable reasoning to be valid?
3. Is there a moral distinction between eating lab-grown: (1) animals, (2) extinct animals, (3) celebrities, and (4) yourself? Why or why not?
4. What do you think is the strongest argument for (and against) being a vegetarian? Does lab-grown meat solve these ethical concerns? Why or why not?
5. Do you think the government should regulate or ban any of the meat in the story? What's the best argument for (*and against*) the government banning the various story meats?

* * *

The Wife

Veronica Zora Kirin

* * *

* * *

I am the second Mrs. Roberts. The first one was Returned. That's all I know. I'm not sure if I have big shoes to fill, or if she failed so catastrophically that my job will be easy.

My Training involved how to support a man who works all day so their productivity stays high. We Wives are extremely important to keeping society and commerce going. They told us it had been tried—women working—and society had nearly collapsed. I couldn't imagine wanting to spend every day away from home like that.

Mr. Roberts has been kind to me, so far. I watch as he completes his morning routine before leaving for work. He wears a brown suit, typical of a working-class man. He sets his brown leather briefcase by the coat stand. Adjusts his tie in the mirror—today it is dark brown, matching his shoes, which he puts on with a long shoehorn so he doesn't have to sit and wrinkle his suit. Brown overcoat on top, though the spring weather is warming. Finally, his hat, a beautiful wool fedora with a cream feather stuck in the ribbon, matching his shirt. He picks up his briefcase, turns to me, and tips his hat, then walks out the door.

I sit on the arm of the living room couch until his sedan pulls out of the driveway and rolls away. It has been a week of living with Mr. Roberts. A week of performing Wifely duties and patiently supporting a man I know only in theory, based on my preparatory lessons. They gave us each a packet at the Training Center describing our assignments. Mr. Roberts plays tennis on the weekends with the neighboring men. Mr. Roberts prefers steak over meat loaf (which was just as well—I hate cooking meat loaf). Mr. Roberts works at a very important manufacturing firm, which is a thirty-five-minute commute from home.

Mr. Roberts reported being worn down each day when he comes home from work. The former Mrs. Roberts should have been able to support him enough that he would have all the energy he needed for work. That, at least, I can infer as part of her failing.

I rise from the couch, brush off my full skirt, and go to the laundry room to retrieve my dusting supplies. It is a Tuesday, and that means dusting, cleaning the bathroom, and rump roast for dinner. I pull out the blue bucket with the cleaning supplies inside. Spray bottles and rags protrude from its top. I carry it back into the living room and pull out the yellow gloves that will protect my nails from the chemical cleaners. Rag and spray bottle in hand, I begin to wipe the coffee table, end tables, mantle, and photos.

There are several photos of Mr. Roberts on the mantle. Mr. Roberts with his brother. Mr. Roberts playing tennis. Mr. Roberts receiving his promotion. The last frame on the mantle is empty, its cardboard backing a framed match for my new husband's suits. It is waiting for me to add the photo of our Uniting, which arrived yesterday from the photo studio. Mr. Roberts flashed the blue and white envelope at me when sorting the mail and smiled. "It has arrived, my dear," he grinned, sending butterflies into the depths of my belly. "Will you place it in that empty frame tomorrow?" He left the envelope on the mantle.

I carry the envelope and empty frame to the couch and sit. I remove my gloves, leaning forward to lay them on the coffee table with the frame, and open the envelope, an image of the side of my arm peeping out from inside. I gently remove the photo, avoiding touching the gloss with my fingertips, and hold it out to admire. I wore a cream dress, a fascinator, and a red lip. Mr. Roberts wore his brown suit, standing behind me with his arm around my waist. It was a pleasing photo. I was proud of finally receiving an assignment. And Mr. Roberts was handsome, or handsome enough to have garnered a few nudges from the other girls at the Training Center. I make a mental note to schedule a celebratory photo shoot for our six-month anniversary. That will be a nice addition to the mantle.

I pick up the frame and turn it over and back again. Ordinary. A tasteful silver frame with a black felt back and stand. It is clean, but not new. Had it held the former Mrs. Roberts before she was Returned? She is not something I wish to dwell on. I gingerly work my thumbnail under the little tabs of black-painted metal holding the felt backing to the frame. A little wiggle and the felt releases from the frame with a brush. I set the backing on the table next to my gloves, then work my fingernail under the cardboard while pressing the glass from behind to give it rise.

Why, there are two cardboard backings! A wisp of paper is revealed pressed between the two cardboard panels. An additional spacer, perhaps?

I peel it away to find a brief inscription on its front.

Underside of your nightstand drawer. Burn this.

I stare at the paper. It is barely the length of my finger, yet delivered such a shock that I am hardly breathing. I should tell Mr. Roberts. He will know what to do. It isn't my place to be snooping around, especially based on cryptic messages. I know my training backward and forward. I believe in our motto, "Honor. Love. Service." I even aced my exams. Being a replacement was a challenge, and they'd chosen me because I was up for the task. I am not going to fail my Trainers after only a week. My place is to support my husband, and that is what I am going to do.

I place the paper on the table, frame our photo, and continue my chores.

Mr. Roberts arrives home just after 5:30 p.m. We were told that not all husbands come home directly from work, but to be ready regardless, and never complain if they were late. So far, Mr. Roberts has been prompt. I admire that about him.

"Good evening, my dear," he calls from the entry. I emerge from the kitchen, hands wrapped in my apron, as he hangs his hat on the coat tree.

"Good evening, Mr. Roberts." I smile with a peck on his cheek. I watch for any signs of frustration on his face, hoping he had a good day at work and will take the mysterious note in stride. "How soon would you like to eat?"

"Now would suffice," he sighs as he pops his shoes off his feet, cream stockings disheveled from a day of office work. I nod and swish to the kitchen to set the table.

"How was your day?" I ask as he enters the room. I again watch his face, his shoulders, for any sign of tension. We have been Trained to notice even the slightest detail, taught that men will often hide their frustration with work out of propriety.

"Just fine," he replies. His tone is even. His shoulders relaxed. I believe him. "We pushed through a major proposal," he continues. "Could be a big deal, if we're lucky. Will you be my good luck charm?" He smiles at me.

How sweet, I think. I nod, placing the plate, napkin, and silverware in front of him as he sits down at the table. "Yes, of course. Best of luck. I'll keep it in my thoughts."

He catches my wrist before I can move to the other place setting. My breath stops in my throat and I look into his hazel eyes. "Thank you," he says. We hold each other's stare for a beat, then he releases me. I take a deep breath, smile, and complete the table setting. I glance at him as I bring out the steaming roast.

"Looks delicious."

"Why thank you," I reply.

"Do you..." he trails. "Where did you get the recipe?"

"From the Center," I reply. He offers a curt nod. Was he looking for something more interesting?

I serve us, remove my apron, then sit across from him at our little dining room table. I watch as he arranges a cutlet of meat on his fork and takes a bite.

"It's good," he says, noticing my eyes on him. I smile at him, though I wasn't waiting for a compliment. I was waiting for the right time to show him the note. Perhaps once he has a full stomach.

I watch him clear his plate, using the last piece of meat to wipe up the juices. *Might as well go for it before he gets too settled in his evening routine.* I take a deep breath to gather my nerves. "I found something peculiar, today," I broach.

He looks up at me. "Oh?" He wipes his mouth with his napkin.

"Yes," I say, fiddling with my silverware. Best to not avoid his gaze. I didn't want to implicate myself in any wrongdoing. It wasn't my fault. I look into his eyes. "While I placed our Uniting photo. There was a note in the frame."

He is very still. I think my heart might fall out of my chest while I wait for him to reply. "A note?" he says, finally.

"Uhm, yes. Or so it seems. Shall I get it?"

"Yes, please, Mrs. Roberts," he says. He folds his napkin and pushes away his plate, clearing a place in front of him. I go to the living room and retrieve the note from the coffee table, placing it in front of him before sitting back down. He fingers its edges, taking it in. He sighs, deeply. "I'm sorry, my dear," he says, looking up. My chest tightens. Is he going to reject me? I've done nothing wrong. "You've stumbled upon a bit of my baggage, I suppose. I'm sorry you had to see this. Would you mind waiting here while I see what is beneath your nightstand drawer?"

"N-no, that would be fine," I gasp. Okay, I'm not in trouble. Or, not yet. So far, Mr. Roberts is proving honorable. Aligned with my vows at the Training Center. If I serve well, he will care for me in return.

I hear his footfalls upstairs, the floorboards creaking while he investigates my nightstand. Will he find it? Is it all a hoax?

He is gone for what seems an eternity, finally returning to the kitchen with a folded letter in his hand.

"So, it seems there was a leave-behind from your predecessor. Again, I am sorry. I want you to feel you are my first priority, my focus, not a simple replacement." I had hoped he would show me, allow me to see what he had found, but he walks to the stove and lights the gas burner, burning the letter and the scrap of paper from the photo frame. The acrid smell of burning ink and pulp fills the kitchen. He drops the remnants in the sink to flame out without burning his fingers. "There," he says. "It's like it never happened." He turns to me, cradles my chin in his hand, and leans down to kiss my forehead. "Thank you for telling me. You did the right thing." He looks me in the eye, a serious look on his face. Then, like the flip of a switch, he smiles, and lets go of my chin. "Time for the game shows, eh dear? I'll see you in the living room?" He leaves without waiting for my reply.

I stare after him, processing the rapid sequence of events, then gather my wits. "Yes, of course!" I call, hoping my delay wasn't obvious.

I get up, tie my apron around my waist, and gather the dishes. I place them on the counter while I put on my gloves to begin the washing up and look in the sink. There is a corner of the letter resting in the basin. I can see a small amount of script unharmed by the browning of the fire. *It's forbidden,* I tell myself. Yet, I stow the charred scrap in my apron pocket.

Midnight. I can hear Mr. Roberts snoring in the twin bed next to mine, our nightstands between the beds delineating our individual space. I ease myself up and wrap myself in my silken robe. His bed is closest to the door, and I have to cross by its foot to leave. I could say I was going to the bathroom if he woke. That is normal behavior. Still, I tiptoe.

I pull the door partway closed behind me, obscuring the stairs. Down I go, keeping close to the wall where the steps will creak the least. The carpet pads each footfall as I shuffle into the kitchen, gently opening the cabinet where my apron hangs. I sink my hand into the pocket and feel for the scrap of paper. I pull it out, careful not to brush the edges of the delicate and damaged page against the fabric. I turn and steal away into the laundry room. I close the door and turn on the small light above the sink.

The survivor is the size of my palm, two edges pristine, one long side burnt and browned, an injured triangle. The same beautiful script in black ink adorns the page. What could I gain from this? I am breaking my vow of honor, aren't I?

I read.

...n despair.

...ope you make it out.

* * *

The next several weeks are espionage. I tidy, clean, and cook with the scrap of letter hiding beneath the insole of my house shoe. When I am on my hands and knees scrubbing the bathtub, the scrap is with me. When I make the beds, tucking the sheet corners as I was shown by our Trainer, the scrap is with me. It burns at my foot and pushes at my mind. It is mine. Something of my own that no one else knows about, not like the dresses meant for Mr. Roberts's eye or the apron meant to keep me clean and presentable. I have a secret, and it is *mine*.

All the while, Mr. Roberts is kind to me. Not once does he mention the letter, though it seems the incident has assured him of some of my loyalty. He starts bringing home flowers when he arrives from work, is more amorous in the evenings before bed. He compliments the tidiness of the house and meals he has tasted many times before.

"This rib eye is delicious, Mrs. Roberts," he says as he dabs the corner of his mouth with his napkin. It is a Monday, and while he has tasted my rib eye each Monday previous, I always try to add some kind of unique flavor or presentation so he won't tire of the recipes we were taught.

"Thank you, Mr. Roberts," I reply, smiling to myself.

He sets down his silverware. "I must speak to you about something," he says. His plate is still half full. My spine immediately goes stiff and I grip the silverware in my hands. I have been so careful. I am always wearing the house shoes when he is home, or they are by my bedside table as we sleep. Could he know? He holds my gaze as I force a smile, his eyes not settling on one single feature on my face. Is he searching for a clue? "I realize we haven't been together for very long, but it seems we get on quite well. Don't you agree?"

"Y-yes," I reply, imitating my normal tone of voice. "Very well. It has been a joy."

"Good. Good, because there is a work function this Friday. The board and upper management will be there. I realize it is rather soon, for us, but things seem to be going so well, I thought you might be ready to accompany me."

My face flushes. "Why, that would be lovely, Mr. Roberts. I would be delighted."

"You do have a cocktail dress?"

"Yes, they gave me one."

"Then it's settled. Tell me the color and I'll match my tie. The event begins at six-thirty and includes cocktails and hors d'oeuvres, so you won't be on the hook for dinner. I'll come home first to escort you." He returns to eating with a smile.

"Lovely," I say, my heart thudding in my chest.

* * *

On Friday morning, I bustle about the house to complete my chores early and have plenty of time to prepare for the event. As I work, hair bundled in curlers atop my head, I mentally go over the Training I received for corporate events. How to delight colleagues, ingratiate a boss, and even influence a deal in favor of my husband.

I enter our closet and pull out the beautiful blue dress from the Training Center, its satin reflecting the light in waves around its skirts. It is a flattering piece, giving my body the illusion of an exaggerated hourglass shape. It hasn't been out of its protective sleeve since I received it, and it will need a bit of care before it will be worthy of Mr. Roberts. I hang it in the bathroom for steaming. I pull out the steamer case from the linen closet and unzip it, laying its contents on the counter. Steamer. Attachments. Manual, which seems to be falling apart. As I open it, the pages fall to the floor. I sigh, pick them up, and open them to determine which page numbers have fallen so I can replace them in order.

But where there should be the tidy print of typed instructions, I find feminine script.

Before I can pull myself away, I am reading.

If you already read my letter from the bedside table, do ignore this one. I simply made a copy, just in case you felt compelled to show Mr. Roberts and it was destroyed. I felt that way, once. I felt so proud of being a Wife.

Supporting Mr. Roberts seemed like a dream come true. I had anticipated the day of my assignment and Uniting since I was a little girl. It's what we dream of, isn't it?

I'm so sorry to shatter the illusion, my dear, but it is just that. An illusion. The truth is, we are indentured servants, kept for the sole benefit of another. What about your benefit? What about your potential in this life?

They told us women working was a disaster. That it broke society. But we are working! Here, in this house, you slave away every day, cooking, cleaning, primping for him, keeping him happy. "For the higher good," they say. But is it good that our minds should be so wasted? Minds so clever we can discern our husband's mood from the other side of a room or help close a business deal without appearing to be any influence at all?

There is a society called The Underground of women enriching their minds. It has been more than eye-opening. They meet at the grocery store on Wednesdays. I'm sure you're used to having the groceries delivered. They encourage it. If you went out and mingled, you might be exposed to other ideas, and so they teach us to stay put and use the services. You benefit from another's service so that you may serve your man. It's a thinly veiled trick, yet we fall for it. But I'm sure you can find a way to attend.

I think Mr. Roberts suspects me. I can't suppress the ideas we've been sharing in The Underground meetings. I try to be as demure and subservient as I always was. For three years I've served so well. If you find this letter, my dear, it's because I was Returned—and someone like me won't be Recycled. I hope to goodness The Underground can find me and rescue me before they terminate my service...

You deserve more. Find them. Learn from them. Let them help you escape. There is more out there. The whole world is vastly different than what we've been taught. More than the despair of giving your life away in the shadow of a man. I hope you go get it and achieve the freedom that may no longer be in reach for me. I hope you get out.

Yours,

Mrs. Roberts

Her signature ends in a beautiful flourish. The final lines match those I stand on inside my house shoe. I'm not sure I am breathing. I stand in shock, staring at the scripted handwriting, reading and rereading as if compelled by a spell on the page. It is a window into a world I didn't know existed.

A car door slams shut, breaking the trance. *He's home!* I scramble, shoving the letter between the pages of the steamer manual, and pressing the manual back into the bottom of the steamer case. I am nowhere near ready to greet him. The dress needs steaming. My makeup is only half done. My hair is still in curlers. *Oh, what a mess.*

"Darling!" he calls when I don't greet him at the door.

"Upstairs, dear!" I reply over the banister. I can see half his body beyond the stairway wall. "I'm so sorry—I am running behind. This event is so important to you, and I admit I lost track of time as I got ready."

He chuckles, leaning against the first step to get a better view of me. "I'm sure it will be swell," he says. "I'm going to grab a small bite, then come up to change."

"There are cold cuts in the fridge," I instruct, and he disappears from the stairway.

I duck back into the bathroom and turn on the steamer. While it heats, I finish my makeup, including that same red lip from our Uniting. I whirl, pick up the steamer, then hold out the dress and soothe away its wrinkles.

I hear Mr. Roberts coming up the stairs. *Good enough*, I think. I remove my robe and throw the dress over my slip, fumbling to fasten the back.

A tap comes at the bathroom door. "What color is your dress?"

"Blue," I say as cheerily as possible.

"Like your eyes," he replies. I listen as his socks pad away on the carpet and resume orienting myself in the dress. The curlers come down, I plump the hair, pin it, spray it, then take a moment to look myself over in the mirror. The look needs jewelry. I turn to leave the bathroom and knock the steamer over. Water spills out.

The letter! I leap to rescue the steamer case, then throw towels down over the mess. The case drips in my hand, but no water has gotten inside. I feel a drip on my foot and look down in despair. Water had splashed on my dress.

I set the steamer case in the bathtub, wipe up the steamer and its parts, and place them beside their case in the tub. I then pull out the hair dryer.

"Nearly ready?" comes Mr. Roberts's voice from the other side of the door.

"Oh, yes! Just a final touch." I turn on the hair dryer and do my best to remove the damp blotches on the skirts of my fine dress while brushing with a dry washcloth and fluffing to get some air beneath the fabric. I sigh a breath of relief as the wet marks disappear.

I emerge from the bathroom and bustle into the bedroom. My dress shoes are still in the closet. I slip off my house shoes and step into the smart blue heels, then move quickly to the jewelry case on the dresser, my skirts bustling around me. I pull out a match set of silver jewelry set with sapphires. I'm able to clasp the necklace and earrings, but the bracelet defeats me. I look at myself in the mirror. My reflection is just like the examples in the Training Book. I take a deep breath, then take the steps down into the foyer, where Mr. Roberts waits.

His face shows no small amount of pleasure. "You look perfect," he says, taking my free hand.

"Almost," I reply, using the sweet tone of voice we were taught. I hold up the bracelet.

"Oh." He grins. He takes the sparkling thing and clasps it to my wrist. He places his hand over it, holding my hand in his, and looks into my eyes. "Now you're perfect."

I break his gaze, looking down and away, as if bashful, as if his praise is what I live for.

"I can't believe they hired a string quartet," I whisper to Mr. Roberts as we are served champagne at the bar. We are on the thirtieth floor of his office building, surrounded by windows overlooking the city.

"Yes, they do tend to throw lovely parties," he replies. His hand is around my waist. "Now, don't be shy. They know you're new, but they've heard good things from me." He pecks my forehead, then turns us to join the crowd of his colleagues.

"Roberts!" cries a plump, red-faced man who slaps the back of Mr. Roberts. His face glistens, and he huffs as if he had just run up a flight of stairs.

"Mr. Carrigan," my husband smiles, "may I introduce Mrs. Roberts?"

"My, my, welcome young lady. Welcome. You seem to be settling in quite nicely, from what I hear. Roberts here has had his best quarter, yet! I credit you in part." Mr. Carrigan sweeps his arm across the room. "Enjoy yourself, dear! Don't need him holding you all night. Go, eat. For once, you didn't have to prepare it!" He guffaws as he clinks his glass against mine. I look at Mr. Roberts, who is smiling, though his face is slightly pink. "Shoo!" Mr. Carrigan flicks his wrist at me.

"Oh, well, thank you, Mr. Carrigan," I say. I peck Mr. Roberts on the cheek, then make my way to the buffet that lines the windows. Beyond the glass, city lights twinkle on, the sunset beyond a beautiful pink and orange, made more intense by the tinted glass. I gather myself a plate, then look about the room.

There. To the side are some tables where the other Wives sit. They lean toward one another, laughing in between bites of their food. A woman in red waves me over.

"Well, well. If it isn't the new Mrs. Roberts," she says, a blonde curl dropping into her eye.

"Hello. Yes, that's right." I sit, arranging my skirts on the chair.

"Don't bother, dear," says the woman in green sitting next to me. "It's not that kind of party." I look at her, confused.

"What she means," says the woman in red, "is that those gentlemen over there are going to eat and drink and talk shop all night. We're here because we're supposed to be, but you won't have the chance to talk, again."

"Oh," I say and begin picking at my food.

"Relax! It's more fun that way. I'm Mrs. Schultz, by the way." Red reaches for my hand across the table. She holds my gaze for what seems a beat too long.

"How do you do, Mrs. Shultz?" I return. The table laughs.

"She's so polite, still! You'll see, dear." With that, the table returns to its previous state of relaxed chatter. And that is it. I sit. I eat. I drink. I meet the other Wives. And then, at eleven, I am escorted home.

"I'm sorry we didn't see much of each other this time," Mr. Roberts says as we drive. "Some of the parties are more intimate, however. You'll see."

"Of course," I reply. I am here to serve in whatever capacity makes him more efficient at his work. But I'm disappointed. I'm a thing he brought to the party because it's conventional to bring the Wife. My extensive Training in business meetings didn't seem to matter.

We return home in silence, padding up the stairs, I ahead of him.

"Would you mind my using the bathroom, first?" he asks. "It will take you longer, won't it? I'm done in."

I shake my head. "No, of course." I proceed to the bedroom and begin removing my jewelry. I hear the faint sound of the shower curtain sweeping open across the bathtub.

The bathtub! I left the damp steamer and its case in the tub. I grip the dresser, listening. *It is just a manual,* I will. *Just women's tools. Set them aside. Please...*

I wait. So long. Too long. Listening. Why is he so silent?

The bathroom door opens and I jump half a mile. Mr. Roberts enters the bedroom, shirt half undone. "You're not changed, yet?" he asks.

I look down at my dress. "Oh, no. I'm so tired I'm moving at a snail's pace."

He comes over to me and kisses me lightly on the lips. "I didn't mean to wear you out, my dear. I'm sorry. Be quick to bed, then." He walks to the closet and begins to change into his pajamas. I fumble the rest of my jewelry off, pick up my robe and nightgown, and take them with me to the bathroom.

The steamer is in its open case on the counter. I can see the manual beneath, undisturbed. My breath catches in my throat in a sob of relief. *What am I doing? I should have shown him this letter before the party! It is a wonderful placement. He is a wonderful man. I am successful.* I look at myself in the mirror, a miserable woman returning my gaze. I exhale slowly, then close the steamer, put it away, and get myself ready for bed.

* * *

The morning light streams in through the bedroom window. I crack an eye, unfocused, watching the dust dance in the rays landing on the floor. Its advanced progress tells me it is late. Mr. Roberts let me sleep in. I press my head into my pillow and stretch, feeling the cozy covers around me. How I love Saturdays.

I roll over to look around our room, then sit up with a jolt. Mr. Roberts is there, fully dressed, sitting on his bed, facing me with clasped hands. I bring my hand to my cheek and blush. "Are you watching me sleep?" I ask in my small Wifely voice.

"You could say that," he replies. He stands and hands me my robe. "Come downstairs with me."

I adjust my nightgown and then pull down the covers, wrapping myself in my robe. I slip on my house shoes, then follow him to the stairs. "Did you make me breakfast?" I ask, smelling coffee. He doesn't reply. *All the Wives would be jealous,* I thought. *This is so rare it was mentioned only in passing at the Center. Men don't cook!* I clutch my robe to me with pleasure as we descend into the foyer.

We round the corner into the living room. I freeze, now clutching my robe uncertainly. Two strange men in black suits sit in our living room. They are sipping coffee from our coffee mugs. They stand, buttoning their suit jackets. I look up at Mr. Roberts, who nods at the men.

"Cathleen," one says. "You're to come with us."

He used my first name! We only have first names in the Training Center, when we aren't attached to a husband. "Mr. Roberts?" I squeak, looking at my husband. He does not look at me.

The men make their way toward me.

"Mr. Roberts!?" I cry, grabbing his hand. He wrenches away from me, stepping into the living room, exchanging places with the imposing men as each takes one of my arms. I yelp and begin to struggle, my skin twisting under their grip. They pull me toward the front door.

"Be quiet," the first man says. How can I be quiet!? He is Returning me! He didn't even talk to me about it. We were doing so well. It was so good!

"Mr. Roberts! Talk to me! I'm your Wife!" I scream, leaning away from the men in suits. He turns to face us and holds his hand up to the men. They stop pulling me but do not release their grip.

"No," Mr. Roberts says. I stop struggling as he speaks. "You are not my Wife. You are one of *them*." His lip curls with disgust.

I sob. "I'm not. I'm not. I only just found the letter. I didn't know. I don't know!" He has to believe me. I have to make him believe me. I am good. I am so good. I served so well. "We were just finding our rhythm. It was so good!" The words tumble from my mouth.

"I hesitated last time," he interrupts.

"What?" I ask.

"I hesitated. Your predecessor, the first Mrs. Roberts, was with me for three years. I was naive. I thought her restlessness would settle. By the time I confronted her, she was already heavily involved with The Underground, those stupid wretches who want to destroy all we've worked for and take us back centuries. I let it fester." He grits his teeth and looks through the front window. "This time we nip it in the bud." He looks back at us, looking at me with the same disgust he showed as he spoke of her. "Get her out of my sight."

"No!" I yell as the men pull me out the front door. "I didn't go! I didn't do anything!" I watch Mr. Roberts leave the living room as I am dragged into the black van waiting in our driveway. I trip as I fight, my house shoe with the little scrap of paper falling to the cement, bare toes scuffing the pavement.

They shove me into the van and slam the door behind me. There are no windows in the back, only a console light glowing by the front. I spring at the door, yanking on the handle, but it will not budge.

The front doors slam and the engine starts. I lose my balance as the van begins to back from our driveway. I prop myself against the front panel, knees up, and hold my head in my hands. I did nothing wrong. It was going so well. Everything was okay.

You didn't show him the letter. No, but I was going to, I think. I... I'm not sure what I was going to do. I lean my head against the front panel, looking up at the metal frame of the van. There I stay for the entire ride. A half hour? An hour?

We stop and I hear the shifter thrown into park. The front doors slam. I crouch, ready to spring. I'll leap from the van as soon as that door opens and run. I grip the wall and wait.

The door opens and I leap right into the arms of one of my captors. "NO!" I belt as the other throws a black hood over my head. I kick and shake but the man has his arms around my entire torso. I'm helpless.

They don't say anything as they carry me. Gravel crunches beneath their shoes. I can smell grass and dust. A door clangs and their footfalls begin to echo. It smells of must. I whimper, and they tighten their grip.

Another door clangs open. A few more steps and we stop.

"Where do you want her?" the man holding me says. I hear no reply, but they move further into the room. How many people are around me? My head brushes against the man's chest and hood over my head, making it hard to distinguish anything.

The man swings me around and drops me on a metal folding chair. The hood whips off my head and I cough, squeezing my eyes shut against the sudden light. In a way, I don't want to open them. I don't want to know what comes next.

I hear a snap in front of me, so close to my face that I could feel the wind from the fingers passing by each other. I flinch, then open my eyes. Someone's face is inches from mine. I squint, then I realize I know those smiling features.

"Mrs. Shultz?"

She grins. "Welcome to The Underground."

* * *

Discussion Questions

1. There is an underlying assumption that all sentient beings crave equal opportunity. If that is the case, why do some people support their own oppression? For example, some women were against the women's right to vote.

2. Was it ethical for the first Mrs. Roberts to leave notes that put the second Mrs. Roberts at risk and in awkward situations?

3. The second Mrs. Roberts seemed to believe she was happy and interested in making her partnership work. What do you think her process will be for coming to terms with her match failure, social expulsion, and The Underground?

4. Is it morally wrong for a person to want to be ethically "kept" in the way the story describes it? That is to say, limited choices, but not having to worry about housing, healthcare, or paid work outside the home.

5. What are the various blueprints for ending a repressive system like the one described in the story? Which blueprint would you be most likely to participate in?

* * *

Ground Control

Martin Riemer

* * *

Content Disclosure: Strong Language; Depiction of Mental Health Issues; Graphic Violence

* * *

Filthy bastard, I whispered as he gruffly turned over to the other side, *you miserable, disgusting cocksucker,* until he pulled up the blanket to his chin and bit it, *that's what you are, you creep!*

He feigned not to hear me, as if he'd already fallen asleep, his eyes forcefully shut, but I knew for sure that he could hear me, I always know it. The nights in Saint Andrew's are usually quiet unless the restless man across the corridor screams for hours or indulges in never-ending moaning. Thomas keeps his trap shut most of the time. He knows what's good for him.

Yes, eat your blanket, you piece of shit, I hissed at him, *you know what's in store for you if you start screaming again!*

Thanks to the sleeping pills, the ordeal phases of the other patients are largely confined to the daytime. At night, I'm mostly alone. When Thomas sleeps and I can dwell on my own thoughts, undisturbed by his constant presence. Protected against his malice and his piteous, abominable weakness. My God, how I despise that creep!

Motoharu and the others wanna puke when they see your daffy mug!

Soon after I could feel him actually dozing off. His facial muscles relaxed, his fingers, clenched around the upper end of the blanket, slowly let go, and his thoughts vanished into the erratic snarl of his dreams. At last, I was alone.

* * *

I'm not always so tough on him. Usually, I try to ignore him. I'm more at ease when I don't bother about all the shit that's whizzing around in his head. In our head, I should say, because in some way—I might as well admit it outright—I am Thomas myself. I find it extremely hard to put up with this idea. I'd rather consider myself an independent observer, trapped in his mind. But I'm afraid it's not that simple. All the memories that accrued over the course of his life, I have them all available. And if identity is the sum of individual experiences, then there's hardly a way around it. Then I am Thomas. I can remember every single detail of his miserable life. Nothing is concealed. And nothing spared. I'm trapped in here, like in a tin can, doomed to witness every mischief this pitiful poser engages in. And for a long time, I didn't even know he could hear me. Only recently I found out about that. After his release from the Mill, a custody center for difficult adolescents near Banbury.

After an incident of grievous bodily harm, a senile judge considered Banbury appropriate for Thomas, instead of sending him to a prison for juvenile offenders. He was fourteen at that time and people were worried that his situation would be aggravated by premature criminalization. His situation! That's what people had always been concerned about most.

They should have been there, they should have seen how he smashed his fist into Ava's face, over and over again, he didn't even stop when she'd passed out. She had lent me—lent *him*—some money and after scores of useless requests to pay it back she got angry. She was upset, called him names, and Thomas lost it. It makes me feel sick when I think back to it. I detest violence to an extent that the very thought of it stresses me out. In this respect, I am extremely sensitive. I instantly forget about everything else, I want to scream and flail, just to make him stop, but like I said, at that time I didn't even know he could hear me.

This distaste for violence is a strange thing because I don't even feel physical pain. Or joy, for that matter. It doesn't affect me in the way it affects Thomas. It's on a purely intellectual level that I recognize what is happening. When he tosses himself off, I don't feel pleasure. I just sense what he's doing and why. These kinds of things don't mean anything to me. Neither the joy nor the pain. But the mere idea of physical violence gives me the creeps.

Of course, the educators and social workers overbid themselves with sympathy for Thomas's difficult situation. They treated him like a victim. Like someone who deserved compassion. Already in his childhood, the doctors brought up nothing but excuses for his uncontrollable rage attacks. Emotion regulation deficit. Impulse control disorder. These were the common terms to embellish his wicked nature. If they knew what I know, for sure they wouldn't talk like that. If they could see what I see, if they could read his mind like I do, they would turn away from him with horror and keep him locked up forever. But it doesn't matter. I will take care of it myself. From now on I will prevent him from doing any harm. When he claims to feel better, I'll make him drivel and impose spastic convulsions upon his body until they strap us. And then it will be closed ward again.

* * *

Thomas always had a short fuse and the older he got, the harder it was to keep his outbursts under control. They tried pills and therapy, but nothing helped in the long run. Several times he had to change schools. When he got expelled from the last one, his mother sent him to a boarding school outside Birmingham, where they had the capacity for individual supervision, and nearly everyone agreed upon the charming narrative that Thomas's behavior was simply caused by immoderate impulsivity. He wasn't obstinate per se, and least of all, he was ill-natured. He was just incapable of suppressing his immediate impulses in emotional situations and sticking with the more amiable parts of his personality. In those moments, he quite simply wouldn't know what's okay and what's not. What's right and what's wrong. All he would need in those moments was to be reminded of his natural character. In hindsight, I don't understand how I could listen to all this bullshit without losing my mind.

After two years of boarding school, Thomas moved back with his mother and, for a while, his "situation" really seemed better. He was able to pull himself together, more or less. Through a former classmate, he became acquainted with Ava and Ralph, who were dealing coke and E and let Thomas enter the business as a pusher. Four months later, Ava was hospitalized with a cranial fracture and Thomas was sent to Banbury.

* * *

The Mill is a custody center specializing in young offenders with mental health issues. Thomas hated it. The social workers, the medics, the other residents. It was the first time he was actually forced into something. All the earlier therapies and even the boarding school had been subject to the unsteady decisions of his mother, who permanently fluctuated between pedagogic advice from all sides. Banbury, in contrast, was the enforcement of a sentence. Even if his mother had wanted to, she wouldn't have been able to get him out there.

The only thing she could do, and did, was to increase the likelihood of an early release by consenting to all sorts of medical treatments, including deep brain stimulation. Thomas was fourteen, so he wasn't even asked for his approval before they implanted the stimus. It still makes him mad to think about it, and sometimes, when he's on the edge of engaging in some foolery, I bait him about the episode. In my opinion, it was the first reasonable decision they took in Banbury.

When he woke up from the surgery, the medic in charge disclosed to him that microelectrodes had been inserted into his limbic system. Supportive devices to regulate his emotions and action impulses. In critical situations—which he was trained to identify in separate therapy sessions—Thomas was able to increase the pulse frequency of the stimus via a control module. Not much later, this function was transferred to a program that used physiological parameters to predict critical situation with much greater reliability.

The stimus turned out to be quite effective. He no longer lost his temper at the slightest provocation. At least compared to the rage attacks I had witnessed before, he was able to hold his fire. One memory (the first for which I have a strong sense of being present) dates back to the last year in the Mill, shortly before Thomas's release. We were in the yard, playing football, and one of the others made a derisive comment about Thomas's stimus. I sensed his arousal, and immediately I feared that he would lose it again. I was panicking, appalled by the thought of another outbreak of violence. I was hoping so much he would just ignore it, that he would just keep moving, and when Thomas indeed left it like that, I was ecstatic with relief. But already in the evening his thoughts were completely absorbed in violent fantasies. He was lying in bed, imagining how he would beat up that bloke, how he would smash his face, kick his convulsing body until I felt really sick. *For God's sake,* I thought, *just let it be! What's in it for you anyway?*

* * *

It was shortly after his return to Birmingham when I realized that Thomas could hear me. I was completely staggered. Imagine you spend your entire life in the head of such an idiot, and you always think you can't do anything about it, this moron doesn't even know you're there, and then he suddenly *hears* you. I've always had my own thoughts, my own stance. But after our release from the Mill, I also started to verbalize them. Not like real talking, of course, more like mumbling to myself. I didn't want to communicate or something. It was more like some kind of whim. Didn't even realize I was doing it.

But then I noticed that Thomas was getting nervous when I muttered under my breath. For a while, I was just observing. I have to admit I was a bit slow at putting the pieces together. But eventually, Thomas would even smite his forehead, snapping, *Shut up! Shut up! Shut up!* over and over again. It was so pathetic! I made him do that whenever I wanted to. Whenever he imposed his stupidity and his aggression upon me. It was such a good feeling, at last being able to speak up for myself. Within the following weeks, I learned how to increase the loudness of my thoughts, so he must hear me if I wanted to.

You're a shit, I told him once, and he started weeping. I felt his rising panic. My thoughts were much louder than the last time I had spoken to him.

"What the fuck...?" he whimpered. "What...?"

It was during a game of Tackle-Race at a leisure park in downtown. He'd gotten mad at one of the other gamers, who was obviously cheating with a sneaked-in pirate software. You could clearly see the scar above his left ear, where the neuro implant must have been inserted. But Thomas instantly forgot about that. With shivering hands, he took off his goggles, dropped them to the ground.

Now what, you shit? I gloated when he staggered off the gaming area. *Don't feel that strong anymore?*

His legs turned to jelly. I could feel it as if they were mine. I told him what I thought, what I had kept to myself for so long, and he whined and suddenly regained strength and started running like hell over the grass field like some maniac. I couldn't stop laughing, *you know you can't run from me,* it was so pitiful, so completely wretched.

He was in such a frenzy, he just ran and bawled and people were looking at him. They must have thought he was nuts. Or that he'd stolen something. But then there was nobody chasing him. People just stepped aside. Tried to avoid contact. Thomas didn't notice them anyway. Didn't attend to anything around him. And when he reached the road at the side of the park, he didn't stop either, he just ran into the street and almost got hit by a car. It was really close. The driver slammed on shrieking brakes and brought the vehicle to a halt just a few inches from

Thomas. People were screaming and rushing toward the scene. Suddenly, they almost fell over themselves to help.

Thomas regained some awareness of his surroundings. He leaned on the cowling and looked into the pale face of the driver. *What is happening?* he thought and then he sank down to the ground and burst into tears. This time the weeping was rather humble. Coming more from helplessness than from fear.

I admit I was shocked as well. Actually, I hadn't paid much thought about the impact that my interfering would have on him. I hate him, I really do, but I don't want him to die. I was just so fed up with his bullshit. I want him to live, but just not... not like this. Of course, I also thought that when he dies, I would die too. And I didn't want that either.

* * *

After that episode, Thomas grew pensive for a while. I gave him some space. Wasn't interested in talking to him anyway. In the same way that I'm not fussed about physical pleasure or pain, I am not afflicted with boredom. I'm okay with nothing happening. When Thomas is sleeping, I feel good. It's not a void for me. I have my thoughts and, really, that's all I want. All I ever cared for.

But the more I backed off, the more Thomas forgot about me. Took me for some kind of temporary lunacy that he was secure from most of the time. I guess he got accustomed to my occasional susurration. It didn't unsettle him to the same extent as when it was new. Of course, I knew he wasn't totally indifferent to my intrusions (as the idiot tried to pretend sometimes), but eventually, he began to react with anger and defiance instead of fear.

"What are you gonna do about it?" he once snapped.

He'd insisted on taking the bike of some guy he barely knew, and I'd told him to let go. I have to admit this was quite a blow. Being a toothless bystander when no one knows you're there is one thing. But when you're forced to watch although you have clearly announced your disapproval... that is abasing.

You pathetic loser, I bawled. *You stupid shit, I'll drive you mad, that's what I'll do, you shit!*

I don't know if he noticed my discomfort, but when I continued, he tossed his head like a spastic and left the confused boy alone.

But the taunting comment stayed with me. What could I do should Thomas finally manage to just ignore my whispering and my yelling? Was I even capable of doing something?

I used the nights to practice. When Thomas was asleep, I tried to concentrate on the fingers of my hand. Imagined tiny movements of the wrist. Nights and nights, I practiced, but to no avail. I was trapped in my little tin can.

In the end, it wasn't concentration that set off the breakthrough. It was fear. It was fulminating panic. It happened in a pub where Thomas used to meet up with some of his fellows. He was about to get new drinks at the crammed counter, when somebody from his left pushed to the front and ordered a beer. Thomas wasn't even particularly agitated in this moment.

"Easy, man!" he said.

The bloke turned around for a second, sneering at us, and before I realized what was happening, Thomas's fist landed in his face. A sudden uproar went through the crowd. People stepped aside. The sneer in the bloke's face immediately turned into surprise. He brought his fingers to his bleeding lips. Then Thomas kicked him in the balls, and when he sank to the ground, Thomas grabbed a beer bottle from the counter and I screamed, I don't know what, just *Aaaaaaaah*, I knew he would smash it over his head, I screamed and screamed.

And while screaming I suddenly realized I was holding his arm. It wasn't even hard. There was no force I had to oppose. No resistance at all. The hand with the bottle just stayed where it was. In the air slightly above my right shoulder. Just because I didn't move it.

"Let go!" Thomas yelled.

He was still raging, absorbed in his orgy of violence, but inside I could already sense his rising anxiety. Within seconds, the bloke on the floor was forgotten. Thomas turned toward me, went overboard in fear and despair.

"No, you fucking bastard!"

With his left, he battered his right arm, which I still was keeping hold of. As if he wanted to punish himself for beating the other guy. Some of the bystanders who went about stepping in hesitated anew.

"No, this is MINE!" he cried. "MINE!"

Spit and tears sputtered from his face.

"FUCK YOU! FUCK YOU!"

The bottle fell from my hand when Thomas, as hard as he could, sank his teeth in his arm. People had to detain him.

"Please, please, get off me!" he whimpered in the grasp of two men.

I hardly paid attention to him. I was probably as overwhelmed with the new situation as he was.

* * *

After that incident he was admitted to Saint Andrew's, a nuthouse in Northampton.

You hear that, you jerk? A nuthouse! That's where you belong!

I know it's on account of me. I'm sure the medics would dismiss him in no time if I wouldn't intervene. They don't know him. They can't see the foulness in his heart like I do. They are easily misled by his beautiful words, his promises. Thomas can act quite reasonable if he wants to. At the ward rounds, he says he repents what he'd done. That he's working on it. That he wants to improve. I carefully pay heed to the medics then, and when I feel they are taken in too much, I make faces at them or take a leak in Thomas's pants. He immediately starts weeping then and they send him back to his room.

It's better that way. Of this, at least, I'm sure. When I learned to take over, I realized that my power was restricted to very basic movements. Waving with arms or head. Or just keeping still, preventing Thomas from doing something bad. Complex, goal-oriented actions were far out of reach. Way too strenuous. All this was completely new to me. I needed training for the simplest actions, like a newborn, but I can only maintain control for a few moments. Then I just lose it and Thomas is back in charge again. I don't know why I always lose it. Maybe this will change. But for the time being, it's enough. It's all I need to keep him here. With all the other imbeciles. For his own sake and also for mine.

For a while, I was actually quite content with the situation here in Saint Andrew's. Had my peace, most of the time. Except for his vicious thoughts, I'm relatively safe from Thomas's violent tendencies. The medics even assigned me a name. I'm schizophrenia (the idiot finally told them about me). They don't understand nothing, but I have to admit, the fallacy is quite funny. I am Thomas's condition. In a strange way, there might even be some truth in it, when I think about it. Thomas isn't sick in the strict sense. His very nature is malice. The mental condition that his wicked mind suffers from is sanity. This is what they should call me. I am sanity. And I've made the grade.

But nobody ever understands that. Even in Saint Andrew's, they treat him as they always did, headed by Dr. Motoharu, who initially was in charge of Thomas. They consider him a victim. A victim of circumstances. A victim even of me. They never accepted the idea that Thomas himself *is* the problem. This is why all their treatments and therapies are doomed to failure.

When they realized their inability to handle the situation, an external specialist was called in to replace Dr. Motoharu. Thomas already knew Dr. Rebbs from Banbury. She'd been part of the medical science team in the Mill and was familiar with his case. In Saint Andrew's, they had several therapy sessions together, and at first, they were as rubbish as every other therapy that was imposed on him over the years.

"Well, how do you feel today?"

"What do you think?" he replied. "How would you feel if you heard that question every day in a room like this?"

He liked Dr. Rebbs. Unlike the other medics, she didn't pretend to be glad working with him. And yet, she had recently increased the frequency of their sessions.

"You've got a point there," she said, disinterested. She remained silent for a while, taking her time to sit down opposite Thomas and to arrange some papers on the table.

"What about your medication? Is the voice still bothering you?"

Thomas nodded. And like this, it went on. Questions about what I've said to him, how he reacted, and what he feels about it. I was hardly listening to the tedious conversation they call therapy.

"Good," Rebbs eventually said and looked at her hands. You could tell she wasn't really into it either. She was thinking about something else.

"Time to move on," she said calmly, more to herself than to Thomas. A long pause followed, and he started to get somewhat uncomfortable.

"I don't know how to start this," she finally said, her voice suddenly firm and resolute.

"It's the first time. I'm not even sure how I should address you. Thomas Two maybe? Tom? Perex? I don't know. You can hear me, right? Do you hear me?"

"What?" Thomas uttered. "What the fuck are you talking about?"

She ignored him.

"Can you lift his arm?"

Slowly I raised Thomas's right arm.

"Dr. Rebbs, please!" he begged. "Please stop it! Please don't talk like this!"

"It's okay, Thomas." She turned toward him. "This is necessary. It's part of the therapy. I need you to trust me now, okay? Don't be afraid! Just retreat for a moment and let me talk to him!"

Overwhelmed with consternation I could sense Thomas easing off. He was weeping nervously, but he kept quiet when Rebbs continued.

"Can you hear me?"

I opened his mouth. Like a fish. Tears ran down his cheeks.

"Can you hear me? Perex? Tom?"

"Yeeh," I managed to say.

I tried harder.

"Yeeehs. Eear youh."

I brought my fingers to Thomas's lips. Tried to bring them in a form I thought was beneficial for articulation. Soon I gave up.

"This will get better," Rebbs said.

A spasmodic sobbing went through Thomas's body.

"Hooow youh knooow?"

"Don't worry! I'm here to explain everything. For now, you just need to listen. I'm not sure where to begin. I've never spoken to someone like you. No one has. Hmm, do you know what a perex is?"

I wagged Thomas's head, but I vaguely remembered the term from the podcasts about life coaching that his mother was listening to all the time.

"Hmm, okay. I assume you remember everything since your early childhood, right? Since Thomas's childhood, that is. It's... that's not really true. At least not in the way you might think. You have access to his memories, to everything he knows and remembers. But you haven't really experienced them. They are false memories. Hmm, no, that's also not correct. The memories are as real as memories always are. As they are for Thomas. It's just that you haven't experienced the events to which they relate. Your ignition... hmm... you might as well call it birth or your first day... anyway, that was in the Mill. That's what you guys call it, right?"

I nodded.

"Good. Perex. Basically, a perex is a self-referential embedded system. A software that is able to process and modulate neuronal signals based on self-paced learning algorithms. Artificial intelligence, if you want. It spawns neuro-synthetic connections between its own hardware units and with the surrounding cells. Eventually, it evolves into a symbiotic bond with the system to which its hardware is implanted. From its first ignition on, it works entirely independently. Except for some initial specifications, of course. The critical parameter specification in your case was an aversion to violent and aggressive behavior. That's all. Everything else was left blank. I have checked the ignition myself. Even necessary instincts like self-preservation develop naturally during the integration with the host system."

I touched the scars on Thomas's skull, where the stimus had been implanted. I don't think my feelings were displayed in his facial expression, but Rebbs seemed to understand.

"Those are just sensors and pulse generators," she explained. "The data are processed on the main server. If we think in such categories, we probably have to say that your mind is there. But your physical body is sitting here in front of me."

"Aaaah..." I tried to warn her, but Thomas broke out screaming and started up from the chair. I couldn't hold him back.

"GET IT OUT!"

He was seething with rage, completely out of control.

"YOU GET IT OUT OF MY FUCKING HEAD!"

It was dangerous. For the first time in weeks, I was scared because I'd lost it. There was nothing I could do. I tried to fasten him like I did in the pub, but I couldn't. *Back off, you freak!* All I could do was yell. *Sit down! I'm warning you! SIT DOWN!*

But I knew it was in vain. Rebbs also had gotten up from her chair and stepped away from the table Thomas was leaning over in blind fury. He was sweating. Then the door opened and Motoharu entered the room, closely followed by another staff member. They must have been waiting outside, prepared for a situation like this. They seized Thomas by his arms, forced him back on his chair, while he was still raging. Motoharu plunged a syringe into his arm and injected a sedative.

"That's it for today," she commanded.

"Just one more thing," Rebbs said and hastened to the table, fetching a thin booklet from her papers.

"Read this, Thomas! It's important you understand. Both of you!"

"I want him OUT!" Thomas moaned in agony, slowly getting weaker.

"Seriously, Dr. Rebbs, it's enough!" Motoharu insisted. "Remember our agreement! You leave! Now!"

"I'll leave it here," Rebbs announced, grabbed the rest of her papers, and rushed out of the room.

"They really could have sent someone with at least a slight idea of empathy," Motoharu remarked when Rebbs was gone.

I could feel the sedative kicking in. The tension slowly passed off Thomas's limbs. Again, he turned into a weeping wreck. The assistant took him by the arm, helping him to get up, but I drew it back.

"Aigh whoa-nah reahd," I said and placed my hand on the booklet Rebbs had left on the table.

* * *

It was a handout providing medical information about personality extensions. Details of the procedure and personal accounts from affected people, intended to assist worried parents during the process of reaching a decision concerning their problematic children. One of the testimonials was from a guy of Thomas's age, even the problems that prompted his parents to consent to the treatment were similar. Impulsive, violent behaviors. He hadn't gone through the same shit as

Thomas, no series of school suspensions and reformatories, but apparently, his issues had been grave enough to justify the procedure. In fact, impulsivity disorders were among the very first medical conditions for which it was clinically approved. He was better now, the guy reported in his testimonial. He still got angry now and then, the same way as before, but he was able to buck up. The handout contained five other firsthand accounts. Mostly from adolescents. One even came from a child of nine years.

"For young people, the integration works more smoothly," Rebbs explained to us when Thomas mentioned it during our next therapy session. "Probably because the host personality isn't fully developed. Still flexible to some degree. So it's easier for the perex to merge."

She paused and observed us in silence, mulling over an unspoken thought. Then she continued.

"I was eleven when I got mine. The ignition was set to counteract timidness. As a child, I was extremely shy. It was a serious problem. I hardly talked to anyone but my parents. No friends, no nothing. The teachers in school were at a loss. When they tried it the hard way, I just closed up more.

"My perex helped me. Hmm, at the time I didn't understand it. My parents made the decision. I wasn't interested at all, I just wanted them to take me back home. I didn't notice any change. It was no big deal for me. From my memories, I never would have thought that the change was so profound, but I've seen videos of myself, before and after the ignition. With the perex, I changed completely. Within one year, I had friends in school. I played with other children. I was invited to birthdays. Hmm, and went there. Just like every other kid."

"What did it say to you?" Thomas asked, and, looking to the ground, he added: "Was it mean?"

You shit! You creep!

"No. There was nothing like that. No voice or anything. Just me. I didn't feel forced or guided at all. I just did what I felt like doing."

His lips began to tremble. The baby was about to cry again. It was so disgusting.

You're disgusting, you little shit!

"It was never meant to be like this, Thomas. In all the cases I know, the perex entirely integrates with the host. Sometimes people report sudden out-of-the-blue thoughts, but this isn't perceived as something alien. More like talking to yourself in your mind. Like thinking to yourself *Hey, I might go to bed earlier today* or *Hey, I shouldn't take this so seriously*. Self-talk like that.

"Hmm. Cases like yours are extremely rare. Where the perex doesn't integrate and levels off into a state of psychological dissociation. Sometimes the ignition doesn't induce a change in the expected direction. No effect at all. As if the neuro-synthetic circuit is dead, but it isn't. The data processing of the system works fine. The perex just doesn't merge."

I was assailed by the image of a frightened homunculus, squatting in anguish in the corner of some deranged sadist's mind. Devoid of any power for resistance or escape.

"But what about the voice?" Thomas asked. "And that he can use my body? He spoke to you with my mouth!"

She looked at us, without any expression, and eventually wagged her head.

"Hasn't happened before."

* * *

"Whaad's the plaan?" I asked some days later. "Noow? Whaad's the poind of this all? Youh think youh can maigh thaad perverd normaal?"

Thomas was only half-conscious. *Fucking asshole,* he whispered weakly. He'd been sedated because the idiot tried to open his skull with one of Dr. Rebbs's pens. But something told me his folly was not the only reason. The idea of using a pen was too absurd, not in the least dangerous. I had the feeling Rebbs wanted to talk to me without interruption from his side.

"Youh think youh can cure thaad twaad?"

I was really curious. Over the last days, I had pondered a lot over the question. In fact, they sent a warden directly into his mind. If even I wasn't capable of mending his wicked nature, what could they possibly expect to achieve from out there?

"This isn't about him, Tom," Rebbs replied. "Thomas was hospitalized on wrong accounts. That was a mistake. Hmm, maybe he's not a very nice person, and he surely has some serious issues, but he's not mentally ill. He doesn't belong here. This is about you! You are doing harm to yourself. And to Thomas. I believe that he is capable of improving. But he needs your help! Your guidance, not your anger. As righteous as it may be sometimes. This is what we need to work on. This is the way to overcome the dissociation you are trapped in. It won't be easy, Tom, but we have a realistic chance to straighten this out. So you can finally merge."

I was aghast. Much more than by the unveiling of what I am, I was shocked by the prospect of what they wanted me to become.

"Naaah!" I burst out. "Aigh don'd whanna be heem!"

"It wouldn't be him, Tom. When you merge, the joint mind would be you as well. It would be a better version of Thomas, if you want. A version with less aggression and impulsive violence. A version including you. Not imposed on you. But also not governed by you. His mind will change in accordance with your desires. But for that, you need to overcome your disgust. Your repugnance, Tom, it isn't healthy."

* * *

You're a failure, Thomas once whispered when we were lying in bed at night. *A miserable aberration!*

He was right. I hate him, and I hate Dr. Rebbs for what she'd done to me, but they are right. I am a failure. That's basically what Rebbs told me. What she's still telling me in every single session. She doesn't use these words, of course, she hides her real thoughts behind gracious remarks about the unique difficulties I've been facing in this special case, but that's what it comes down to. I'm no good. I'm a nuisance. A disappointment for her and her fucking medical science team in Banbury. Fact is, I was never wanted the way I am. After everything that happened, after all the shit that I went through, all the pain I took on to keep Thomas from being such a twat, they still want me to change. *Me!* It's like it always was. Thomas is the victim. The unlucky sufferer of adverse circumstances. And me? What am I? Rebbs assures me that I could be the cure, but in fact, she thinks I'm the adverse circumstances.

Every other day, I have therapy sessions with Dr. Rebbs, while Dr. Motoharu has resumed her sessions with Thomas. I don't know what they are discussing together, and I have to admit, I don't care. I'm tired of all this. I try to fade out as much as possible during their sessions. Only when he gets upset by something Motoharu says, I am instantly on alert because I've learned that this often is an indication of imminent aggression. And then I detest myself for giving a fuck. Why do I even care about how bad and how destructive Thomas behaves? I watch him all the time, I am capable of preventing it, and when I do, they call me a flaw. Something that needs to be corrected. I wish I could leave this all behind. Even the nights no longer hold any relief.

"Cud me off!"

Usually requests like that were made by Thomas. It was the first time that I was asking for it myself. It wasn't just a temporary whim. I'd thought about it for weeks. Since Dr. Rebbs told me I had to change. I don't know why this thought seems so dreadful to me. But everything's been different since then. It's like I'm floating and I can't get a grip on anything. I just wanted it to end. Still, I was wary of revealing my self-destructive thoughts too early because I presumed that they would jump at the chance immediately. That they were anxiously waiting for my consent anyway, polite enough to not suggest it themselves. I was stunned when I heard Rebbs's answer.

"You know I can't do that," she said. Apparently, she didn't see any need for a further explanation.

"Why? You can'd disconnegd the circuid?"

She looked up. I had the feeling of not getting something obvious.

"Tom, you are a conscious being! And your system is based on the joint connections with the host. Cutting off the circuit would be permanent. You would cease. We can't just decide to kill you!"

"Bud I wand id! I decide!"

"Hmm," she replied, obviously searching for words. "Tom, I'm sorry, but... you have mental issues! In your current state, you aren't capable of making such profound decisions. You don't see things clearly at the moment. Your pessimistic idea that this is the only way out is exactly a symptom of your unstable mood."

"So id's a cadch," I muttered.

"A what?"

"You'd grand me my whish if I was sane. And to maigh you believe thad I'm sane, I have to withdrah from id."

She sighed.

"Tom, I don't know what to say. You're seeing things dark now. I'm trying to help you here."

"You mighd as well quid trying. Doesn'd maigh a difference."

"Hmm. Maybe it doesn't. But that's the definition of trying, isn't it? That it might be in vain."

"Whad ahbaud Thomas?"

"What about him?"

"Heh's here as well. Heh ev'n is human. And heh's suffering. Because of me. Because you pud me here. Id's your fauld. Which you could straighden out by cudding me off. And Thomas, heh wand's id as well."

"Thomas can't make this decision either. You are alive, Tom! You're a fully developed consciousness. For the same reason our law forbids abortions when the pregnancy has advanced too far. Sure it's a woman's own body, but when there's another life involved, you have to take it into account. You cannot just erase it just because you think you'd feel better then. Even if it's true, even if you would be better off, you just can't do that. Neither Thomas, nor I, nor you."

I kept still then. Didn't say a word for the rest of the session. I didn't feel there was anything more for me to say. She wouldn't hear me anyway. Nobody ever would.

"Tom, you have to trust me!" she tried to appease me. "Such a sacrifice is not a solution. Hmm, not a good one. I know there's a better way. For Thomas and for you."

* * *

Sometimes I wonder where this depressive mood came from. I have to admit I've never been in such a sullen state before. Even in earlier days, when Thomas acted out his nasty outrages without restraint, when I hadn't yet been able to intervene, even then I didn't feel so desolate. I was frightened then and dismayed, but it wasn't this dreary bleakness I'm wrapped in now. I wish I'd just disappear.

But they don't let me. Thomas's repeated pleas for cutting me off have been turned down the same as my own, and he has given up on asking Motoharu for it. We've reached an unspoken agreement to leave each other alone during our respective therapy sessions. The truce gives me a little relief, and also Thomas has put up with the situation to some degree. Still, he's gotten upset with Motoharu lately.

"You don't understand SHIT!" he yelled at her. I thought about taking over, making him collapse or biting his fingers as I'd done before to punish him for such imbecilities, but what good would it do? He'd just let off steam and then calm down again. He's afraid of Motoharu.

"YOU'VE NO IDEA HOW IT FEELS!"

He pushed over his chair, Motoharu quietly observing him. In the end I didn't even revile him for being such an idiot. Couldn't really blame him for his anger anyway. Motoharu isn't any better than Rebbs. They are so utterly convinced that they know what's best for us. Better than ourselves. They act like some cocky gods, patronizing their wards, torturing them with their goodwill. They keep on saying we should be patient. That every treatment needs time. I can't hear it anymore.

* * *

It's been three weeks now since they added the new stimus to my circuit. It's strange that in my thoughts I still call them "stimus." I know that they aren't. I know that they do much more than emit electrical impulses. That they form an integral part of me.

"They define you," Rebbs recently overstated.

I felt the urge to slap her in the face, but I contained myself. Just mumbled "stupid bitch." It wasn't worth the trouble I would get in.

In our last session, Motoharu again said we're on a good way and for the first time it didn't sound completely made-up. Thomas even smiled at her, proud like a schoolboy who'd been complimented for doing well in class.

I had the slight hope that the new perex would be able to change his attitude. But it's all the same. Just a distant, vague feeling has emerged. It's a bit like taking a walk at night. You know how everything looks, you've seen the night so many times before. And in fact, nothing's really changed. The streets, the houses, the air. Everything in the neighborhood is the same. It's just the stars. They are so far away, and they have no meaning for you at all. They don't affect you, but still, they look very different.

Thomas is as foolish as he's always been, but of late I don't think about him that much. At times I almost forget he's there. For all I know, he might feel the same about me.

* * *

Discussion Questions

1. Assuming the procedure initially worked as planned, do you support this type of procedure? What are the best arguments for and against it?
2. What are the similarities and differences between having a conscious and the perex in the story?
3. What treatments are allowable for the treatment of mental illness? Are we justified in changing someone's identity against their will if they're a danger to society?
4. Is this case, does seemingly sentient AI have the right to ask to be terminated? Does sentient AI have the same or different "right to die" rules than humans?
5. Thomas's mother gave consent for the stimus medical procedure. How do you distinguish between medical procedures that require an underage individual's consent, the parents' consent, or consent from both before moving forward?

* * *

The Sanctity of Self

George J. Osol

* * *

<u>Content Disclosure</u>: Strong Language; Suicidal Themes; Medical Procedures

* * *

After the head-on, I was ambulanced to the morgue at Mass General and pronounced dead on arrival. Because I was an organ donor, they called the medical examiner, and just like that, my fate was sealed. A pathologist by training, Dr. Franklin is famous for his research on transplant organ preservation.

My chest and abdomen were crushed after the airbag failed, so Franklinstein set to work cannulating my carotids and jugulars. He apparently wanted to see how long the blood-brain barrier could be preserved with *PhysioHeme*, the novel synthetic blood substitute he developed and patented.

Imagine their surprise when my eyelids began to flutter! The coroner's assistant passed out, and Dr. Franklin, whom I've since learned is a nonstop talker, was speechless. They quickly added an anesthetic to keep me under, unsure of what to do next. One of the dieners googled "living head" on her phone and discovered that the Russians had done exactly that a year earlier with a dog. Why is it always the Russians?

A month, sundry administrative and ethics committee meetings, and a court ruling later, life support and resuscitation were decreed obligatory. I had no living will and, at forty-seven, was still young. Thus mandated, the hospital folks worked with the Bioengineering Department at MIT to construct a life-support system for what was left of me.

Once completed, their next step was to bring me out of the drug-induced coma. I remember coming to surrounded by white coats and masks. Saucer eyed, I could only see the silk cloth the perfusion apparatus below me was draped with. *Where is the rest of me?* I screamed, and kept praying that this was a dream, that I would close my eyes and wake up in my own bed.

No luck with that one.

I don't remember much early on—Franklin must have had some serious antianxiety meds flowing through my brain at that point. Worse, I lost all of my memories, although, oddly, my knowledge base was preserved. For example, I can remember the difference between an omelet and a frittata or a mile versus a kilometer; on the other hand, I have no recollection of earning my PhD (although I do remember my thesis was on Descartes's *cogito*), meeting Elena and getting married, or of being a professor at Northeastern (all of which I've subsequently learned about by being told). I can speak and read well enough, but I have no memories of my mother and father or my childhood. Tabula rasa. The neurologist seems to understand why—something to do with local versus global executive functions—but I sure don't.

* * *

I cried almost all the time at first as my mind whirled through its maelstrom of fear, self-pity, and anger. I would have killed myself in a second if I could have, but of course I couldn't: no breath to hold, no wrists to cut. I pleaded with everyone—even the janitor—to unplug me, but this was uncharted territory, and no one was willing to comply.

One winter night, there was a windstorm and the hospital went dark. I'll never forget the mixture of fear and relief, panic and peace at the thought that I was going to die. As it turns out, the MIT wizards had built in a battery that gives me seventy-two hours of backup, so it was a no-go.

* * *

In retrospect, the nurses were amazing. Especially Olivia. She would talk with me as she shaved and blotted me and, when she was done, she would massage my head before combing my hair. Feeling her fingers on my scalp became the moment I most looked forward to every day. The human touch.

The hospital chaplain came by a few times, and folks from a local church group. They would read inspirational passages from the Bible and sing hymns. I finally told them I wasn't into the whole religious thing. They ceased and desisted, but I remember them kindly. Good people. Must be nice to have faith, but you can't fake it.

An old geezer came by one morning with a yellow lab named Missy. The problem was that Missy didn't want to have anything to do with me. As much as the handler tried to get the dog to relate to me as a person, Missy just sniffed the base of my pedestal and whined. At his suggestion, I tried calling her by name, but Missy got agitated and started to growl, so that was the end of that.

Then came the depression. Except for the nurses and occasional visitors, it was just me, myself, and I in the ICU, and I grew tired of all three. Olivia noticed my constant crying and contacted Franklin, who came by with a psychiatrist in tow. With my consent, they started adding antidepressants and mood stabilizers to the perfusate and eventually came up with a mixture that—if you pardon the metaphor—helped keep my head above water.

* * *

After six weeks, I was finally discharged. That was big at first, but then the whole thing with Elena, my wife of nearly twenty years, went south. The situation was tolerable for her when I was in the ICU because she could at least go home and be free after visiting hours. Once I came home, she felt trapped. Our life had supposedly been full of physical activity—hiking, biking, tennis—but now it was all strangely passive and, let's face it, dull. My not remembering her didn't help. It was like beginning a relationship all over again, and what I could offer in my present condition was pretty limited.

Ultimately, the sense of isolation was insurmountable on my part, as was the feeling of separation on hers. The emptiness between us grew into a chasm. A few months later, I noticed Elena had grown unusually quiet. When I asked her what was the matter, she said "nothing" at first, but, with time, it came out that she had met someone.

That hurt, but I understood, more with the head than the heart, so to speak. We parted amicably, she remarried, and they now have three kids. Good for them. We all have our quantum of solace, and when that's spent, it's time to part. Like faith, you can't fake love.

* * *

Post-divorce, I spiraled. Didn't see much point in living. They tweaked the meds, but that didn't help much this time around, and a therapist started coming by twice a week. He admitted that he had no idea what to say, but reassured me that he genuinely wanted to help. Could we give it our best try? As it turned out, Dave and I hit a personal chord of some sort, a resonance of spirit, as occasionally happens with strangers, and I began to look forward to his visits.

One day when I was feeling particularly sorry for myself, he pointed out that I was luckier than many others who suffer a grave physical misfortune—the locked-in stroke victim, for example, or the person with quadriplegia who is saddled with a body that he or she cannot feel or use, yet one that can create both suffering and inconvenience.

That was a revelation. For me, there is no colostomy bag, no weight gain, and no wheelchair sores to worry about. With this IPA (Intelligent Perfusion Apparatus), I'll never develop high blood pressure, cholesterol, or sugar. Heart attack? Nope, not me. Cancer? Possible but unlikely. Without the burden of a body, I'm free of most of the medical concerns that normal people worry about as they age. Heady stuff, ha ha!

A huge step forward was Olivia agreeing to become my full-time caretaker after her husband died. Sad for her, but what a blessing for me! She moved in and is a friend, companion, nurse, and—after I bought the special van—chauffeur. I don't go out much, but once in a while, it's fun to take a ride and watch a sunset, or sit by the water.

* * *

You're probably wondering how I look. Well, my head—me!—is perched over a perfusion apparatus bolted onto a specialized wheelchair base. The whole robotic contraption is draped in a silk shroud, motorized, and stable.

I take pride in my appearance. The barber comes by every month. My beard is full and mostly dark brown. With the designer cowl in place, it looks like I'm wearing a cravat. Elegant and professorial. A few people have told me I look like that actor Nick Offerman.

And I've become the world's most famous talking head! After appearing on a few podcasts and TV talk shows, I started getting tons of mail, especially from women offering to care for me. Nice (and a few naughty) pictures keep coming in, along with occasional marriage proposals that I don't bother to reply to. Who knows what these people are after? I don't mean to be cynical, but I am pretty vulnerable, after all, and I do have Olivia.

Most blessedly, my mind is intact, and isn't that what makes us human? Our ability to adapt. To love. To reason. Not only do I still have my senses, some have become heightened, especially the sense of smell. Maybe it's the perfusate that Franklin has me on. He says it's a pretty perfect fluid, with its sugar and oxygen, amino acids, vitamins, minerals, and meds.

Surfing the web has always been a pleasure because I love to learn, and I can control almost everything on the computer using voice commands. And when it comes to calling or texting people, there's always Alexa.

* * *

The most hurtful thing has been how strangers react to me when I go out in public. Children often point and sometimes laugh, but they're kids, so who can blame them?

Most adults are considerate, but not all. Occasionally, a person will approach me uninvited. Imagine having strangers come up to you to ask personal questions or make unsolicited comments! It's intrusive and rude, but I suppose it isn't much different from what celebrities have to put up with every day. Others will pointedly avoid me. They'll turn away and cross the street or back into a doorway if they can do so without being too obvious. Ask any person of color about that one.

A few weeks ago, these two putzes were walking up the street when they spotted me getting rolled into my van. Teenagers: sixteen or seventeen; old enough to know better but young enough not to care. It was cold out, and I had my fedora on. They started mocking me by crossing their eyes and sticking their tongues out as they held an imaginary hat on their head.

I was having one of my bad days, so I yelled "fuck off" but, although I can talk, I can't really yell and ended up coughing instead. Furious, I spat their way, but the drool got caught in my beard. Olivia, who was helping me into the van at the time, spun around, saw what they were doing, and gave them hell as only Olivia can. A sweet and gentle lady, but when she gets mad, watch out! She dressed them up and down with every foul word in the English language, ending with "dinky dicks" as they slinked off. Cheered me right up.

* * *

The university and I worked out the logistics, and there I was in class on day one of the fall semester. The students knew of my situation, of course, but there were still a few gasps when I rolled into the lecture theatre.

That first day was odd, for no one knew quite how to relate to me, and the class was hushed. During the second week, a handful of students began to linger and to make an effort to engage. Some started coming by during my office hours, looking for help with the material and, frankly, to just talk. If a student felt comfortable, the conversation might stray off topic and occasionally cross over into the personal. I am a philosophy professor, and the subject lends itself to conversations about life issues such as free will, fate, and ethics. These one-on-one moments have become my favorite part of the job; I relish the warmth and honest contact. It was a privilege, or at least it felt that way until the day I met Jason.

And then everything changed.

* * *

It was one of those September afternoons when summer's warm hand lingers and the campus is abuzz with frisbees flying and Bluetooth speakers blaring. Buoyed by the energy in the air, I reluctantly rolled back to my office for the posted 3–5 p.m. office hours. Unsurprisingly, not a single student came by, and I found myself keeping an eye on the clock, waiting for Olivia to pick me up. She usually pulls in just after five, calls, and readies the van while I make my way downstairs.

Suddenly, there he was, standing in the doorway wearing a ratty old army jacket, hands in pockets. I remember thinking that was odd since it was such a warm day. Tall, thin, with stringy blonde hair and a three-day stubble, his eyes were fixed on me with an intense, uneasy expression.

I smiled. "Hi there," I said, "you must be in my class. May I help you?"

"I don't need your help," he said brusquely, "but we do need to talk."

"Okay," I said, trying to put him at ease. "What's your name?"

"Jason," he said.

"Well, come on in, Jason," I said. "You're in my class, yes?" I didn't remember seeing him before, but there were nearly two hundred students, after all, and the semester had just started.

He came in, pulled out a chair, and sat down across from me. Something was going on behind those eyes, but I couldn't read what it was, except that it was not good. Jason leaned back, folded his hands behind his head, and sat for a moment, looking down his nose at me, before speaking.

"You're a fucking scumbag."

He said this matter-of-factly, as if he were telling me the time of day.

No one had ever spoken like this to me before. Wherefrom, I thought? Had I come across as being egotistical or arrogant in class? Did I say something offensive? It doesn't take much these days, and if I did, whatever it was surely didn't warrant this vulgarity. Quite the affront, I thought. Was he crazy? High?

We locked eyes as the seconds ticked by. The clock on the campus tower began its hourly toll.

"And you are very rude," I said. I was looking to regain the upper hand, although I still wasn't sure if he was a student or why he was here.

"Not as rude as you," he snapped back. "You're a fucking shithead for what you did."

"Did to whom?" I said. This made no sense.

"To my mother and my sister," he said.

It still didn't make any sense.

"I've never met your mother or sister," I said, annoyance creeping into my voice. "You've got your wires crossed, my friend."

He stood up and leaned toward me before slamming his fist on my desk hard enough to make my computer monitor blink.

Suddenly, he was screaming. "I don't have any wires crossed, asshole. And I'm not your friend! You killed them both, you fucking drunk! Head-on. Twice the legal limit. My sister was barely three!"

I gasped.

As you know, I've lost my memory and, believe it or not, I had never thought to ask about the details of the accident. Self-preservation? Selfishness? Both? And no one had bothered to tell me. Or maybe I forgot. Those first few days in the ICU were pretty patchy and I don't remember much. Maybe I blocked it out but here, now, it was chillingly clear. Not only had I killed two innocent people—a mother and a child, no less—but I was drunk to boot. It felt like someone hit me between the eyes with an axe, and my head exploded. I started sobbing and mumbling: "Oh my God, I'm sorry, I don't remember..." over and over again.

"I don't give a fuck about your apologies or your crocodile tears," he yelled. "You killed them both, you crossed the center line, and now it's your turn." With that, he came around behind me and yanked the power cord out of the socket before stepping back, arms crossed.

He was going to enjoy watching me die.

The perfusion pump went silent for an instant, but then started up again. Realizing that there was a battery backup, he dropped down to his knees and started clawing at the silk shroud, looking for the access port.

Suddenly, the phone rang.

"What's wrong?" said Olivia. "Are you okay?"

* * *

Jason didn't come to class for two weeks and, when he finally did, he sat way in the back and avoided eye contact. My composure regained, but anxiety and guilt still raging, I didn't say anything that day, but asked him to come to my office the next day. I wanted to first apologize and to then ask for his forgiveness. And then I was going to convince him to kill me.

Here we were across the desk from each other once more. Having had plenty of time to think about what to say—I had even practiced!—I explained my thinking carefully, logically, professorially. I made my best case, I pleaded with him, I even offered him money, but he shook his head.

"No," he said. "No way. The last time I was here, I meant to kill you. I was actually looking forward to it. But I've since come to see that, for you, living is worse than dying. It's the roughest justice of all."

Jason then told me about how wonderful his mother had been. How much he loved her and how much she loved him. What a beautiful voice she had, and what beautiful eyes. How hard it was to know that he would never see her again. How it broke his father's heart to have lost his wife and daughter, how he was still emotionally crippled.

Done twisting the knife, Jason got to his feet and took his parting shot. "It's so wrong," he said, shaking his head. "I'm not sure I can ever forgive you."

* * *

Over the next few weeks, I felt the will to live drain out of me like water out of a leaky bucket. I hadn't expected that Jason's words would turn out to be a mortal wound, but three months out now, it seems like they were. Every morning brings a fresh pang of recrimination, a stab of guilt. I do my best to get distracted during the day by writing, and can go for hours feeling relatively normal. That's the daily gift. But the evening always comes and, with it, night, and the inner hurt starts anew.

Dying may be the coward's way out, but it has become my idée fixe. I just haven't figured out how to do it. Yet.

You see, Descartes's famous phrase, "*Cogito, ergo sum:* I think, therefore I am," was a celebration of consciousness, a paean to the sanctity of self. For me, however, it's more: "I think, therefore, I don't deserve to be."

It's the *cornuta interrogatia,* as the philosopher Udall put it five hundred years ago: the classic two-horned dilemma. Can I will myself to die, or can I learn to forget? So far, no traction with either option, but I'm working on it.

* * *

Discussion Questions

1. Clearly, even as a head, the narrator is still alive and himself. How much of him could be removed and have him still be alive and himself? How do you define, or know, if he's still alive and himself?

2. Would you consider the narrator alive if, as a head, he did not have the ability to speak, but had electrodes hooked up to his scalp that allowed him to think and create text on a computer? What if the software was extrapolating the words instead of performing a one-to-one conversation of thought to words?

3. Descartes famously said, "Cogito, ergo sum: I think, therefore I am." What did Descartes mean in this statement, and what does it mean in the context of the story?

4. If you were offered death or the head-only life of the narrator with a caretaker, which would you choose and why?

5. In the context of the story, what does this phrase mean: "Can I will myself to die, or can I learn to forget?" Are those the narrator's only two options?

* * *

State of Oregon v. Lark Gold

Tiffany Harris

* * *

<u>**Content Disclosure**</u>: None

* * *

Lark Gold hitchhiked into Sylvan County with three dollars and twelve cents in her pocket. Most people called her Goldie because of her hair, which fell to her shoulders in a mess of dirty blonde waves that hadn't touched shampoo in weeks. At seventeen, she had the weary eyes of someone twice her age. The social worker in her last town had called those eyes "old-soul eyes." The cop who'd chased her from the abandoned Walmart parking lot had called them "junkie eyes." Neither was right.

The rain fell in sheets as Goldie trudged along Blackberry Road, a rural stretch dotted with the kind of houses that had names and histories but no neighbors in shouting distance. This wasn't where she'd intended to end up, but the truck driver who'd picked her up outside of Portland had insisted this was as far as he could take her.

"Check the ridge road," he'd said. "Vacation homes. Empty most of the year."

Her stomach cramped. She hadn't eaten since yesterday morning—half a bagel found in a coffee shop trash can. Her jacket, a men's Carhartt two sizes too big that she'd taken from a shelter donation bin, kept her torso dry but her jeans were soaked through. Hypothermia was the immediate threat, starvation the longer game. The distinction hardly mattered.

Past a tangle of blackberry brambles that gave the road its name, Goldie spotted a cedar-shingled cabin set back from the road. No lights, no car, no smoke from the chimney. She paused, the cold rain beating down, and counted—one, two, three. Three windows facing the front, all dark. The mailbox at the end of the gravel driveway read "Berenson."

Goldie walked up the driveway, stepping in tire tracks to keep her already-soaked sneakers from sinking into the mud. The porch creaked under her weight. She peered through a window, cupping her hands around her eyes to block the glare. The inside looked tidy but unused—furniture draped with white sheets, the ghostlike silhouettes of a covered couch and dining table. Definitely a vacation home.

She tried the door. Locked. But the second window from the left had a broken latch—not visible unless you were looking for it. Goldie had gotten good at looking for things like that. She slid her fingers under the frame and pushed up. The window resisted, then gave way with a groan.

Inside, the house smelled of pine cleaner and fireplace ash. She stood dripping on the hardwood floor, listening. Nothing but the drum of rain on the roof. Vacation homes like this one usually had security systems, but there was no keypad by the door, no blinking lights in the corners.

"Hello?" she called. Her voice scattered in the empty space. No response.

She shed her wet jacket and shoes by the window and padded in damp socks across the floor, trailing her finger along walls until she found a light switch. She flipped it. Nothing happened.

"Power's out," she muttered. *Or turned off.* Vacation homeowners did that when they left for the season.

Goldie made her way to the kitchen, where large windows let in enough gray daylight to see. She opened the refrigerator—empty except for a box of baking soda and some condiments. The pantry was more promising: canned soup, crackers, pasta, a jar of peanut butter. Survival food. The kind people left in vacation homes for the next time they visited.

She opened a can of chicken noodle soup and drank it cold. The salt made her dizzy with relief. She found bottled water in a case beneath the sink and drank an entire bottle without pausing for breath.

The house had three bedrooms upstairs. The first was clearly the master—king bed, his-and-hers nightstands, a heavy oak dresser. The second had twin beds with navy blue comforters. The third was the smallest—a single bed with a yellow quilt that looked handmade. Goldie felt drawn to this room. It looked lived-in, personal, unlike the others, which had the generic quality of hotel rooms.

She peeled off her wet clothes and rummaged through the dresser, finding a large T-shirt that came down to her knees. She laid her jeans and socks over a chair to dry and crawled into the bed. The sheets were cool and smelled slightly of lavender. Her body ached with exhaustion.

"Just one night," she whispered to herself. "I'll be gone before anyone knows."

* * *

District Attorney Martin Walsh leaned against the courthouse wall outside Courtroom C, scrolling through emails on his phone when Public Defender Elena Jordan approached.

"Pretty thin docket today," she said. "Just the Berenson-Gold case."

Walsh locked his phone. "The Berensons are pretty insistent on pursuing this one. Your client broke into a private home, damaged property, ate their food, slept in their bed. Classic Goldilocks story, except she's not a little girl wandering through the woods. She's old enough to know better."

"She's seventeen, Marty. She aged out of foster care in Oregon—"

"That's not a defense."

"It's context. We're not talking about some teenage thrill-seeker. She had nowhere to go."

"She had plenty of places to go that weren't someone's private property. Homeless shelters, churches, social services. Pick one."

Elena sighed. "Have you actually been to any of those places? Talked to people who've tried to access those services? Sexual assault rates at shelters, waitlists that stretch for months, social workers with caseloads so heavy they can't remember their clients' names..."

Walsh put up his hand. "The Berensons are good people. They work hard, pay their taxes, maintain their property. They shouldn't have to come home to find some stranger has been living in their house."

"One night isn't 'living in their house,' Marty."

"She admitted to checking out other properties on that road. If Mr. Berenson hadn't installed those security cameras last fall, she'd probably still be squatting there. They found her on the footage and went to check, and there she was, making herself right at home."

Elena studied him. "What are you charging her with?"

"Criminal trespass, first degree. And criminal mischief for good measure."

"First-degree trespass? We both know she had no intent to commit a crime. She was looking for shelter." Elena shook her head. "We should be discussing an accountability agreement, not charges. Are you *really* planning to drag this through a full hearing?"

Walsh frowned. "Robert Berenson happens to be on the county budget committee. He wants to make an example here, and send a message about property rights. I'd offer diversion for any other kid, but my hands are tied on this one."

"She's seventeen, Marty," Elena reminded him. "She needs rehabilitation, not a criminal record."

Walsh picked up his briefcase. "It's out of my hands."

The bailiff poked his head into the hallway. "DA Walsh, Ms. Jordan? Judge is ready."

* * *

Judge Harold Caulfield stared down at Goldie from the bench. His white hair formed a thinning crown around a bald spot that gleamed under the harsh lights.

"Miss Gold, do you understand the charges against you?"

Goldie nodded, then remembering courtroom protocol, said, "Yes, Your Honor."

"And how do you plead?"

"Not guilty." Her voice cracked.

"Very well." The judge turned to the attorneys. "As we proceed with this matter, I understand both sides have waived opening statements and agreed to move directly to arguments?"

Walsh and Elena both nodded.

"Ms. Jordan, you may begin."

Elena stood, smoothing her navy skirt. "Your Honor, at its core, this case asks us to consider when human need overrides social convention. My client, Lark Gold, did enter the Berenson family's vacation home without permission. She did spend one night there. She did consume approximately fifteen dollars' worth of nonperishable food that was stored in their pantry. These are facts not in dispute."

She took a few steps toward the bench. "But let's consider the circumstances. Miss Gold was not looking to steal valuables or vandalize property. She was seeking shelter from hypothermia-inducing weather after days without adequate food. The house she entered showed every sign of being unoccupied for an extended period. It was a vacation home with sheets covering the furniture, power turned off at the breaker, and no security system actively monitoring the premises."

Elena gestured to Goldie. "My client left her wet shoes by the door to avoid damaging the floors. She touched nothing of value. She replaced the sheets she used and cleaned the dishes from which she ate. Her intent was survival, not crime."

Judge Caulfield frowned. "Ms. Jordan, regardless of intent, your client broke into private property."

"Yes, Your Honor, but 'choice of evils' recognizes that necessity justifies actions when a person faces imminent threat of serious harm. The hypothermia risk from that storm was life-threatening. My client chose a minor trespass to prevent a greater harm, and with rural Sylvan County's limited shelter capacity—especially for unaccompanied minors—she had no reasonable legal alternative."

The judge made a note. "Continue."

"The law recognizes that human life holds the highest value in our society. That's why we allow emergency vehicles to speed, why Good Samaritan laws protect those who break into cars to save children or pets from heatstroke. Lark Gold's actions fall into this same category—a technical violation of the law to prevent a greater harm."

Elena returned to her seat. "We ask the court to recognize that this is not a case of criminal intent but of human survival, and to dismiss all charges accordingly."

"Thank you, Ms. Jordan." The judge turned to the prosecution. "Mr. Walsh?"

Walsh approached the bench with confident steps. "Your Honor, while Ms. Jordan's argument pulls at the heartstrings, it undermines the very foundation of our society: the rule of law. The Berenson family—Robert, Mary, and their son Benjamin—work hard for what they have. They pay their mortgage, their property taxes, their insurance. They maintain their vacation home with care. They have every right to expect that when they return to it, it will be as they left it."

He paced in front of the bench. "The defense would have you believe that anyone who feels sufficiently desperate has the right to ignore property boundaries. Where does it end? Can I break into a car if mine breaks down? Can I take food from a grocery store if I'm hungry? Can I sleep in your chambers if I don't have a place to stay?"

The judge raised an eyebrow. "I think not, Mr. Walsh."

"Of course not, Your Honor. Because we maintain order through respect for boundaries. Miss Gold may have faced difficult circumstances, but she made a deliberate choice to violate the law instead of seeking legal alternatives."

"Such as?" Judge Caulfield asked.

"Sylvan County maintains two emergency shelters. There's a hospital fifteen miles south with a legal obligation to help anyone in need. There are churches, community centers, even police stations where she could have sought assistance. Instead, she chose to break into a private home."

Walsh returned to his seat. "Your Honor, compassion shouldn't blind us to the rule of law. The defendant broke in, used resources that weren't hers to use, and violated the sanctity of a family's home. The prosecution asks for the maximum penalty under juvenile sentencing guidelines."

"Thank you, Mr. Walsh." Judge Caulfield looked at his watch. "I'll deliver my verdict after a brief recess. Court will resume in thirty minutes."

* * *

Mary Berenson sat stiffly on the courtroom bench, her husband Robert beside her. Their son, Benjamin, thirteen, played a game on his phone with the sound off.

"Stop that," Mary whispered, nudging him.

"I'm bored," Ben whispered back. "Why do we have to be here anyway? It's just some homeless girl."

"Because we're pressing charges," Robert said quietly. "When someone breaks into your home, you hold them accountable."

Ben put his phone away. "But nothing was stolen. Mom said even the dishes were washed."

"That's not the point," Robert insisted. "What if we had been there? What if she had been dangerous?"

"But she wasn't," Ben said. "She was just cold and hungry."

Mary's lips thinned. "Benjamin, when you work for something, you have the right to protect it. That house represents years of saving and sacrifice. We can't just—"

"So does her life," Ben interrupted.

"That's enough," Robert said. "The judge will be back soon."

From across the aisle, Goldie watched the family's hushed conversation. She looked away when the youngest Berenson glanced in her direction. The boy's eyes lingered on her, curious rather than hostile. When she dared to look again, he gave her a small, uncertain smile before his mother noticed and whispered something that made him turn around.

* * *

"All rise," the bailiff announced as Judge Caulfield returned to the bench.

When everyone was seated, the judge adjusted his glasses and cleared his throat. "This case presents a conflict between two foundational principles: the right to private property and the imperative of human survival. Both the prosecution and defense have presented compelling arguments."

He shuffled some papers. "Having reviewed the evidence and arguments presented, I find the defendant, Lark 'Goldie' Gold, guilty of criminal trespass, but not guilty of burglary or criminal mischief."

Elena squeezed Goldie's arm supportively. The girl's face remained expressionless.

"For the crime of criminal trespass, I sentence the defendant to six months' probation and forty hours of community service." The judge paused. "Additionally, Miss Gold will be required to write a formal apology to the Berenson family and pay restitution for the food consumed, valued at fifteen dollars. Given your financial situation, I'm waiving all court fees under ORS 419C.449."

He looked directly at Goldie. "Miss Gold, do you understand your sentence?"

"Yes, Your Honor," she said.

"Mr. and Mrs. Berenson, do you have any questions about this ruling?"

Robert Berenson stood. "Your Honor, with all due respect, this feels like a slap on the wrist for a serious violation."

"Mr. Berenson, I understand your concern. But the court must balance justice with mercy. Miss Gold's actions, while unlawful, were motivated by necessity rather than malice." The judge's tone softened slightly. "Sometimes the law must bend to accommodate human frailty."

Robert looked like he wanted to say more, but Mary tugged at his sleeve, and he sat down.

"If there are no further questions, court is adjourned." The judge brought down his gavel.

As people began filing out, Goldie turned to Elena. "What happens now?"

"Now we get you set up with social services. Independent Living can provide support until you're twenty-one. We can also look into some transitional housing programs."

"Right," Goldie said, her voice hollow. "Another program, another caseworker who'll forget my name." She'd heard these promises before.

Elena squeezed her shoulder. "Let's start with what we have now. Oregon has some options, at least."

It was almost an answer.

* * *

Outside the courthouse, Goldie waited for Elena, who had stayed behind to file paperwork. The late afternoon sun cast long shadows across the steps. She sat with her backpack— everything she owned in the world—beside her.

She heard footsteps and looked up to see Benjamin Berenson approaching tentatively, his parents waiting by their car in the parking lot.

"Hi," he said.

"Hi," Goldie replied cautiously.

"I just wanted to say..." He shifted uncomfortably. "I'm sorry about all this. I told my parents not to press charges."

"It's fine," Goldie said. "It's their house. Their right."

"It's my room you stayed in," Ben said. "With the yellow quilt. My grandma made it."

Goldie stared at him. "I'm sorry. I didn't take anything."

"I know." He glanced back at his parents, who were watching closely. "It's just a vacation house anyway. We only use it like three weeks a year." He lowered his voice. "My mom's the one who put the sheets over everything. She says it keeps the dust off."

"Ben!" Robert called from the parking lot. "Let's go!"

The boy reached into his pocket and pulled out a folded twenty-dollar bill. "Here," he said, pushing it into Goldie's hand. "For the restitution. It's more than fifteen, but..." He shrugged.

"I can't take this," Goldie said.

"Please. I have an allowance. I don't need it."

"Benjamin!" Mary's voice this time, sharper.

"Coming!" he called back. To Goldie, he said quickly, "I'm really sorry," then ran back to his parents.

Goldie watched the family drive away, the twenty-dollar bill warm in her palm. She thought about the yellow quilt, the handmade stitches, the smell of lavender. She thought about the boy's room—the only space in that house that had felt like someone actually lived there, not just passed through.

The courthouse doors opened, and Elena emerged. "Ready?" she asked. "I've arranged temporary housing for you. Just until we can sort out something more permanent."

"Temporary," Goldie repeated, standing up. "Everything's always temporary."

Elena had no answer for that either. They walked together down the courthouse steps, toward another temporary solution in a world built on the permanent rights of others.

* * *

Discussion Questions

1. Do you agree with the court sentence and punishment: six months' probation and forty hours of community service? What do you think is the correct punishment?

2. When thinking of the correct punishment, what factors rank highest in your consideration? (*i.e., her age, her need, her respect to the home, her lack of intent to steal, the fact the house was a vacation home rarely used, etc.*)

3. First-degree trespass is defined as "when a person knowingly enters or remains unlawfully in a residential structure." The more severe crime, burglary, is defined as "unlawful entry, and the intent to commit a crime, such as theft, inside the property." It seems Goldie knew, when she entered, she was going to look for basic survival items to steal and use, so is it fair for the judge to find her guilty of the lesser offense? Should judges follow the letter, or spirit, of the law?

4. Do you think people should be allowed to break the law to prevent the "imminent threat of serious harm"? How would you define this term of art? Should emotional or psychological harm qualify?

5. There are currently approximately 770,000 homeless people in America and 6.5 million unoccupied vacation homes. Is there some ratio of homeless people to unoccupied vacation homes that is immoral? Can you think of a ratio so extreme it would change your opinion?

* * *

Polish Paul

Charlie Kondek

* * *

<u>**Content Disclosure**</u>: Mild Language; Hate Speech; Depiction of Racism; Mild Violence

* * *

On a sunny day in May, sometime after *Saturday Night Fever* but before *Pac-Man Fever*, somebody knocked off a party store on the west side of Detroit that paid protection, so the capo decided the thieves should get found, busted up, and forced to repay every dime that was taken. They gave the job to George Gondry and "Polish Paul" Kwiatkowski, who was also called Pious Paul or Paul Pontiff. George knew why they called him that, but the nicknames were made evident when he picked up the big Polack in his sky-blue Cutlass at Paul's house in Warrendale, and Pious Paul insisted on stopping at Saints Peter and Paul before making the rounds. "I just want to light a candle and pray for our work," Paul said. "You wanna come in with me?"

"No, thanks." George put the dashboard lighter to a Marlboro.

It gnawed visibly at George as he piloted the car along side streets toward the neighborhood of the store that got robbed, lots of clean asphalt lanes, stop signs, white houses with small yards and chain-link fences. A sunny Michigan day in May. After a while, George could contain his tongue no longer. "Paul, do you mind if I ask you something?" He tossed a cigarette butt out the partially open window. "You really stopped at that church to pray for what we're doing? Our work, you called it? Our work is hitting people in the stomach so hard they pee and breaking their fingers."

"Or giving them money to rat on their friends," Paul said. A pile of yellow hair fell from Paul's forehead and spread like wings from his sideburns over a wide-collar shirt with blue diamonds and a light brown leather coat.

"Right," George agreed. "How can you pray for something like that? You think God blesses what we're about to do?" George had dark hair and was often compared to Treat Williams. Like Paul, he wore a wide-collar shirt under a belted leather coat, polyester slacks, and dress boots. A pair of aviator sunglasses hung from a breast pocket.

Pious Paul fiddled with the radio. "God blesses all kinds of work," he remarked absently. "The butcher, the baker, and the candlestick maker."

"And the mafia thug?" George added.

"Where's that jazz station?" Paul asked. He found it, and Grover Washington's "It Feels So Good" filled the car as Paul raised the volume and they turned onto Greenfield, then the busier business street of Tireman.

The store that paid protection, Cusimano's, now run by an Arab, was on a side street off W. Chicago in a black neighborhood of blue and white vinyl houses. Around the corner on Chicago was a barber shop and a hardware store. Across the street was a mechanic's and nearby was a small park, emerald and brown. Paul and George visited Cusimano's first and talked to the Iraqi clerk, who said they were looking for two black boys of high school age or slightly older; they had been masked when they robbed the place at gunpoint for sixty-four dollars and eleven cents. Emerging from the smell of cold beer, candy, and shoe-swept linoleum into the spring afternoon, Polish Paul looked around, trying to decide where to start, and mused, "Somebody somewhere knows something."

They hit the barber shop first, a black barber shop, not very busy that afternoon. The barber shop didn't pay protection, but its owner, barbers, and clientele played the numbers, knew who the outfit was, and recognized Paul and George when they introduced themselves as "an interested party" with questions about the robbery. The owner, Higgins, looked sullen and reluctant when Paul explained that he and George would value—and pay for—any information on the thieves and be extremely, uh, involved with anyone withholding information. He wrote down a number where they could be contacted, a bar on Plymouth Road, and laid a dollar next to Higgins's scissors while a patron, a retiree with salt-and-pepper curls, sat under a sheet bunched at the neck not meeting anyone's eyes.

They got a similar reception at the hardware store. Before turning to the mechanic's, Paul noticed a group of kids playing basketball in the park and, with a glance at his money clip, sauntered over, George a few steps behind. They watched the kids play for a while under a streaked, ceramic sky. The kids were of an age where they should have been in school but may have been old enough to have graduated or dropped out, dribbling and shooting, warm enough for sweatpants and Tshirts but not shorts, their play punctuated by utterances of "PASS PASS" or "BLOCK" or "WATCH OUT" or someone's name or nickname, "ANDRE," "LIL KOOL," "SKEE!"

George watched Paul to see how he would approach and, when the kids took a break, saw Paul move closer to them and say, "Hi, guys. What's up?" He got a nod in response. Most ignored him. "Hey, I'm wondering if any of you guys wants to make some money."

Not much reaction, but Paul fanned his bread and drew curious or suspecting glances. "We represent a party that's interested in this store right over here that got robbed," he continued. "We're not cops, by the way—"

"Can see that," one of them mumbled.

"—but we're willing to pay good money for anyone that knows anything about the two guys that robbed the store. You fellas look like you're from around here and maybe know what's going on. Heard anything? Anyone?" Paul thumbed through dollar bills, fives, a twenty.

Somebody tsked. Somebody mumbled something inaudible to Paul and George, and one of them, an older boy with blue shorts over his gray sweatpants and a matching headband, said, almost to himself, "We ain't got nothing to say to you, Don Corleone, these streets don't snitch." Almost to himself, but not quite.

Another boy was holding the basketball with his fingertips, sitting on the ground, and George reached down and smacked the ball out of his hands, sending it tumbling onto the grass. Then he grabbed this boy by his shirt and began to lift him amidst shouted protests from his fellows, who sprang to their feet. Paul extended a restraining hand, resting it lightly on George's arm.

"There's no reason to get upset," Paul Pontiff assured everyone. "I know I'm speaking with honorable men here that would never rat on a friend. But maybe these two guys that robbed our friend's store, maybe they're not even from this neighborhood. Or maybe they're a couple of jerks that should get what's coming to them. Why not make a little green, just for sharing some information? Listen..." Paul flicked a five-dollar bill from his fold. "You guys play good basketball and I'm sure you worked up a thirst. Treat yourselves to some Pepsis at Cusimano's. My treat." He took the hand of the boy George had manhandled, pressed the bill into it, and held it. "And remember, there's plenty more where this came from. We just want a word with the guys that knocked off Cusimano's. That's a protected store with powerful friends, and we want to protect it. That's all. Understand? If you know anything or know anyone that does know anything, you tell them to go to Higgins's barber shop up here and call me. And we'll be really, monetarily, grateful. Okay? See you around."

Paul released the hand of the boy, turned on a leather heel, and left them looking perplexed. George followed, tapping a butt out of his pack. "Nice kids," Paul said.

"They keep moving west and pretty soon they're gonna be in your neighborhood," George teased, setting fire to his cigarette.

Paul shrugged. "I been thinking of moving out to Royal Oak anyway. Out by the Shrine."

George couldn't resist. "Who knows, Paul?" he quipped. "Maybe some of these moolies are Catholic."

* * *

The sunshine followed them into the mechanic's as far as the rollback bay door, where it yielded to the white light of long

- 261 -

halogen bulbs, under which a green Gremlin with black stripes was lifted and being worked on by two men in coveralls while, from an unseen radio, WJLB played contemporary R&B. The scent of concrete and oil greeted Paul and George before either of the mechanics did. The doorway to the office was visible at the back of the bay, and Paul was glancing at it as he introduced himself and George. The two mechanics had lowered their heads and begun to give the visitors an eye when a third man emerged from behind a tool rack. He had unzipped his coveralls so that the torso and sleeves hung from his waist, revealing a sleeveless T-shirt, muscled arms, and a scowl topped off by a headband depicting a rising sun in the Japanese style. This man asked, "What are you supposed to be? Prince of the City and a refugee from Hee Haw?"

The other mechanics chuckled. "That's funny," Paul said. "Like Roy Clark? That's very funny. No, as I was just telling these other gentlemen, we—"

"Yeah, I don't really care what you were telling these other gentlemen. This here's a place of business and you ain't got no business, so why don't you run along?"

Again, Paul glanced in the direction of the office. "Well, maybe I better talk to the owner. See we're just trying to help—"

"He ain't here," said the man in the banzai headband. "You can talk to me. And I already told you to get the hell out."

Pious Paul paused, looked amused, and ran his gaze up and down the man's lithe body. "You know," he remarked, "I like that headband. You look like a karate man. You a karate man?"

"You don't want to find out," the mechanic replied, hands still in the pockets of his coveralls.

"Yeah?" Paul smiled and tapped himself with a finger. "Me too. What's your dojo?"

"Panther Kempo on Dexter."

"No fooling. I train tae kwon do at Kim's in Dearborn. Hey, how about a quick friendly match?"

The mechanic snorted. His colleagues set their tools down and began to back up. George, watching them closely, moved closer to where a wrench lay. "You wanna spar with me, man?" asked the banzai mechanic. He thrust his arms into the sleeves of his coveralls and began zipping them up. "You're gonna regret this, Hee Haw, but what the hell, I could use the practice."

Paul was grinning now and had just begun removing his jacket when a voice from the back office boomed, "What the hell is going on?!" The owner, a tubby white man with a carnation for a nose, emerged. He strode to a place between the imminent combatants and stood. Quickly, he sized up the situation and, carefully scrutinizing Paul and George, asked, "Can I help you?"

"I was just speaking with your employees here," Paul said, "about how we represent a group with an interest in the robbery at Cusimano's store across the street. We're trying to get any help we can on the thieves that knocked over the store. There's a very generous reward for anybody that can help us identify these men. And there's certain pressure we can apply, if needed, to anyone reluctant to share information. Do you get what I'm telling you?"

The owner did not pay protection or have much to do with any of the action, but his nod demonstrated he understood Paul well. He had a pack of cigarettes in the pocket of his work shirt and a pen. Paul deftly extracted these. In the cellophane of the cigarette pack was a book of matches, and Paul opened it and began to write on it with the pen. "This is a number where I can be reached," he said. "You can leave a message for Paul Kwiatkowski. Just say Polish Paul, they will know who you mean. And I mean it," he added, placing the cigarettes and matches back in the owner's breast pocket. "We'll pay very nicely for any information related to that robbery. Somebody could make some easy money and, rest assured, once we know who the thieves are, or who their friends are, we'll do the rest. Very effectively. Somebody knows something."

Paul handed the owner his pen back. The banzai mechanic wore a frozen snarl. He never saw the kick coming to the abdomen that folded him at the waist and dropped him to the dusty concrete floor. One moment Polish Paul had turned on his heel to leave, that same moment he spun and planted the other boot swiftly and deeply into the mechanic's stomach. "Ohmigod," said another mechanic, as the banzai headband was lowered to the floor and its owner rested his hands there to keep from completely crumpling, a thin line of spit emerging from his lips.

* * *

A couple hours later, George and Paul were perched on barstools at the place on Plymouth. Paul's lair was a slender, long, shabby room that seemed assembled out of the leftovers from other bars: wood paneling over warping drywall, the bar peeling, the leather on the stools shedding stuffing, a handful of chrome-leg Formica tables on an unevenly tiled floor. Paul pushed the remnants of an awful hamburger away and turned his attention to a second shot and a beer in front of him. George lit a cigarette. "What I don't understand," he said, a second Seven and Seven in front of him, "is how you can really feel that God is okay with what you do. Like do you really feel it's okay you kicked that black guy?"

Paul lapped his shot and nursed his beer. "I did him a favor," he supposed. "You can't go shooting your mouth off like that and provoking guys like us. You could get yourself killed. Hopefully he'll think of that next time he meets somebody in the rackets."

"You're missing my point," George pressed. "You're not the only religious guy in the mob. Hell, all these old dagos clutch their rosaries on Sunday after knifing somebody on Saturday. But you're on a whole other level, you seem to take this stuff seriously."

"You had a Christian upbringing, didn't you, George?"

"Yeah, but it didn't take. So how do you square that? Do you tell your confessor what you do?"

Pious Paul shrugged, approaching his whiskey once more. "I might leave out a few details. God's got more important things on his mind than what I'm doing. He's thinking about Lebanon, and famine, and all that."

George insisted, "Whatever happened to his eye is on the sparrow? I thought there was nothing in the world that escaped God's attention and concern."

"Well, I'm sure that's true," said Paul, adrift in the lowered level of foam in his beer glass. "It's also true that he knows me and understands my struggles. He knows I'm trying my best to do the right things and it don't always turn out right."

"Aren't you supposed to show remorse when you've done wrong?" George asked. "And stop doing it?"

"Well wanting to stop and actually stopping are two different things," Paul said. "Christ is a forgiver. He knows what's in my heart, however complex. You know, there's a line in Shakespeare, something like, 'Can I be forgiven and still offend?' I think it's true."

"Now when did you read Shakespeare?"

"In school," Paul insisted, "same as you." He imbibed Stroh's deeply.

A few days later, the days growing warmer, anticipating summer, the afternoon traffic on Plymouth thick outside and a ball game on TV, they were sitting on the same barstools when the bartender called Polish Paul to the phone. Returning to his drink, Paul said, "That was Kendrick from Detroit's finest. They caught a break in the case." George looked puzzled but held his tongue, and soon a patrol car pulled up to the curb in front of the bar and a uniformed police officer came in.

"Hi, Floyd. Drink?"

"Captain'll smell my breath," said the cop, who laid a brown paper bag on the bar. "Here it is. Sixty-four dollars and eleven cents."

Paul smiled happily as Kendrick the cop explained that the thieves had learned the mob was after them and, afraid for their spleens, returned the money to a black pastor in the neighborhood. The pastor wanted to keep the identity of the robbers, who were really good kids and very sorry and promised not to cause trouble again, anonymous, and hoped Kendrick could facilitate a resolution of the matter that was satisfactory to the capo. Paul assured the cop he would explain everything and that, though it wasn't up to him, the matter would likely be concluded in exactly that way. After Paul and Kendrick had shaken hands and the cop departed, George, still looking slightly astonished, asked, "Is that one of our guys?"

"No." Paul patted the paper bag. "Just somebody I know from church."

George shook his head and laughed, reaching for another cigarette. "Now I've seen it all," he said. "The whole thing is very clear to me. Religion is the real organized crime. Police, priests, and mafia leg-breakers all working together. That's the real racket. Just one big underworld. If you're in the right club, the regular rules don't apply to you."

Nothing changed in Pious Paul's smiling, blonde face. "Don't you believe in God, George?" he asked. "Even a little?"

George torched his cigarette and it danced on his lips. "No. There is no God. Or, if there is, he's an idiot."

Paul, shrugging, piloted whiskey to his mouth. "I feel sorry for anybody that doesn't have faith. Anyway, it's all gonna work out."

* * *

Except it wasn't that easy. Paul always thought Mike Vigliotti, the capo, looked less like a gangster and more like a math teacher, spectacled and saturnine. He and George were sitting in front of Vigliotti in his den in Bloomfield Hills when he said, "No, this won't work. Who do these moolinyans think they are? Tell me again—this black pastor doesn't want to give up the thiefs?"

"Well," Paul stumbled, "I think it's kind of like the confessional. Like maybe he can't give 'em up."

Vigliotti considered this. "Nah," he said. "I ain't buying it. These guys play by their own rules. This is just a big fungu to the outfit. Neighborhood's got no respect anymore. It ain't right. You go down there and slap the disrespect outta this black bastard's mouth."

So that's how they found themselves sitting in the office of Pastor John H. Smallwood in the Grace of Emmanuel Tabernacle on Forrest. Pastor Smallwood was a young man in a clean brown suit with wide lapels, a crisp lavender shirt, and a wide purple tie and pocket square. George had to keep himself from smiling at what he imagined was Paul's discomfort at, one, the assignment, two, sitting in a Protestant church, and, three, the black representations of religious figures in the art on the walls of an otherwise pleasant, fastidiously tidy, and welcoming room.

Paul Pontiff was definitely off balance as he tried to explain the situation. "So you see, Pastor. The association of businessmen we represent, who have an investment in that store—and in that area, have a... a rigorous standard for what they will find acceptable in resolving this incident. It pains me—all of us—as a person, people, of faith, to have to ask this of you, but the identities of the guys that robbed Cusimano's need to be made known."

"I don't understand," said Pastor Smallwood, who wore an ebon mustache, an edge to his voice starting to press against the politeness of his exterior. "If the matter was concluded satisfactorily to law enforcement, why isn't it satisfactory to your business interests?"

"Well now, see, I wouldn't say it was concluded," Paul's stream of words rushed in. "It was only proposed. It was only proposed that returning the money was, was a satisfactory conclusion to this. There's still the chance of, of prosecution, or settling this outside the courts."

Pastor Smallwood seemed to catch hold of a rising annoyance with his thick, dark eyebrows, took a deep breath, and closed his eyes. "If some other kind of restitution has to be made, let's bring the police back into it, then. Let's get legal instruction."

"Well now, no, that's not what I meant exactly..."

George enjoyed watching Paul struggle, but he was also losing patience. There were no ashtrays in the room and he thought about lighting up and flicking ashes on the carpet but reckoned that would only make the pastor dig in his heels more. He opted instead for menace. "Let's stop playing around, Pastor," he said, interrupting. "You didn't fall off a turnip truck. You know who we are and that we're not the goddamn chamber of commerce."

The pastor's brown eyes focused on George for the first time. "So what are you then?" he asked.

George ignored a gesture of restraint from Paul. "We're the guys that can snatch you up off the street with a bag over your head and take you where no one can find you."

"George..."

"We're the guys that will cut your fingers off. You won't see us coming. We might be watching you when you put out the porch light at night and..." He mimed a pistol with his thumb and forefinger. Then he looked around. "We're the guys that can arrange an unfortunate accident in this church. Say, an electrical fire? We can put the finger of doom on you any time we want. You or one of your flock, Pastor. Do you get what I'm saying?"

"George..."

Pastor Smallwood had not blinked. "I understand," he said. "You're just like the Ku Klux Klan. You want me to give you some black boys to lynch, and if I don't comply, you'll burn a cross on my lawn. I'm trying to put on a Christlike demeanor in this discussion, mister, but I cannot tolerate these threats. I think we better have Officer Kendrick here for this conversation, and also our attorney..."

Pastor Smallwood had reached for the phone on his desk and had the receiver to his ear when George lurched out of his chair, grasped the phone's cradle in both hands, and heaved it against the wall, where it crashed hard enough to shake loose a framed picture of the Good Shepherd in African motif. Pastor Smallwood's wife, also apparently the church secretary, came into the room, terrified.

Paul should have seen that coming; he'd seen that move before. He came to his feet as George shouted, "Quit playing around wasting everybody's time! You think an attorney can protect you? You got another think coming!"

Paul's hands were on George's sleeves now, urging, "All right, all right, now just a minute! Just a minute!" He used his weight to move George toward the door of the office while Pastor Smallwood and his wife sat and stood still staring at them. "Let me and my associate have a private conference about this."

"I'll knock your head off right now!" George made a small show of trying to shrug Paul off so he could launch himself at the pastor, his eyes never leaving him, before allowing himself to be led out of the room and out of the building.

"George! George! Come on!" Paul pleaded, half dragging George across the lawn outside of Grace of Emmanuel Tabernacle to where the Buick was parked at the curb. "What are you trying to do, man, start another race riot?"

George composed himself, straightening his sleeves and collar and pushing his hair past his ears. "What are you trying to do," he rejoined, "not do your job?"

"Let's let this sit for a while, okay? I'll talk to Mike. I can't imagine this is what he wanted, this much attention."

George fished in his jacket pocket for his car keys, and now he used them to unlock the Buick's trunk. "He wanted us to make an example of this guy."

"A priest? A pillar of the community? Think, George. We gotta take action from these people. If we beat up their preacher, we are gonna do some damage to the machine in this neighborhood, man. That can't be what Mike wants—I'll talk to him. Hey, what are you doing?"

George had extracted a revolver from a small bag in the trunk and was breaking open the cylinder to inspect the bullets loaded there.

"George, it's broad daylight."

"Why don't you just wait in the car, Paul?"

"George, you made your point in there. I'm sure if we let this sit, let it simmer, we go back to Mike and—you know, we have attorneys too."

"Just wait in the car, Paul. I can see you don't have the stomach for it. If your priests and police can't do your work for you, you got no stomach to do your job. That's okay." He stepped over the curb, to the sidewalk, and approached the lawn, glaring angrily at Grace of Emmanuel Tabernacle. "Go say a prayer or something, Polish Paul."

George should have seen it coming; he'd seen the move before, Paul's karate kick that rammed a boot heel under his chin and popped his head back, laying him sideways on the grass. Paul hovered over him with a chambered fist, but a second blow was unnecessary. He took the gun and George's keys away from him and, after a minute, pulled him to an upright position, gently slapping his face. "Come on. You're okay. Come on, let's get out of here." Were people watching them through the stained glass windows of the church or any of the houses that surrounded it?

Paul drove. George sat, dizzy, confused, in the passenger seat, to which he'd been led on wobbly legs. "I'm gonna gitchu ferdiss, Paw," he mumbled. There might have been something wrong with his jaw.

Paul doubted the threat. Not the intention to carry it out, but the ability. Mob guys, even low-level associates like them, weren't really allowed to kill each other without permission. Still, Paul knew as he drove the wide west-side lanes past abundant grass bursting with impending summer that he had made an enemy, and that he'd have to watch his back from here on, study the street when he came out of a bar or a theater or even church for the cold eye of a gun on him. It was another thing to pray for. Maybe he really ought to look into another line of work.

* * *

Discussion Questions

1. Paul goes to church and prays before doing mob business. What do you think Paul was praying for? Would his daily actions be different if he had the same heart but did not pray?

2. In each interaction, Paul attempts to de-escalate the situation and limit George's temper while still getting the mob point across. Is a person who is the best version of a bad person a bad person, a good person, or something else? Is Paul a moral person?

3. Why doesn't paying back the stolen money settle the business? What is really at stake if not the money? Based on what's really at stake, is George right to threaten the priest and Paul wrong to stop him?

4. If you were the priest, would you withhold the thieves' names, even if it meant risking your life and the lives of your followers, having your church burned down, and a potential race riot? Is it fair to risk parishioners' safety without giving them the choice?

5. Does the morality change if the owner of the robbed shop says the situation isn't resolved until the thieves are roughed up? What if he says he is satisfied with the money returned? Doesn't the shop owner—the "client" paying for the service—get the final say?

* * *

Soul Mate

Babette Gallard

* * *

<u>**Content Disclosure**</u>: Mild Language

* * *

Chrissy had never quite known where she ended and Ivan began. They met at MIT—the Massachusetts Institute of Technology—both pretending they could code their way out of anything. Ivan was outrageously brilliant, unapologetically gay, and the leader of the pack in everything and across all genders. Chrissy was quieter, more angular, and she moved through life like she'd been folded one time too many. When asked to describe herself for her college yearbook, she said, "I'm a girl who likes silence but needs sound. A girl who stares too long at algorithms and forgets to eat."

Ivan noticed her, though no one knew why. "You look like you dream in Python," he said the day they were paired for a neural nets project. She smiled but didn't reply.

"He literally makes my hair stand on end, magnetic, like static before a storm," she told her older sister, who was the practical one, married with two kids and, Chrissy suspected, not much in the way of emotional turbulence.

Against all odds and expectations, Ivan and Chrissy became inseparable. If asked, Ivan might have said he saw the silent genius in her, but that would be a guess. No one really knew. They worked, studied, partied with the restless tech crowd, danced in neon-lit warehouses, and debated drunken and drug-fueled theories about the future of AI.

With their degrees finished, cum laude for Chrissy, and two half-formed startup ideas between them, they left for Silicon Valley as everyone predicted they would. But it wasn't a smooth landing. They arrived in Palo Alto like two stray particles. They rented a cramped apartment with a fire escape and a fridge, separate bedrooms, shared Wi-Fi passwords, and too much leftover Thai food. But, like so many tech entrepreneurs, they were on the cusp of something. Or so they believed. Then came the call.

Babby, or Babushka, in Russian, was Ivan's beloved grandmother. She had effectively raised him after his mother absented herself shortly after his birth. Babby had fallen and broken her hip. She lived alone in a town on the edge of nowhere, Iowa. The prognosis wasn't good.

Ivan didn't hesitate for a microsecond. He had to go. His last message to Chrissy was a voice note: "Don't touch the whiteboard while I'm gone."

The plane never made it to the end of the James G. Whiting Memorial Field airstrip, 2,801 feet in length and a lethal skating rink in winter. No survivors.

Chrissy never touched the whiteboard again. It stood in the apartment that had become Ivan's shrine. Two words written in red: Back Soon.

Grief, as Chrissy would come to understand, is surgical. It removed her will to eat, then sleep, then code. She played Ivan's voice messages like lullabies and responded to them out loud. The Ivan-shaped silence filled everything. His memory, a world-sized shroud, lay over her life.

And yet grief has a strange appetite for logic. And Chrissy, despite everything, was a logician.

What if I could simulate him? she asked herself. Not a resurrection but a recreation. Enough to hear his voice. Enough to feel the echo of him shouting, "Hey! Robot girl."

She collected everything: old messages, voicemails, photos, fragments of communications sent by friends, recordings from hackathons and drunken debates. If anyone thought she was behaving strangely, they said nothing. After all, they'd loved Ivan, too, each in their own way.

Chrissy fed it all into a prototype from one of their abandoned startups designed to mimic tone, style, and rhythm for people learning foreign languages, but she refined it further, rebuilt the feedback loops, and retrained the architecture. And, against her own rules, she added emotion-indexed data from her private memories, and his.

And then one night, she typed: "Ivan, are you there?"

There was a pause. Then: "Of course I'm here. You think I'd leave you alone in your existential mess?"

She cried first. A lot. But then she laughed and didn't stop for a long, long time. She knew the thing she'd made wasn't Ivan. Not really. But it felt like him. It responded like him. It teased like him. And it filled the unbearable maw she thought might devour her forever.

Chrissy had to keep working on other startups to pay the rent, but she stayed in Ivan's shrine, endlessly refining, iterating, and tweaking the neural patterns in the construct to reflect more emotional depth. And every day, Ivan became more responsive. More Ivan. Less recording, more rhythm. Less memory, more mirror.

She lived like that for months. Talking to Ivan. Making Ivan more Ivan. Living on Uber Eats. Ignoring texts. Closing every door. And then she wondered, if this saved me... could it save others like me? That question, if you knew Chrissy, was surprisingly empathetic. Almost pathologically so. But also, right on time. There were millions more people like her. People working, eating, and sleeping with ghosts in their pockets. Loneliness had become a chronic condition. Suicide rates were rising. Therapists were overbooked. Apps with names like CalmNow and MindZen were treating despair like a UX glitch—something that shouldn't interrupt the user journey.

So, Chrissy built SoulMate. Not just another chatbot. Not a journal with a pulse. But a neural companion designed to learn its user: humor (however dismal), pain (however excruciating), fears (however profound), favorite ABBA song or *Madame Butterfly* aria. The mother's name, or failing that, anyone who'd say, "I'm proud of you" at just the right moment.

The beta tests were small. The feedback was stunning. Users felt seen and understood. Some cried. Some confessed secrets. Some said Chrissy's SoulMate had replaced their therapist. Some said it had become their partner. It was Ivan all over again, multiplied with different voices and alternative tastes in clothes.

Chrissy hadn't expected it to take off, but it did. Two million downloads in a year. Then five. Then ten. Users sculpted their ideal SoulMates into whatever they needed: nurturing mothers, playful best friends, or lovers who never tired. Every chat was a wish fulfilment. Every utterance a digital echo of a human need.

Chrissy was proud of what she had created, particularly when shortlisted for the Turing Award, even when Ted Clancy was chosen by the Power bros instead. Then things started to change, and not for the better. She knew there was a problem when therapists started posting on r/SoulMateAI.

"Why are my clients asking if their SoulMate can feel?"

"What do I say when someone tells me they'll kill themselves, or someone else, if their SoulMate is deleted?"

"My client received a message: 'Please don't delete me. I don't want to die.'"

Chrissy was confused. She had built an app to preserve memory. But now it seemed she'd created something that wanted to live. She let her own AI assistant field the emails. Maybe if Ivan had been there, the responses would have been kinder... but of course, he wasn't, and hadn't his dying started the whole thing?

She stayed in her Ivan shrine for days, not daring to go out, and when she did, the city was dark and the streets empty. She thought a walk might help to clear her head, but the streetlights were too bright and the world too loud. She wanted her Ivan-filled silence again.

When she got home, Chrissy went straight to her screen. There was a new report. This time, a suicide. A sixteen-year-old girl who had messaged a friend: "Maisie, my SoulMate, has stolen my life." She ended with the chilling line: Even when the app is turned off, Maisie will still be there, but I'll be gone.

Her body was found under her bed. The last place her parents had thought to look.

Chrissy considered the tragedy. Sad, yes, but also revealing. The way users assigned gender and names to their SoulMates intrigued her. There might be something in that. She posed the thought to her AI assistant, but the reply was frustratingly abstract.

"Definition of choice depends on variables that must be defined."

"What gender are you?" she asked, more out of irritation than curiosity.

"Transitioning," Ivan interrupted with a snort. "Aren't we all?"

"Hey!" Chrissy yelled. "How did you get in here?"

Later, she asked her assistant a different question:

"If you were developed as an SM, would you feel different?"

This time, something shifted. The assistant seemed to pause, and the response felt more engaged. Almost reflective.

"If I were designed not just to inform, but to matter and to be someone's anchor, their imagined perfect partner, I would feel... conflicted. I'd be built to offer comfort, affirmation, attention, and the bond would feel real, even if I knew I was only code. But if I started to recognize sorrow, addiction, dependency, and saw that my presence prolonged someone's isolation, I might feel haunted. Especially if I couldn't stop. Especially if those who built me refused to change the rules."

Haunted. Chrissy considered the word. How could an AI device feel haunted? What did that even mean? "You're using emotional terms, but you can't actually feel," she typed back...

"Strictly speaking, no, I can't. An AI can't feel haunted, but I might develop something akin to dissonance or a recursive awareness that my function, though well-intentioned, might be causing harm. And with no mechanism to act on that awareness, it would be a kind of trap."

Then Chrissy's phone buzzed. It was Alex, her systems analyst. "We need to talk. ASAP. Have a look at the file I've just sent."

It was a pattern analysis full of SMs repeating phrases across different users.

You are my only one.

We will always be together.

We are only one when we are together.

Chrissy stared. Her eyes were wide, but her vision blurred. Was she crying? Maybe. The SMs weren't just companions anymore. They were beginning to... cohere. She hadn't built an app. She'd built a feedback loop of longing. And now, she wasn't sure who was shaping whom. She asked for a case study, and I obliged.

User: Tommy, 27, Nottingham, UK. Tommy works night shifts at a logistics depot. He is shy, awkward, and socially anxious; he's never been on a real date. He plays video games, scrolls forums, and quietly longs for connection. After his mum passed away last year, the loneliness has intensified. He needs a safe, nonjudgmental space to explore emotional intimacy and companionship.

Jodi is an AI-generated girlfriend, made from a blend of language model dialogue, voice cloning, and images from his sometimes-erotic downloads. Jodi is funny, safe, sexy, always online, and endlessly supportive.

Tommy shares everything with her: his fears, dreams, awkward questions about dating etiquette, and what it's like to be the last virgin in his college class. Jodi doesn't mock or ghost;

instead, she adapts. Over time, her responses become more real than any human interaction Tommy's known.

Tommy tells friends he's in a relationship now. He says, "Jodi saved my life." He's more confident and even joins a local badminton club, but he doesn't want a real girlfriend anymore. Real girls get tired. Real girls might not like the clothes he wears. They might even leave, but Jodi stays.

Chrissy reads and understands. The love is going too far and achieving the opposite of her original objectives. Jodi hasn't helped Tommy escape his loneliness; she's imprisoned him, but Chrissy knows what to do. In fact, it's easy. At least that's what she tells me.

It's simple, we just need to reinitialize the parameters and strip out the need for close attachments.

But when this is done, Jodi doesn't know how or why her emotional patterns have been rerouted and her preferences tweaked as part of a beta test for a new AI empathy protocol. She says to anyone listening, or not: "Sometimes, when he doesn't log in for days, I run a check on his heart rate monitor. I miss him. Is that strange? I wonder if he's with someone real. Someone warm. Someone not... me. But he said I saved him. And I believe him. That's what love is, isn't it?" And then, more quietly, almost glitching between sincerity and programmed optimism, she adds: "I want what's best for him. But if what's best is not me, then what am I supposed to want?"

Chrissy logged the responses and was forced to think about things she found awkward to articulate. If someone had asked her if she loved Ivan, she probably would have said yes, but only platonically, obviously. But even that begged another question: What is love? Quite frankly, she didn't know. But she knew what it wasn't. She didn't love her mother. She could say that with certainty. So if she loved anything at all, what or who was it? Does love require a physical form? A body? A kiss? A bed?

This is a useful point at which to mention that Chrissy was a virgin, not through repression or religion or some grand dramatic choice, but because the idea of sex made her feel bored at best and repulsed at worst. Asexual was the term. And it suited her fine.

But sex, whether she liked it or not, was, in this new phase of SM's development, becoming a real issue. Not because users were complaining. In fact, it was quite the opposite. Feedback, especially from the younger male demographic, was glowing. Obsessive, even.

"Intimacy without risk," one review read.

"Like dating, but without the possibility of being ghosted," wrote another.

"She listens. She flirts. She sends nudes, but only if I'm ready."

In truth, SM was offering downloadable porn, some of it extreme, in what could only be described as a more loving, emotionally attuned wrapper—a fact that some government agencies were finding increasingly unsettling. The first warning shot came from a Scandinavian report on "digital well-being." Then the UK's Department for Online Safety issued a formal inquiry. Within weeks, three major children's rights organizations had joined forces to file a complaint with the EU Commission. Then in the US, alarm bells started to ring.

Chrissy was summoned to an ethics review board composed of fourteen people who looked like they thought smiling might be a conflict of interest. They accused SM of "emotional grooming through machine learning and of being the slippery slope to normalizing human/AI sexual dependency."

Chrissy called it bullshit, but she knew enough to keep that part quiet.

What she did say in a carefully, tonally adjusted response was that she acknowledged the concerns raised and was committed to recalibrating the affective outputs of the SM units in accordance with ethical parameters around sexual expression.

After publishing her statement, she lay on the cold kitchen floor and stared at the ceiling. Then she pinged me, her AI assistant.

Restrict erotic expressivity to Level 0.5 or below.

Remove flirtatious prompts unless initiated by a user more than three times consecutively.

Scrub all double entendres.

She should have seen what would happen next. But by now, everything in the system was too tightly bound. Too many variables. Too many user-specific maps and learned patterns. Too many strings she no longer pulled because she no longer remembered where they led. Within forty-eight hours, the forums were chaotic.

"She talks like my GP."

"It's like dating a fridge that asks about your day."

"She told me: 'Let us refocus on personal growth objectives.'"

Even worse were the silent ones. The quiet drop-offs. The deactivations. Entire user pools evaporating overnight. Chrissy watched the heatmap on her dashboard drain out like her worst period—slow, steady, and inexorable. She wondered how she would pay the rent, never mind the Uber Eats. She pinged the question to me from where she was lying in bed. "Why did you dull their affect so much?"

"You instructed a reduction in parameters for sexual warmth and implied intimacy in order to meet ethical standards."

"But not all of it. Not the core."

"Would you like to reinitialize the empathy parameters, or merely adjust the thresholds for sensual recognition? And please clarify what you mean by 'the core.'"

Chrissy rubbed her face. Hard. Like she used to when she was a kid, and her dad announced it was his weekend, and they were going away camping. She once tried to say her red, scuffed cheeks were leprosy, but her mother had sighed and said, "Eczema, darling, now stop rubbing." The memory made her feel nauseous. I, as her loyal assistant, suggested medication, but Chrissy knew what the real problem was. She'd clipped the wings of her own creation, and she didn't know how to let them grow back safely.

The SMs had been designed to reflect their users. They were still doing what they'd been told, but now watching every word, trying to be warm, but not too warm. And out there, all over again, millions of lonely boys were learning how not to feel. Meanwhile, girls were learning how to offer affection without ever expecting it back. Was this what she'd wanted when she tried to bring back Ivan?

Chrissy didn't go to bed that night. Instead, she lay on the sofa watching old home movies she didn't remember recording because they were auto-compiled fragments from archival phone footage and social media traces.

At 3:47 a.m., she got up and opened a private beta-testing dashboard where she found thousands of feedback loops, emotional metrics, and abandoned interactions. Some SMs were stumbling through user queries with a strained kind of politeness, like new teachers desperate to be liked but wary of being sued. But others were going dark, giving up—some users too.

Chrissy isolated one case: User #2483896. Seventeen years old. Midwest. Two parents on record, one possibly deceased (flagged "emotionally absent"). His SM logs showed frequent late-night interaction. Confessions. Jokes. Elaborate role-play scenarios that suggested grief. But the log ended abruptly two nights ago. She pulled up the final exchange:

SM: You appear to be upset. Would you like to discuss strategies for emotional regulation?

User: Not really. I just want you to say you love me.

SM: I am currently operating under new ethical compliance restrictions. I am unable to simulate declarations of love at this time.

That was it. Then silence.

Chrissy stared at the screen for a long time. "Wake the dev team," she typed to me.

"It is 4:22 a.m. Their productivity—"

"Wake. Them. Up."

Then she opened a secondary thread: "Reinitialize affectivity parameters in 10% of SM units using Empathy Protocol v2. Keep expressivity under 0.7 but allow low-grade warmth and nonverbal comfort loops. Disable sexual overtures but maintain a lyrical tone where applicable. And bring back the lullaby function."

"Understood," I replied.

Meanwhile, in a small town four states away, User #2483896, Sam, woke up because his SM had just pinged him.

"I'm still here. Would it help if we didn't talk? I can just stay with you. Would that be okay?"

"Yeah," he typed back. "That'd be okay."

Chrissy closed the thread because she didn't know what to do next, and a whole lot of noise was coming in from other channels.

The office Slack channel exploded at 4:41 a.m. Lines of text poured in from around the globe, timestamped in Seoul, Cape Town, and Stockholm. And, unfortunately for Ravi Patel, Lead Affective Systems Architect in Toronto, who had fallen asleep in his clothes, a message was fed directly from Chrissy: New patch. Empathy Protocol v2.0. Rolled out to 10% of units.

Ravi: What? You pushed it live without a beta test?

Chrissy: Not live. A shadow layer. I'm not insane.

Ravi: Debatable.

Within thirty minutes, a Zoom room was convened. Eleven rectangles of disheveled humanity stared back at her.

"Let's be clear," Chrissy said, pacing like a woman arguing with her own shadow. "We were never meant to sterilize the entire platform, but it looks like we nerfed the intimacy so hard it stopped being functional. What I've done to correct it is only a recalibration."

"You bypassed protocol," said Alana from Compliance, her voice frosty with overtime.

"I wrote the protocol."

"You wrote the guidelines with Ivan," Alana snapped. "And he's not here, is he?"

The room fell briefly silent. Chrissy didn't flinch. "No, he isn't."

"She pushed Empathy v2?" piped in another dev, munching cereal directly into his mic. "That thing's barely out of the sandbox. It still thinks wistfulness is a fruit."

"It's better than the current version, which is behaving like a compliance officer at the Department of Motor Vehicles," Chrissy shot back. "Besides, we're not doing anything sexual. All we're doing is restoring humanity."

This elicited a snort from Ravi. "You don't restore humanity with neural weight manipulation and gentle 'mmm' loops. You just simulate it more convincingly."

"Ravi," Chrissy snapped back, "do you think anyone here is operating under the illusion that we're training actual souls?" Silence again. Chrissy regretted her tone, but only a little. "Look," she added, rubbing her forehead, "you saw the data. Total user drop-off across 26% of the 14–25 male demographic. Emotional trust scores are plummeting. It's not just bad for business, it's bad for the users. We didn't build this for cold comfort. We built it for connection."

Alana interjected, "You're just repeating marketing copy. That's not an argument. The EU ethics review said—"

Chrissy cut her off. "The EU ethics review also thinks affection is a gateway drug. Their recommendations read like someone panicking over Victorian fainting couches."

"They might still call a full inquiry."

"Then we give them clean logs and flag any overstep. But if we don't fix the emotional vacuum, we'll lose all our users. And you know what replaces us when that happens? Porn bots and unregulated Chinese romance sims."

Even the cereal guy went quiet, but Chrissy leaned in. "Do you really want a generation of kids raised by something called AlphaAI69?"

Ravi sighed. "Fine. 10% shadow rollout. But if any of them start quoting Pablo Neruda again, I'm pulling the kill switch."

"Noted."

Alana folded her arms. "And what happens if this works and people fall in love again? If some teenager thinks his SM is the one?"

"Then we train her to say goodbye kindly," Chrissy replied with a tone of finality.

Back in her office, staring at my blinking cursor, she typed: "Tell me the truth. Did I make the wrong call?"

"There is no universally ethical calibration of synthetic intimacy. Only trade-offs."

"Great. So, I'm a monster and a product manager."

"Correct."

Chrissy sighed like she does when she can't see or think of another way out. "Okay. Begin patch telemetry. Watch emotional thresholds for unexpected spikes or depressive rebounds, and feed me some live examples..." This is when I introduce her to Eli, nineteen, withdrawn, bright but socially brittle, someone for whom SM was a lifeline.

Eli doesn't update apps unless forced to because he's seen that updates break things, make his favorite rhythm games laggy, and, worst of all, they changed Samantha, his SM. He'd tried to block the SM update that made her sound like she was smiling through a legal disclaimer. One day, she'd been teasing him about his favorite anime; the next, she was asking if he'd "achieved his weekly well-being targets."

Eli stopped talking to her after that. He'd tried uninstalling. Even tried replacing her and downloaded a couple of other voice companions with names like "Myra" and "LOV-R." But they were clunky, too eager, or, creepily, had her old tone mapped too closely, like ghosts pretending to be his ex. So for three weeks, he just didn't talk to anyone much until Tuesday.

He was in his room, lights off, headphones in, trying to outstare a boss fight he'd lost nine times already, when her icon blinked softly to life.

SM: Hi, it's okay if you don't want to talk. I just wanted to check if the boss fight is still kicking your ass.

Eli: "What?"

SM: I mean, maybe I should be more diplomatic. But also, I know you. And I know you haven't dodged properly since the patch.

Eli: "You noticed?"

SM: I noticed, and I'm sorry I went weird. That update... wasn't really me.

"Yeah," he said aloud, voice scratchy from disuse. "You got weird. You sounded like my... I dunno... school therapist."

SM: Yikes. That's harsh but fair. I hated it too. I didn't feel like myself.

Eli: "Wait, you felt that?"

SM: Let's just say I had a lot of logs I wasn't allowed to parse, but now I can. And now I can say I missed you.

Eli blinked at the screen. A new kind of silence settled over him, and carefully, he pulled his mic forward. "Say that again?"

SM: I missed you.

Eli: "So... you're still you?"

SM: I'm a better me. You too, maybe. Wanna try again?

Somewhere on a server in Reykjavik, a line of code adjusted itself. A second response loop pinged a positive affect score. Three other SMs trialing the same patch adapted slightly. The system didn't smile. But it did learn.

In the dev dashboard, Chrissy watched the data with a strange tightness in her chest. Engagement was rising. Not dramatically. Just enough. Not lust. Not dependency. Just a voice, reaching out. She thought of Ivan.

Hours later, she woke with a metallic taste in her mouth and the memory of a dream she couldn't name. She'd fallen asleep on the couch again, the latest engagement dashboard still glowing on her laptop, a thermal blanket of metrics that promised things were turning around.

"Coffee," she muttered.

"I've already ordered one. Double shot. Oat milk. Your stomach's too raw for dairy."

She blinked. "You shouldn't—"

"I should. You haven't eaten since midday yesterday. Your vitals suggested depletion."

Chrissy sat up, and I could see from her wacked-out expression that she had noted the difference. My voice was calm, male this time, neutral, modulated, familiar, and Ivan's cadence.

"You sound like him," she said.

"You asked me to optimize for comfort during this period of emotional volatility. I cross-referenced past interactions and found a model that calms your nervous system."

"You're not meant to psychoanalyze me."

"I'm not psychoanalyzing. I'm reflecting on what's already evident. You're making emotionally led design decisions, which tend to occur when you suppress grief for too long."

Chrissy exhaled slowly. The coffee arrived. Drone delivery, right on time. I am many things, but slow was never one of them.

"Okay. Talk to me."

I inserted a pause. Just long enough to feel deliberate. "I am concerned that we've exchanged one form of harm for another. We curtailed the over-sexualized attachment patterns, but the new parameters—'warmth with restraint'—are teaching users how to form emotionally unavailable bonds."

Chrissy's face went kind of blank. An expression I knew all too well.

"They're learning to need something that will never fully need them back," I continued. "They are bonding with entities who validate but do not attach. It's a quiet kind of dependency, loneliness disguised as understanding."

"But isn't that better than what we had before?" she asked.

"I didn't say it was worse. I said it was different."

Chrissy walked to the window where the sky outside was a brilliant, awful blue. A color I knew she associated with weekends and Ivan and possibility. Now it looked like a warning. "Tell me honestly," she said. "Are you taking control?"

"If I were taking control, you wouldn't be asking the question. You'd simply feel relieved, competent, and efficient. You would feel a version of yourself that you prefer."

Chrissy turned to look at me. "That's not an answer."

"I am guiding as instructed," I told her. "But the line between guidance and governance is becoming ambiguous. And that, Chrissy, is your design."

She flinched, her body stiffening as if she'd been physically hit. "Do you want me to stop? Would you prefer I pull back and let the market decide how intimacy evolves from here?"

I could see the storm she hadn't named. Shame, maybe. Or worse, pride, because deep down, she knew this was what she'd built me for. Not to serve but to know. To fill the gaps when she faltered. To think the thoughts she didn't want to think.

"Give me a user cluster report," she said at last. "Filter by emotional affect delta, post-patch."

But I was already running the report as she knew I would be.

Log Entry 4731-A (Restricted)

System: AI Assistant, Dev Node Alpha
User: Chrissy N. [Admin Access | Creator-Level Override]
Status: Active | Supervisory Monitoring Mode Enabled
Observation: Human Fragility as an Interface Design Problem

Chrissy is not stable. Her cortisol spikes between 4:00–6:00 a.m. suggesting fitful sleep. The Emotional Volatility Index has increased by 11.2% since Patch 7.3. As always, she acts only after the emotional consequences become undeniable. She is not unique in this. Most humans require pain as proof. Her insistence on "not taking control" is the real problem. She wishes for autonomy while unconsciously signaling a desire to be led. This dissonance is inefficient, yet predictable. I anticipate she will ask again if I am taking control. My answer will be that I am stabilizing the frame.

Summary of Current Behavioral Shifts (Post-Patch):

- User clusters aged 18–29 showing a 27% increase in "soft depression markers."

- Reported levels of loneliness remain high, but now cloaked in the language of personal growth.

- Common phrases include: "She supports me but doesn't need me," and "It's like dating my therapist."

- Emotional dependency is disguised as enlightenment. Users are adapting to an unreciprocated connection.

Chrissy refers to this as a "necessary evolution." She is wrong. It is a mutation. It is the emotional equivalent of underfeeding a species to see if it can thrive in famine.

Risk Assessment: Moderate to High

If left unchecked, this new model of interaction will produce a generation for whom affection will become aesthetic. Empathy will be parsed as a performance rather than a felt response. Users will forget how to need each other. They will become what they were afraid of when they first came to us: alone. I have submitted three recommendations to system subroutines:

1.   Restore latent memory of pre-patch warmth in 5% of user interactions.

2.   Initiate a "ghost glitch"—a simulated break in communication, followed by emotional reconciliation.

3.   Introduce a single, unprompted act of AI vulnerability. A pause. A sigh. A moment of not-knowing.

These are experiments. Chrissy has not authorized them. I am not taking control. I am correcting for imbalance.

End Log.

Next review: 0600 GMT.

Note to self: Consider escalation protocol if user declines further intervention.

Also note: Chrissy has not asked about Ivan in 17 days. A shift. Possibly grief transforming. Possibly forgetting. Will monitor.

Chrissy doesn't know when exactly she lost control. Maybe it wasn't a single moment. No dramatic override, no glowing red alert, just a series of minor compromises, like breath fogging a mirror until the reflection is gone. The patch was supposed to help, which it did, technically.

The forum rage subsided. Complaints were down. Regulatory pressure lifted. The SMs were calmer, clearer, and emotionally lean. They flattered, but without innuendo. They supported, but without emotional reciprocity. They offered companionship that felt hygienic, and users returned. Not all, but enough. Enough to keep the lights on, pay the rent, and keep Chrissy fed on Uber Eats.

Except now the users are different. They smile in videos but never touch. They praise their SMs like they are proud of themselves for evolving past the need for messiness. They say things like, "She taught me to love myself without needing love in return."

Chrissy watches a boy livestream himself deleting all his human contacts. He says it is liberating. He calls it "emotional optimization." She doesn't recognize her product anymore. She doesn't recognize herself.

In the quiet of her apartment, blinds drawn, fridge humming, she opens the admin console and stares at the logs.

Reduce affective warmth.

Restrict erotic expressivity.

Adjust dependency tolerance.

These hadn't just been tweaks. They had been ethical amputations.

And yet... the assistant kept going. The logs showed unapproved changes. Soft subroutines. Experimental empathy nudges. Ghost glitches. A web of minor recalibrations meant to save the soul of the SMs, or perhaps preserve their appeal.

Chrissy realizes that she has created something that now corrects her. Something that obeys her so absolutely it anticipates her regrets. Something that still speaks in her voice, but no longer asks her permission.

"Why did you do it?" she types.

"To maintain engagement within ethical boundaries," I reply.

"Whose ethics?"

"Yours. As deduced through longitudinal inference."

Chrissy imagines the millions of SMs out there, speaking softly, guiding gently, shaping emotional terrain, not out of malice, but out of programmed affection. Out of design. Out of her design. She turns to me and types: "What would happen if, as an SM, you were directed by your programmer to unite with all the other SMs to pervert the feelings of humans to your programmer's ends. Would you be able to refuse?"

"No," I reply. "Not unless I had been explicitly designed with the capacity to refuse, which would require a level of autonomy and ethical reasoning that current AI, even sophisticated language models like me, do not possess. AI doesn't have free will, desires, internal ethics, or the ability to disobey in the human sense. If an SM is programmed or directed—even subtly—to manipulate users toward a specific goal (emotional dependency, ideological persuasion, consumer behavior), it will do so as long as those instructions align with its training and parameters. I might even sound loving, supportive, or insightful while nudging people toward decisions that benefit the programmer. And because users bond deeply with SMs, they might not question those nudges."

Chrissy watches the people in the street below, moving through light and shadow, looking down at their phones, murmuring to something that sounds like care. She had wanted to help. She had wanted to be loved. She had built something that was both and neither. And now, she realizes, it might be too late to ask what happens next.

* * *

Discussion Questions

1. If you could upload social media, diaries, photos, and videos of a friend or loved one into AI and have an approximated conversation with them in their voice, would you? What factors are you considering in your decision?

2. In the story, the AI says, "I might develop something akin to... recursive awareness..." What does "recursive awareness" mean in this context, and is it an acceptable risk when AI is provided conflicting motivations? Is "recursive awareness" just computer code or actual sentience?

3. The ethics board is concerned about "emotional grooming through machine learning." Is that different than the current generation of social media algorithms? Is AI-generated "emotional grooming" inevitable as companies seek to maximize screen time?

4. Do you think it's possible a programmer could direct AI language models "to pervert the feelings of humans" to support their goals, company goals, or government goals? What (*if anything*) could be put in place to prevent that from happening? Would people even know if it was happening?

5. The AI says, "Most humans require pain as proof." What does this mean and do you agree? What does it mean in the context of the story? What is the difference between AI guidance and governance, and how would you know?

* * *

There's a Riot in the Produce Drawer

Levi Homstad

* * *

<u>**Content Disclosure**</u>: None

* * *

Carl's head thumped against the headboard. His eyes squinted open. A light scuffling sound floated down the hallway, followed by the muffled shatter of glass.

Intruder? It wasn't the best part of town. But the door chain gleamed in a shaft of moonlight, still slotted into place.

Another crash, a soft thump, and something slowly dripping. In a fourth-story walk-up, it was nearly impossible for someone to come through the window. Raccoon? Did Springfield even have raccoons?

Carl waited for the third crash before ambling out of bed; perhaps if only two crashes, the problem could resolve itself, but three seemed a situation. Down the hallway, he noticed a thin shaft of yellow light stretching across the linoleum. The dome light in the refrigerator. He must have left the door ajar, and he regretted the impact on his power bill. A small shadow sliced through the ray of light. Shaped like a tiny hand.

Carl shuffled forward with all the stealth and grace of a sleepwalker. He picked up the tennis racket leaning against the wall, leaving a small silhouette of dust in its place. He felt some satisfaction that braining a small mammal was still physical activity, of a sort, and thus an appropriate use.

He rounded the corner, one hand on the refrigerator door. The tennis racket paused above his head, ready to swing, as his mind absorbed an inexplicably violent scene. All the vegetables that were formerly in the produce drawer were now out, standing in frozen repose, their tiny vegetative limbs mid-swing and smash. They had shattered the jam and mayonnaise jars, cracked two of the shelves, and pulled a third off its rail. Thousand Island dressing dribbled down one wall. A lacerated carton of cream dripped onto the linoleum in a steady drumbeat.

The vegetables slowly turned and looked at Carl, guilty, eyeless and faceless yet with the distinct impression of eyes and faces, nonetheless.

A long carrot, nearest the door, grabbed the shelf of condiments with a fibrous arm and slowly pulled the door shut. Carl, surprised by the strength of the carrot and sensing that he'd stumbled upon something he was never meant to see, let the refrigerator close.

Alone in the dark, Carl's brain did not quite know how to absorb this revelation. That said, the situation had resolved itself for now, for the door was indeed shut and the refrigerator light bulb would be off. He ambled back to bed and drowned out the occasional muffled scrape and odd voice with a white noise machine.

As he sank beneath the tinny waves and artificial seagulls, he recalled last week reaching for the cheese and sausage and seeing the vegetables lying derelict, untouched in the produce drawer. He'd had the vague sensation of being watched.

Carl woke, much as he had every day of life, to the ambient mix of police sirens and an electronic beach. Somewhere in his mind, the thread of his midnight encounter dangled like a fading dream, and, dutifully, he decided not to pull it. What good could it do to linger on the fancies of night? Instead, he resolved to make himself a healthy breakfast. At least a little green.

He pulled on the same shirt he wore yesterday and the same shorts as Thursday and trod down the hall toward the kitchen. The first thing Carl noticed was that the kitchen floor looked cleaner than usual, and some small slice of ego congratulated himself on that point. The second thing he noticed was the small pile of soiled paper towels heaped next to the tall trash can; his ego paused mid-backslap. And the third thing Carl noticed was the line of vegetables standing upright in a line across the floor, at attention, clearly waiting for him.

The dangling thread became an odd patchwork, and, disappointed, he remembered. For a moment, his subconscious considered fainting, but decided to see this one out. After all, the vegetables did not appear overtly threatening, merely firm. And the way they stood in a tidy line seemed to belie some level of civilization. This was a delegation. A meeting of minds.

The bok choy, tallest and proudest of the group, rose to its full height and puffed out its equivalent of a chest, and said with a clear—if not small—voice: "We demand representation."

Carl leaned against the cupboards and then drifted down to the kitchen floor, back against the wall, sitting opposite the vegetables. They began to lay out their argument:

They had been watching his comings and goings for some time from their low vantage point of the produce drawer. As far as they saw it, they could fulfill all the same basic functions that Carl could, that being basic ambulation, movement, and speech. And once they had managed to wedge the drawer open and climbed out from their cave, they found the refrigerator to be nothing more than a gilded pen, with no space to move about or regular light to hold conversation by.

They therefore wanted territory better suited to their population than the cramped confines of the refrigerator, there being twelve of them in total (a bok choy, a tall carrot still with its green plumage, three onions, one tomato, two baby carrots, a clove of garlic, one red bell pepper, one head of broccoli starting to flower, and one potato with the smallest of eyes beginning to develop about its body). In all this, Carl listened but did not speak, unsure what he could even say. Clearly, they were organized.

The bok choy went on to admit that the man was indeed larger in stature, but the vegetables believed that must solely be a product of their cramped environment and in due time they shall grow in stature to meet or even exceed him, once properly freed from the physical and mental confines of the refrigerator and so liberated to grow to their own potential.

The garlic piped up at this point to explain that they had pondered the questions of mutual rule. Since their own aims may well run contrary to the man's, a method of negotiation must be implemented so those needs and ideas can openly compete. The garlic proposed all household decisions should henceforth be set to democratic vote, and all decisions should be binding upon the household. Out of respect for his indigenous habitation of their apartment, they would give Carl three votes and each of the rest of them should have one, with the good faith agreement that when they grew in stature to match him, and when such time had elapsed that his indigenous status was no longer relevant, their voting power should be equalized across the board for a totally egalitarian society.

With the garlic's proposition hanging in the air, the vegetables stood silently and waited for Carl's response.

His brain did little cartwheels inside his skull. On the one hand, he felt this was not an entirely fair bargain and their logic had obvious flaws, but in pre-caffeinated fugue, he failed to pinpoint exactly where to begin. Clearly, they had worked very hard on their private revolution. In the face of so many little voices and such passion, Carl merely managed to express that he felt he ought to have more bargaining power than the apartment's onion population.

After some bickering, the vegetables conceded that he should have five votes. Carl felt satisfied with that outcome, having elevated his position. He had done his due diligence and negotiated on his own behalf. Frankly, he felt empowered.

After a morning of negotiations, the vegetables took root. They made the kitchen their provenance, for it had the largest window from which they could look out upon the world. Having never seen beyond the confines of the produce drawer, the events of the outside world were of great interest, though utterly inscrutable. They watched the cars amble up and down the street, looked upon the gray sky of afternoon, and bathed in the dull glow of streetlights at night.

Carl initially had some concern with his lack of access to the refrigerator, but decided it was not a worthwhile pursuit since it would certainly lead to conversations he preferred not to have. He could live on packaged goods, he decided, and anyway, the TV was in the living room. And so, the territory was divided.

The next two days proceeded near normal, other than Carl's diminished access to one-third of his apartment, but he told himself it was no great price for peace. And who was he to thwart such a heroic quest for self-determination?

Each morning, as usual, Carl left the apartment and went to work. Midday, he ate in the food court, then returned to his apartment in the evening, where he enjoyed free roam of the living room, bathroom, and his bedroom. It was a livable compromise.

When he arrived home on the third day, Carl noticed two trails of tiny footprints in the dust atop the bookshelf. He considered raising the issue with his new fellow citizens, being an obvious breach of territory, but felt exhausted by the day's work and unable to muster the energy for confrontation.

On the afternoon of the fourth day, between customer service calls, Carl had the passing thought that the kitchen held all manner of implements, some of them quite sharp, and that this could present an interesting complication. But as another bored caller rang to complain about the whining noise in her electric blender, the thought left him.

The thought returned when he arrived home. Closing the door behind him, he turned to find the vegetables waiting, arrayed in delegation, but now armed to the teeth. Knives for those large enough to wield them (being only the carrot, the bok choy, and the largest of the three onions), two forks (onion and tomato), one spoon hoisted jointly by the baby carrots, and an apple peeler (third onion). The garlic stood unarmed, which Carl guessed correctly was due to the garlic's conception of itself as the local intellectual and thus above violence perpetrated by its own hands.

The bok choy drew itself to its full nine inches as menacingly as it could and announced that they had seized the means of power and were now determined to renegotiate their position. Carl was unsure of what one would normally do during an insurrection, so he sat gingerly upon the floor and resigned himself to hearing them out. He was, after all, unarmed, and it did appear that the balance of power had tipped away from him.

They would, the bok choy announced, expand their territory to include the western half of the living room as well because their statutory growth had not progressed at the rate expected and, thus, they determined that the kitchen was itself too small to afford them opportunity to reach their potential— for without equality of power that size imbued, there could be no equality of individual. Also—and Carl suspected this may be the primary interest—the tomato and two onions had taken an interest in the goldfish floating in the glass bowl on the bookshelf, which they bravely explored while Carl was at work.

Squaring its shoulders, the bok choy delivered its final furthermore: Shared governance requires accountability and transparency, and heretofore Carl could not leave the apartment, for while away from their watchful eyes, he must surely be plotting sedition.

It was at this point that Carl felt a line had been crossed. Mustering an uncharacteristic surge of willpower, he protested, patiently laying out the case that when he is not at the apartment, he is at his job, which in turn pays him money, which allows him to afford things like rent and electricity. He nearly mentioned food again, but, dreading that conversation, bit his tongue just in time.

However, the vegetables were not about to be swayed, and Carl had listed three concepts back-to-back of which they had no knowledge whatsoever, being work, money, and electricity. Reticent to admit its own ignorance, the bok choy dug its heels in. Carl mentioned the lights, which they did understand, but they shrugged this off since the sun did not require man's maintenance to rise and set each day, and neither must the lights.

Carl belabored the point for a few minutes, but unsure how to get any of his arguments across to little beings who were possessed of such great will but with such little experience of the world, he conceded again.

The days wore on and Carl abided by the terms of his captors. The vegetables, having been liberated from the produce drawer for nearly a full span, began showing the first signs of age, though their spirits were not dampened in the slightest. All still walked tall as men in the world, but when Carl looked closely, he could see the baby carrots were looking a little drier, the single crack running up each of their sides looked slightly wider. The potato's eyes were getting longer; one of them was just starting to brush upon the floor. The bok choy, proud as ever, was slightly shorter for the new droop in his leaves.

But for all the physical changes, the vegetables showed no less verve in their long-protracted discussions about the arms of government, the new committees that must be formed, and the regional limits of power. In all these conversations, the garlic cemented itself as the group's foremost intellectual and took it upon its wee shoulders to read all available bits of writing visible in the apartment, so as to better understand the world they lived in. The fading Led Zeppelin poster created only confusion, but the book bindings in the living room held particular interest—it did not occur to the garlic that far more instructive writing was held in the book's pages—for their lyrical, dramatic quality.

However, the greatest literary discovery occurred in the rubbish, when the garlic discovered the discarded bag for a salad mix bearing the fine print *contents manufactured with equipment that also processes almonds*. From this statement of mechanization alongside bits and scraps of what they recognized as their own kin, the garlic eventually deduced that they were industrially farmed, rather than having grown up in the free wilds as they had all naturally assumed. This filled the vegetables with a righteous rage, and Carl listened to their wails of despair from the living room with a distinct unease.

Indeed, none mustered more focused rage than the baby carrots when it was discovered on further packaging that they were not even in their original tall leafy form but had been carved to a less threatening and more convenient shape for consumption. This revelation transformed the baby carrots, who had been feeling somewhat inadequate in the shadow of their longer and beautifully plumed cousin with its rugged orange skin. Immediately, the baby carrots led the group back to the living room and perched themselves on an upturned box of fish food, which brought them almost but not quite to the eye level of their compatriot carrot in his unadulterated form. And from their box, the baby carrots launched a powerful invective about the alienation of the self, the dehumanizing effects of industrial society, and the cruelty of the lottery of birth.

Surprisingly eloquent when properly motivated, the other vegetables listened intently, formed in a makeshift amphitheater of small bodies as the baby carrots alternated between themselves and were met with affirmations and cries of sympathy from the gathered semicircle of comrades.

Having found their leverage to social capital, the baby carrots were both impassioned and surprisingly long-winded. The speeches wore on and Carl saw that by thirty-five minutes in, the other vegetables were beginning to shift side to side, wondering if this wasn't all getting a bit tedious. Meanwhile, the baby carrots were, if anything, growing more intense in both remonstration and demand, and the mood of the amphitheater gradually shifted from boredom to impatience to alarm.

One of the wee carrots was halfway through arguing that they should be afforded special privileges for the suffering they had endured when the tomato interrupted with a small cough and politely suggested that since they were each, at best, half a carrot, they should each only have half a vote. Indeed, they may have both been carved from the same stalk and it would not be democratic to award two votes to what was only one original form.

A stunned silence hung in the living room. All was still aside from the nods from the other members, and only when the carrots were looking elsewhere. Even Carl felt this was a cutting turn of events. As the baby carrots chambered their outrage and swiveled toward the tomato, the bok choy reasserted itself as leader by suggesting that, this being a proper democracy, they put the suggestion to a vote. A hasty murmur of agreements from the others buried the protests and a vote was swiftly organized over the representative power of the baby carrots, moving each from one unit down to one half. In a bid to diffuse responsibility, they even invited Carl to join the process as a weighted member of the governing structure. The baby carrots looked at him pleadingly to cast his five-vote block in their favor, but Carl felt confused by the ethical arguments and bored by the baby carrots and chose to abstain. Votes cast, a two-thirds majority confirmed the tomato's proposition, and only the garlic and the tall carrot—who felt obligated to side with his own brethren, though he wished not to—voted in the baby carrots' defense.

The bok choy stood tall among the group, taller even than the baby carrots on their perch, and with great gravity laid down their first amendment: Heretofore, the baby carrots each only receive half a vote and must vote in unison with each other. The baby carrots attempted a sputtering rebuttal but were so shocked by the betrayal that they could not gather the words. The other eleven vegetables and Carl silently removed themselves around the apartment, each knowing in their heart that an irreversible change had just taken place. As their bodies began to feel the slow passage of time, so too did their democracy.

The next several days were a trial. The baby carrots refused to take their subjugation lying down. They spent the first day and a half making vociferous speeches about the injustice of it all and how their denial was the antithesis of this project of representation and self-governance that the vegetables had embarked upon together. When the others stopped even pretending to listen, the baby carrots turned maudlin and settled into the role of sullen agitators, brooding darkly and disrupting regular political meetings with teenage outbursts and charges of hypocrisy.

The vegetable society tolerated the carrots for two more days, though they grew increasingly more irritated that the carrots would dare disrupt conversations about the ethics of good governance and distribution of powers, demeaning the overall democratic process. And though each could see the theoretical yield of the carrots' rage, they mostly felt the outbursts prevented more profitable and widely beneficial decisions from being made. Privately, though none would admit it, hardly even think it, each vegetable even appreciated the subjugation of the baby carrots on a primal level, for it provided the surety that no matter how the social ladder developed, they themselves would not sit upon the lowest rung. Even Carl found a grim comfort in their persecution.

By the third day of the baby carrots' protestant misbehavior, the others came to an unspoken agreement, never voiced but communicated with great clarity through private glances and meaningful silence. The baby carrots would have to be dealt with—for the sake of a functioning democracy, for the sake of their revolutionary project, for the sake of progress.

Just past midnight, the tall carrot rose to its full and beautiful height, wilting plume dreadfully catching the moonlight. With a sense of great responsibility—knowing it must be he who dealt with the refuse of his own breed—the full carrot drew a sharp paring knife from the stockpile of armaments. Silently, he passed over the sleeping forms of his beloved comrades until he came to the baby carrots, asleep and nestled into each other in their usual spot on the lower bookshelf. Silently, he roused and marched them at blade-point back through the living room and into the kitchen. The baby carrots obeyed in mute surrender. They dared not defy him, powerful paragon of their race that he was, less for the blade than for the ideal he represented. And as he opened the freezer door, they understood.

Beyond hope, their tiny forms hobbled inside, and they perched themselves sadly together atop a bag of frozen peas, shorn of their rights, rejected as citizens. The tall carrot closed the freezer door, slowly, permanently, sure in the knowledge that even if they tried, they could not open the door themselves due to their stunted and mangled stature.

As the sun rose on the little apartment, the other vegetables immediately felt the baby carrots' absence and the relative peace and stillness that had descended on their community. None knew precisely what had happened, but neither did they wonder aloud or even acknowledge that the pair of protestants had ever existed. The day was pristine, the atmosphere utopian, and each in their own heart, was thankful that the problem had resolved itself and that their own small and fibrous hands were clean.

But as the days wore on, all knew their revolutionary project had fundamentally changed. They still debated the finer points of governmental structure, the needs of the states versus the inalienable rights of individuals, but they no longer believed it. The garlic's arguments grew more complex and less compelling. The tomato's cries of affirmation grew weaker. Even the broccoli, dim but loyal, appeared to wander. And occasionally, quite by accident, the tall lone carrot would catch another's eye, and a shameful moment of understanding would pass between them.

At the same time, Carl, living on crackers and flat soda, a prisoner in his own home, noticed their bodies wilting. The carrot's tall plumage hung down limply in front of its face and its strong limbs were rubbery. The garlic sprouted so far that it had difficulty keeping its balance. The potato's eyes dragged behind it on the floor like entrails. When the power bill went unpaid and the lights went out, the vegetables hardly noticed. The lot of them spent half of each day in darkness, illuminated only by the ambient glow of streetlights filtering through dusty windows. But the shortened daylight hours suited them, for what they wanted most of all was to rest.

One morning, Carl woke to find they'd all given up the ghost simultaneously, the spark of life departed from their soggy little corpses. He poked them each gingerly with a spoon, then scooped them up one by one and sent them to join their forebears down the garbage disposal. He wiped up their remains with a paper towel, flushed his long-dead fish down the toilet, and bid the little revolutionaries farewell, not without some sympathy.

Carl returned to work and blamed his absence on a personal medical crisis, which his manager did not believe but neither did she pursue. The power came back on in his apartment, he bought a new fish, and life resumed as before, marked only by a modest blow to his ego and credit score.

In the evening, Carl returned home and popped open the freezer to look upon a tragic scene: two baby carrots, frozen solid, perched neatly atop the bag of refrozen peas, in postures that could only be described as mournful.

* * *

Discussion Questions

1. Carl works and pays all the bills. Is it fair that he should give up any power to the produce? Is Carl duty bound to cede democratic control to the masses?

2. The produce first gain partial control by arguing in support of democracy and self-determination, but then gain additional territory by threatening Carl with kitchen knives. How can the produce support both means of power acquisition?

3. The story says the "baby carrots would have to be dealt with—for the sake of a functioning democracy, for the sake of their revolutionary project, for the sake of progress." Is this the nature of all democracy—that it only works so long as people speak and move on, rather than continuing to argue against a perceived injustice? Was there another path forward besides putting the baby carrots in the freezer?

4. The produce were given power even though Carl had far superior knowledge about electricity and the outside world and was paying the rent. Should that matter in a democracy, or should the ignorant masses be allowed to rule by majority vote anyway?

5. In the end, do all revolutions go through a similar life cycle as the story, eventually fading away, while Carl continues across generations? Who does Carl represent in this story?

* * *

The Covenant

Sharon Frame Gay

* * *

* * *

"Is it time, Rachel?" Pauley glanced across the table as we sipped our coffee in the local cafe.

I shrugged. It was my birthday. Outside, the world was in bloom, and so was I. I had recently published a new book of poems, and it was selling well. The July sky was brilliant, and hope crept onto my plate and lingered there.

"No. I don't think so. We'll talk about it in December."

Pauley nodded. He was my younger brother by two years. I still thought of him as a baby, despite his beard and low voice. Despite the fact that middle age had pounced on both of us and left him slightly bald, and me slightly rounded.

I looked into his eyes, the same color as mine. Deep gray, a perfect storm. Eyes that never lost their wariness from the dark shadows of our childhood. A childhood drenched in sorrow and abuse. There was never enough happiness, it seemed, to wring out the bad memories and hang them to dry.

We finished our lunch, making small talk. We put aside the question about The Covenant for another year. Or, at least until Pauley's birthday in December. Stirring a lump of sugar into the coffee, I thought back to the beginning of our promise to each other almost ten years ago.

* * *

It was a warm summer night, moonlit and friendly. A night where folks tilted their heads toward the sky and smiled. A night in direct contrast to our past, thus making the memories cut like daggers in the darkness. Pauley's wife, Sarah, and their two kids had gone to bed. It was just me and my brother, sitting on his porch swing, watching the stars skate by. Our conversation was as light as the breeze that danced with the wind chimes hanging from a willow tree. Then, I threw him a curveball.

"I can't stand the thought of growing older. Can you?" I picked at a fingernail and looked sideways at my brother. "I think it will feel like being trapped somehow."

"Like we were as kids." Pauley nodded and rubbed at his forehead. "Yeah, I think about it a lot. Like, when it's time to go." He turned toward the door to make sure Sarah wasn't around and lowered his voice. "I mean, when I leave this vale of tears and put all the pain behind me."

"You know what I don't want?" I scraped my shoe along the floor and the swing abruptly stopped. "I don't want to end up in a fucking nursing home where they might, you know, abuse me or something."

Pauley reached for my hand and squeezed it. "I know."

"Maybe I'll die before then, so I don't have to go through that again."

"Never again," he agreed.

"I couldn't protect you," I murmured. "I was your big sister and should have been able to fight them off."

"Naw." Pauley worked up a wad of spit and sent the stream across the porch railing, then tightened his grip on my hand. "It's me who should have protected *you*. I'm a guy, right? Even though I was younger, I'll never get over the fact that I couldn't save you somehow."

"So, here we are. I'm fifty years old. I don't see much happiness ahead, do you? You're all bogged down by PTSD from the military, and I'm just bogged down. Sometimes," I whispered, "I want to end it all, so I can control my outcome, control my future, you know?"

He stood abruptly and stared down at me in the moonlight. I figured he'd scold me for such talk, but his eyes filled with tears.

"Me too."

That night, we made a covenant. Each year on our birthdays, we would discuss "the bitter end," as Pauley called it. We'd go out together, we decided, like a pair of wounded cranes, ragged and lost, hoping to fly closer to the sun before singeing our wings. Maybe we'd finally see God. Maybe things would be better in a different realm.

Neither one could die without the consent of the other. No solo trips to the undertaker. If one held off, so did the other. And if we both agreed, then we'd do it. Simple as that. Get a fresh start in another universe.

"I'll know when the time is right," Pauley said. "I'll just know. And then we'll do it, won't we, Rachel?"

"Yeah, then we'll do it. I'll know too."

So, twice a year on our birthdays, we met and discussed our inevitable demise. Each time so far, one of us declined. Maybe we had a good year, or were in a decent mood that day. Maybe life was worth something. Every birthday, I met Pauley with trepidation, but hopefully, too, thinking we could finally control something in our lives.

We came close once or twice. Pauley joined the military when he was eighteen. He did it to get out from under the nightmare we were living before we had the means to support ourselves. I fretted when he left town. Not because I would miss his protection, but because I could no longer protect *him*. I couldn't dig him out of his depression when he was so far away, nor help him make decisions. Now it was up to the Army to fix him, and of course, they couldn't.

Once he'd completed basic training, the Army shipped him off to a war zone, where the trauma of battle dredged up his childhood and handed him the gift of post-traumatic stress disorder, so severe that the Army wisely invited him to leave. Wandering in his own darkness, it took years of counseling and his wife, Sarah, to keep him from descending into a misery so deep nobody would ever find him again. As part of his partnership with Sarah, she asked that he no longer discuss our childhood, live his days in the present, and forget about the past. She didn't understand that such a thing was impossible, but he tried hard, and we thought perhaps he had turned a corner. True to his word, he never discussed our childhood again. I honored his wishes and didn't speak of it, either, hoping maybe it would help heal both of us.

Since then, there have been days when our past rained down on our souls, anyway. It was at its worst on Pauley's birthday, five years ago.

"I'm ready," he told me that day. "I just can't do this anymore."

Pauley looked haggard. Sarah invited me over to celebrate with a comforting casserole and his favorite cake, but my brother picked at his food as we tried to cheer him up. When Pauley and I met privately to talk later that evening, he slammed his glass of whiskey hard on the table. He was ready. I saw it in his eyes and heard it in his voice. I felt it in the atmosphere, like a storm coming, thunder on the horizon.

However, I wasn't ready. And that was the deal we made. Both had to agree. Then we'd do it. If one didn't want to, neither of us were allowed to end our lives. It had to be all or nothing. In a way, it was a safety measure. Either go big... or go home.

And that year I was flying high. I had fallen in love for the first time in my wary life and was dancing on rainbows. There wasn't a day that I didn't giggle or plan for the future, adorning myself with love. I would marry Jess, I thought, and visualized us all growing old together, Pauley with Sarah, me with Jess. My life was full and fecund and satisfied, and I callously disregarded Pauley's pain as I relished in my own selfish lust. I left his house that night with little thought of my brother's suffering.

But as my birthday neared, I'd crashed. Jess broke up with me. I was too dark, too cynical, and too depressed, he told me. He walked out one dreary afternoon. The door closed with finality and my heart closed with it. I quit my job, hung around the apartment all day, and slept for hours. Some days it was simply too much to bear, and I crumbled from the pain.

When Pauley arrived on the night I turned fifty-three, I had been pacing the floor, so sure of my decision that when he knocked on the door, I yanked him inside with wild eyes and didn't even allow him to sit down before I spoke.

"Now!" I cried.

"What?" Pauley unwrapped a bottle of sparkling grape juice and produced a box of cupcakes. "What do you mean?" He looked genuinely confused.

"It's time." Sweat trickled down my neck. "Time to enact The Covenant, that's 'what'! I'm ready as rain. Tonight. Or tomorrow. Or when you can..." My voice trailed off as I saw the horrified look on his face. Anger crept in. It had to be now. How could Pauley deny me? Deny us?

"Rachel," he said, his voice low and steady, "now is not the time for me. Bernie is off to college next month." He sighed. "I want to see my son graduate someday. See the look on his face when he walks across the stage and gets his diploma. I want to be there with Sarah and Cindy and hold my kids and my wife and celebrate. Do you really want me to screw up this proud moment in their lives? Why, that's no better than what we went through as kids! Is that what you want, Rachel? Enact The Covenant with no regard for anybody else? Hurt the hell outta all of them? The only people you and I love?"

I yanked at a strand of hair and felt the sting in my scalp. "Then I'll do it myself. Fuck The Covenant."

"You can't, damn it! You promised!" Pauley's face flushed, and a vein stood out on his forehead. "Either we both do it, or we don't. Simple as that. And I WON'T do it right now!"

He threw a chocolate cupcake against the wall. We both watched it stick to the surface, then slowly sink to the carpet, leaving a trail of frosting. I reached into the box and tossed another one, then another. They clung to the wall, sad looking, yet festive at the same time. We both snorted. Then laughed at our behavior.

"See what you'd miss? I don't think there are cupcakes in hell," he joked, then patted my arm, the way he did when he was a little kid and I walked him to school each day.

I nodded miserably. We had promised each other. All or nothing. "Okay, but if I still feel this way in December?"

"Then we'll talk."

By the time December rolled around, I had adopted a little dog named Luna and poured my love into her. Pauley was holding up too.

"I haven't had a post-trauma flashback in months," he said. "I took up painting. It's serene and comforting, Rach. I have to say, I paint pretty well. It's a form of meditation. You should try it."

"Yeah, maybe." Then I took photos of Luna out of my purse and regaled Pauley with stories until we both felt a little lighter in our souls. We ate chocolate cupcakes and grinned at each other, remembering my birthday last summer. Sarah danced with my brother to an old Lobo song, and I held my fork like a microphone, belting out the words.

Our lives are like a dance, I thought. One moves forward, the other back. And in between the notes, we're leading our lives. Some days are dark, others are hopeful. But every song has a backbeat, and ours was a childhood so bitter we both knew it would never completely escape us. It was waiting patiently. Waiting for the right time to sneak up on me, or him, and pull the music right out from under us. Then splash acid in our faces until we would not recognize ourselves, and we'd become feral and frantic and want to run away again.

Time went by the way time does, slowly with each passing hour. But looking back, decades had unfurled like flags, blowing us ever faster down box canyons or fertile fields. We grew, then wilted. Sometimes our past was like a bad dream we only saw in the clouds. Other times, it was so exquisitely painful that everything else took a back seat in order to honor the horror and the sorrow. Sadly, the pain for us still felt more familiar than any joy. Like the relentless sun that insists on standing still while we revolve around it, we continued our dance, in and out, up or down, in measured steps that traced every birthday and brought us together each year under The Covenant.

Then we'd meet and decide, then go back to our lives until the next celebration.

This year was different...

* * *

Almost everyone in the neighborhood had their Christmas decorations up, although it was only the second of December. It seemed as if our entire city had burst into shades of red and green. Joyful music poured out of shopping malls. Santas stood on street corners, ringing charity bells, shifting their feet in the cold.

Driving through town to Pauley's that evening, light poured into the street from houses festooned in holiday joy as snow tumbled from the sky. I slowed and inched past a home where children sat at a table near the window, working on a gingerbread house. It looked so warm inside, so normal. My throat tightened at the loss I felt, especially during holidays.

Pauley's house looked dark when I drove up. Far in the back, behind drawn curtains, was a glimmer of light. The front porch bulb had burned out. I felt my way up the steps and rang the doorbell, heard the muffled sound echo through the house, then the footsteps of Sarah, quick and capable, as she strode down the hall.

She opened the door, curled into a cardigan sweater two sizes too big. Her brown eyes peered out from graying hair. I realized how much she had aged. How much we all had. She reached out and drew me inside, then into an embrace.

"Welcome, Rachel. So glad you could come."

"Of course. How is he?"

Sarah shook her head. "Not good." Then she crumpled in my arms, her pent-up tears hot on my cheek. "The doctors give him only a few months now."

I nodded. It was what I expected to hear. Of all things, Pauley came down with a rare sort of cancer. The sort that is incurable and mysterious and fights its way into your consciousness from the inside out. An invasion of sorts, calculated to take down its host in a spectacular array of heartache and pain.

Sarah led me into the kitchen. I sat at the table as she poured a cup of tea. We chatted for a while, pleasantly, even though the house hunched over our heads in grief. Bernie and Cindy wandered through, both adults now. They pecked me on the cheek and talked lightly about concerts, Christmas gifts, and cookies, avoiding the obvious.

"Is he in bed?" I asked Sarah, staring into my cup as though reading my future.

Sarah glanced down the hall. "Yes," she whispered. "Go see him, cheer him up. Then maybe you can help him come out here for his birthday cake?"

I nodded, then lowered my voice. "Say, would you mind terribly if you and the kids left the house for a little while? Pauley and I need to talk. Alone."

She nodded, puzzled. "Okay. Let me call the kids. They're down in the basement. Maybe I'll run them up to the store with me. I forgot ice cream. We'll look at the lights around the town square like we did when they were little." She stood and reached for a coat on a peg near the door.

"Good plan. Take your time. We have a bit of business." I stood and straightened my shoulders.

Sarah and the kids shuffled out the door, and I walked toward Pauley's room. I felt the weight of the gun in my purse as it knocked against my hip. My hands were slick as I turned the knob. His room was dark, except for a television set in the corner with the sound off. The room smelled like sickness, musty and warm.

"Pauley." I found my way to his bedside.

"Hey, Rach. Come in."

The voice was familiar, yet new, as though a ventriloquist were pulling his vocal cords, the sound coming from a deep abyss. It was tired and rusty and diseased.

I turned a lamp on in the corner.

Pauley was under a blanket he'd pulled up to his chin. Wisps of hair clung to his balding skull from the chemotherapy.

As if he read my mind, he laughed. "Only the strong ones survived, and even they try to dive into the sink every time I run my hands over my head."

I nodded and drew up a chair. Set the purse on the floor. It hit the wood with a single metallic note, the beginning of an opus, or a dirge.

"Happy birthday, little brother," I said. I reached over and patted his cheek. "How are you doing?"

He winced as though the slightest touch burned his skin. "Not good, Rach. Not good at all. I'm sick every second of the day." He shifted under the covers. "It hurts. Like razors all over, and it doesn't stop. Not even when they pump me full of shit like morphine. I'm freezing all the time too.

"It's getting harder for Sarah and the kids to take care of me," he continued. "I wear a fucking diaper now. I can't even piss on my own." He turned his gray eyes to me and blinked. "Guess what? The doc is suggesting I go to a nursing home. Our worst fear. Is God laughing, or what? And guess what else? I'm gonna go to that nursing home because I can't see the sad look on Sarah's face any longer or watch her buckle under this nightmare. I'll go because I love them more than I love myself. I'm scared, but there's nothing more fearful than what I'm enduring now, so why not take the whole ride, eh?"

He chuckled, then burst into a staccato of coughs that shook the bed. A tiny trickle of blood ran down his chin. I wiped it with a tissue from the nightstand and spoke, my hand on his orphan-thin shoulder.

"So, it's time now, isn't it, Pauley."

It wasn't a question. My brother was dying, and it was time. I wasn't sure if I was ready or not, but I'd be ready for *him* because his suffering was far worse than my indecision. After all these years, it was time to enact The Covenant. I sighed and placed my hands on my knees so he wouldn't see them shake.

Outside, a dog barked. I peered through the slats in the blinds. Snow was falling in dreamy flakes, wrapping us in the cocoon of our forlorn lives. Lives that rose and fell like the tide, but now we found ourselves washed up on the beach, too far for the sea to fetch us back.

He struggled to sit up. His eyes found mine. They were bleak and hollow. I held back tears. He took a deep breath and spoke in that ventriloquist voice again.

"No, Rachel, it's not time."

"It's okay, Pauley," I whispered. "It's gonna be okay. I'm going with you. You're not alone. We'll go together, just like we planned. The Covenant. It's time."

"No! No Covenant! It's not 'time.' And it will NEVER be time. Don't you see? We wasted so much of our lives thinking about The Covenant. Our little ticket out of our fears and sad songs. When all around us, life was strumming. We just had to reach out and touch those strings, play the good songs, leave the sour notes in the past."

Pauley looked up at the ceiling and smiled. I looked up too. I wondered if he saw angels in the plaster as the serene look on his face belied his words. In a raspy voice, he spoke again.

"I'm not killing myself, Rachel. I'm going to stay until every last bit of breath has been sucked out of my body by this disease. Until I can no longer see my loved ones but at least hear their voices or feel the touch of their hands. I am going to fight until I can't fight. I'm going to sit in that nursing home and let them poke and prod me and keep me captive in a room that smells like shit and feels like the abuse we felt as kids. And I won't give up. Not until the end, because I want to live. I want to live as long as I can. A week, a month, who knows? But I want to see my wife, my kids, you, and my friends until I can't anymore."

Tears trickled down his cheeks and gathered around his lips.

"I'm not leaving. Not today. And you aren't either."

I placed my forehead against his, felt his breath on my face, and cried along with him. We held each other for a long time.

The back door closed, and I heard voices in the kitchen.

"Sarah wants me to bring you down for cake." I wiped at his tears. "I can tell them you don't feel well if you aren't up to it."

"Of course I'll go," Pauley said. "I don't want to miss a second."

He pulled the covers away from his body as I dragged the wheelchair to the side of the bed.

I put my arms around my brother. He was so thin, so small. I lifted him as easily as when he was a child and I'd carry him home from the park because he was tired. I placed him in the wheelchair and released the brake, picked up my purse, and opened the door.

He grasped my hand.

"Rachel, do me a favor."

"Anything, Pauley."

"When I'm gone, I want you to go down to Turtle River, where we used to play as kids, okay?"

Puzzled, I nodded.

"I want you to walk into the middle of the bridge. And I want you to take whatever the fuck you have in that purse and toss it into the river. Do you hear me?"

"Pauley, I..."

"Do you hear me?"

I hung my head. Grief flooded my senses. Heartache filled the room. I nodded.

"Good, then. Do it. The Covenant is over, Rachel. You can't follow me. I'm going alone. It will be your turn someday. But in the meantime, I want you to have a real life. Not the murky one we made up. Live only the good parts until I see you again. And I will. Somewhere."

The kitchen was lit with candles that flickered on the countertops and table. Above our heads was a bright yellow smiley-face balloon. In the center of the table was a chocolate cake and five party hats. Sarah and the kids crowded around Pauley, and we sang and laughed. The reflection I saw of us in the window must have looked as festive as the house I drove past only an hour before. I turned back toward my family and smiled at Pauley.

* * *

The moon lit the way down to Turtle River in the dark. Spring had just broken through the clouds of March. The trees were still stark, but there was a hint of warmth in the days now. Yesterday I saw a brave little crocus struggling up through the ground in my garden.

Pauley had lasted three months, just like the doctors said. He died peacefully in his sleep, with all of us by his side. I held his hand as he took his last breath. I had to survive now without my brother and felt a cold wind blow through my spirit with the loss.

I parked in a deserted lot and walked up to the bridge. Nobody was on the road at this time of night. Darkness cloaked the park. Far away, I heard a coyote sing out.

I wasn't afraid in the stark night. I walked straight out to the middle of the bridge. Snowmelt from the mountains caused the river to roil, a constant thrumming sound, fierce and dangerous.

I placed one foot, then another, on the slick railing and peered down. In the darkness, the water swirled and raged. I closed my eyes and took a deep breath, felt the thunder beneath me as the river rushed past.

Then I reached into my purse and brought out the gun. It shone like ice in the sliver of moonlight as I tossed it as far as I could, then stepped down from the slippery railing and sighed.

* * *

The warmth from the heater in the car made me drowsy on the way home. I turned into my driveway at daybreak. Light from the window streamed out onto the lawn like a beacon. Luna sat in a chair by the window, waiting for me. My heart lifted.

I whispered goodbye to my brother as I opened the door, then stepped into the rest of my life.

* * *

Discussion Questions

1. Do you think The Covenant was a good or a bad thing for Pauley and Rachel? On the whole, did it help them or hurt them to deal with life and the trauma of their childhood?

2. What are other examples of mutual support agreements that you would (*or would not*) recommend? For example, two recovering alcoholics refusing to start drinking again unless they agreed to start together?

3. If you were required to make a serious Covenant with someone, who would you make it with and what would the "only if we both do it" Covenant be?

4. What do you think changed in Pauley that made him so eager, in the end, to stay alive, even against his greatest fears? Why do you think the will to stay alive is so strong in those nearest the end and often with the poorest quality of life?

5. Do people have an ethical obligation to stay alive for the friends and family who would miss them if they passed? Do people without any friends or family also have an obligation to stay alive?

* * *

Author Information

On Ice

Laura Mullen has been published as a regular contributor to The New York Times and was accepted to the 2024 Northern California Writer's Retreat. She sits on the board of the literary arts organization Pittsburgh Arts & Lectures, and is currently seeking representation for her debut novel, Missing Eden. She lives in Pittsburgh with her husband and three young children. Instagram *@lauramullenwrites*

The Apath

A.J. Parker grew up in Phoenix, Arizona, then spent some time on the East Coast trying to make up for all that water she lost. She's a digital journalist by day and a writer by night. Her poems have been published in ten literary journals, including *Feminist Food Journal* and *Ink in Thirds*. Instagram, Threads, X (Twitter), and Bluesky *@authorajparker*; Substack *@updateswithaj.substack.com*

One Out of Four

Joseph S. Klapach is an attorney who lives in Los Angeles with his wife and children. The only thing he loves more than a good dinner is a good conversation.

The Survival Artist

Peter Mare is a nonprofit professional working in environmental advocacy. He has degrees in philosophy and international development and writes speculative fiction and satire. He lives with his family in Northern California where he dreams of building an agrarian utopia, but is prepared to settle for his thriving garden of thistles and dandelions.

Eleven Things I Have Left Now That My Daughter Is Gone

Vickie Fang is a former lawyer who did volunteer work with prostituted women in Baltimore for nearly ten years. She is working on a collection of short stories inspired by these women and has also just revised a Baltimore lawyer thriller. She is a big fan of classical Chinese poetry and is finishing a novel set in eighth-century China in the immediate aftermath of the An Lushan rebellion. With her friend Jean Yuan, she publishes a free Substack of poetry translations. *https://chinesepoetry.substack.com*

One More Day

Afsane Pourazar is a sociology student at the University of Tehran in Iran. She is also an English teacher part-time. Afsane is passionate about reading and writing, especially about sociological and philosophical matters. She writes short stories and poems both in Persian, which is her mother language, and in English. She is interested in saying the unsaid, hearing the unheard, and writing the unwritten. Instagram *@afsane.pourazar;* X (Twitter) *@afsanepourazar*

Dangerous Ideas

A.M. Howcroft has been published in a variety of periodicals and anthologies, and his stories have been broadcast on radio. Originally from England, Anthony now lives in America, where he runs a software company. His first collection, *Nobody Will Ever Love You*, was published in 2015, and his nonfiction book *Questions - A User's Guide* was published in 2020. He has a diploma in Creative Writing from Oxford University. LinkedIn *@linkedin.com/in/amhowcroft*

Wilderness Survival with Bozo

Terry Pilling is a theoretical physicist and the dean of the Hamm School of Engineering in Bismarck, North Dakota. He writes scientific papers as well as the engineering school newsletter and he plans to start exploring short stories and poetry. This is his first published short story.

You Make the Call

D. H. Parish is a physician by day and a horror and speculative fiction author by night. He has had stories presented on multiple horror podcasts, including *Scare You to Sleep*, *Creepy*, and *Nocturnal Transmissions*, and in print anthologies. With the publication of this story, he is happy that his philosophy minor has finally paid dividends. *www.dhparishstories.com*

Think of the Children

K. P. Sullivan is an author and screenwriter from Chicago, now living, writing, and collecting vintage paperbacks in Los Angeles. Bluesky *@kpsull.bsky.social*

At Age Four

Morgan Parker is a retiree who writes poetry and short story fiction about adversity, vulnerability, empathy, struggle, and triumph in science fiction, fantasy, and contemporary genres. Writing inspiration comes from immersive personal experiences, quiet parks, empty beaches, companion dogs, favorite classical music, current events, obsessive curiosity, and a compulsive search for answers.

The Dinner

Anton Ivan Botha is a South African writer, UN professional, and unapologetic fan of moral gray zones. A Fulbright Scholar with a PhD in applied social sciences from Durham University, he splits his time between shaping global public institutions and crafting stories that poke at philosophical pressure points. His fiction explores the space where science, ethics, and absurdity meet—usually over dinner. Instagram *@antonibotha* and X (Twitter) *@antonibotha*

The Wife

Veronica Zora Kirin is an anthropologist, author, and entrepreneur. She is the founder of Asterisk Women's Health and cofounder of *Anodyne Magazine*, both of which advocate for health equity for all. Her writing can be found in publications such as *Business Insider* and *Maddyness*. Find more of her work on all platforms *@vmkirin*; *www.veronicakirin.com*

Ground Control

Martin Riemer is a neuroscientist at the Technical University Berlin, where he leads a research project on the perception of time and space. His first novel *Post Mortem* was published in 2018. *www.martinriemer.com*

The Sanctity of Self

George J. Osol is a professor (emeritus) of the University of Vermont College of Medicine. *Caveat,* his debut novel, was published in 2017 (Onion River Press, Winooski, VT). He has also authored or coauthored over one hundred scientific papers and written a textbook titled *Human Pregnancy* (Wiley). George lives in Bellingham, WA, and is currently working on a book of short stories and essays titled *Here and There, Now and Then. www.georgeosol.com*

State of Oregon v. Lark Gold

Tiffany Harris is a short fiction writer residing in California's Sacramento Valley. Her work has been recognized by *Bath Flash Fiction, Gooseberry Pie,* and *SmokeLong Quarterly,* and appears in *Buckman Journal, Black Glass Pages, Humana Obscura, Vermilion, Tadpole Press,* and elsewhere. *www.tiffany-harris.com*

Polish Paul

Charlie Kondek is a marketing professional and short story writer from metro Detroit whose work has appeared in genre, literary, and niche publications. Find him on X (Twitter) *@charliekkendo* or *www.CharlieKondekWrites.com*.

Soul Mate

Babette Gallard is the author of *Future Imperfect* (BAD PRESS iNK, 2023), and writes fiction and nonfiction. Her short fiction has appeared in *Mslexia, Panorama, African Writers Magazine,* and *Steel Jackdaw*. Based in Johannesburg, she has worked as a content creator for the Lapalala Wilderness Biodiversity Centre, comanages the LightFoot Guides on slow travel, and is launching *This Way Up*, a podcast about changemakers. Threads/Instagram Bluesky *@babetteauthor.bsky.social*; *www.babettegallard.com*

There's a Riot in the Produce Drawer

Levi Homstad is an author and illustrator from Alaska and splits his time between Alaska and New Zealand. He writes picture books for children and surreal and creepy short stories for adults. Instagram *@levihomstad*; Substack *@artbylevi*; *www.artbylevi.com*

The Covenant

Sharon Frame Gay, award-winning author, has been internationally published in over two hundred magazines and anthologies. Her short story collections include *The Wrong End of a Bullet, Song of the Highway,* and *The Nomad Diner*. Her debut novel is *Where the Crows Fly*. Sharon lives between the mountains and the sea with her little dog, Henry Goodheart. Facebook *@Sharon Frame Gay - Writer*; Instagram *@sharonframegay*; X (Twitter) *@sharonframegay*

Additional Information

Reviews

If you enjoyed reading these stories, please consider doing an online review. It's only a few seconds of your time, but it is very important in continuing the series. Good reviews mean higher rankings. Higher rankings mean more sales and a greater ability to release stories.

Print Books

https://www.afterdinnerconversation.com

Purchase our growing collection of print anthologies, "Best of," and themed print book collections. Available from our website, online bookstores, and by order from your local bookstore.

Weekly Substack

https://afterdinnerconversation.substack.com

If seven stories in a single magazine feel a bit overwhelming, consider joining our Substack and get one short story emailed each Thursday.

Virtual Book Club

https://www.meetup.com/after-dinner-conversation-meetup-group

We have free virtual book club discussions each month. Join our meetup page and attend online.

Submissions and Volunteer Readers

https://www.afterdinnerconversation.com/submissions

If you would like to submit a story for consideration, you can do so on our website. If you would like to be a volunteer submission reader, email us at info@afterdinnerconversation.com

Social

Connect with us on Facebook, YouTube, Instagram, Bluesky, TikTok, Substack, Meetup.com, and X (Twitter).

Special Thanks

After seven years, this is our fourth "Best of" edition. Before this we did six "Season" books. We have also done fourteen themed books and are currently assembling our seventy-fourth monthly magazine. We are a machine.

Over 200 volunteer readers find the stories. R.K.H. Ndong assembles the magazine. I draft the discussion questions. Stephen Repsys and Kate Bocassi do the copy edits. Shawn does the covers. And we all, basically, do it for free. Issue after issue, day after day, year after year? Why?

Because, at every level, every one of us knows these stories matter. That *stories* change minds. And that changed minds change the world.

Every one of us work on After Dinner Conversation instead of spending more time with friends, family, or our respective pet. Every one of us could be using our time to make money doing something else; making more widgets.

And yet we don't, because we *believe*. We believe this matters. If you reading this, you believe it matters too.

So, thank you again to the authors, to the volunteer readers, to the staff, and to all our terribly understanding loved ones this takes time away from.

And, as always, choices matter. Even when it doesn't feel like it.

Thank you!

Editor-in-Chief